Her eyelids fluttered as she tried to open them, but their heaviness daunted her, and she let herself drift, wanting to know only the warmth of the water, the comfort of the tub. Peace.

She sensed his presence—his energy and promise—even before hard lips covered her startled cry. His kiss, unlike any kiss she had ever experienced, filled her with heat. A hard body slid intimately between her legs, slippery with soap and warm water. A hard hand pressed against the back of her head, keeping her face above the water and a hard, determined tongue dipped into her mouth. She sighed, accepted the stroke of that tongue against hers, sucked on it, tasted it and found it to her liking. Her heart rate climbed. He demanded her tongue, received it, toyed with it, treasured it, then returned it to her safekeeping. Her hands, cupped over warm, taut skin covering muscular shoulders, trembled.

"Yes," he murmured, lifting his golden head. "Come to me.

"I need you," he said, his words whispers on the wind. "You must come. We have great need of each other."

Other *Love Spell* books by Judy Gill:
NO STRINGS ATTACHED

WHISPERS ON THE WIND

JUDY GILL

LOVE SPELL   NEW YORK CITY

*For the Egmont Retreaters,
with love and thanks.*

A LOVE SPELL BOOK®

May 2001

Published by

Dorchester Publishing Co., Inc.
276 Fifth Avenue
New York, NY 10001

Cover art by John Ennis.
www.ennisart.com.

ISBN 0-505-52435-X

Visit us on the web at www.dorchesterpub.com.

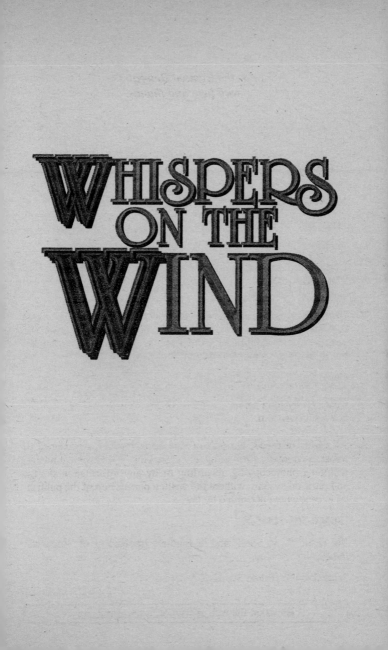

WHISPERS ON THE WIND

Prologue

Steady now . . . Smoothly, feel the translation approach, glide from one into the other. Slide along, down, wait for the point. Keep the pattern. No fear. No wavers. Come with me, meld, hold, and push!

There! *She's there!* Joy, satisfaction, elation crackled through the members of the Octad. *Zenna, we come! Fricka! Hold the surround and gather . . . now!*

And over. We are through. Stay tight. Vanter, repel the storm! It comes too fast! The static! Pain! My people! No! Falling away into the noise, the clutter, the spinning maelstrom of the tempest. Oh, hold, please, hold with me!

Reaching, searching, finding . . . nothing. None to touch, none to perceive. Gone, all gone, swirling away, scattered, lost in the vortex . . . Alone. Alone. Alone. But for that. There! Again! The small warmth. The soft touch. Not Zenna. But . . . safety? Kahniya, help me. Guide me in. "I'm coming!" *Reach out. Reach out. Clasp and . . . hold!*

7

Chapter One

Lenore tossed, disturbing the covers, and the man's hands pushed the comforter back, molding her shape as he followed the flowing curves to the flare of her hips. "Come to me, come to me," he whispered, trailing his fingers over her bare shoulders. He spread her hair across the pillow, then drew one long, curling tress down her chest, feathering the tip of the lock around her breasts, over her nipples.

She murmured a plea. As his caresses found the undersides of her breasts, her nipples hardened, ached. His breath fanning over them did nothing to ease the sweet pain. She wanted ... She needed ... He must ... Her soft moan became a demand. Her body arched. She heard herself begging for his mouth, his lips, his tongue, for all the pleasures his touch promised.

And unvoiced was a deeper need, a buried longing her body asked for, and he offered to fulfill. . . .

"Yes, yes. Come to me," he said again, and she kicked back the sheet and the ancient, heavy quilt. Heat scorched her body from within as his hands seared her skin from the outside. His light stroking smoothed over her abdomen, leaving a trail of embers in its wake, embers that sparked into a wildfire so powerful the flames threatened to incinerate her where she lay. Heat traveled down her legs to the tips of her toes. She burned all over and rolled facedown as if obeying an unspoken request.

The sensual assault continued over her back. Fingertips walked lightly up her spine, filtering through the thickness of her hair, kneading her scalp. Flat, hard palms spread over her shoulder blades, massaging expertly, pressing her into the mattress, spanning her waist. Fingers slid under her hipbones, lifting slightly, then moving down her legs to her knees, parting them. Whispers of hot air fluttered across the small of her back and over her buttocks as the man knelt by her, surprising, teasing with tiny, intermittent kisses and shocking little nips of teeth. His ministrations sent wave after wave of incomparable sensation coursing through her, leaving her teetering on the verge of a climax she knew would be of shattering proportions.

She ached for it, needed it. It was too much to bear, going so far without completion. Within, her barren womb contracted, begging for . . . for his seed? Yes! Fill me, her soul cried. Mate with me. Give me your child.

The craving became a hunger knowing no end, and dimly she recognized the desire as one having long gnawed at her. A baby to hold, a child to love. The logical outcome of these intense feelings, of the union yet to come. The want left her gasping, aching, all but weeping with urgency.

With an inarticulate cry, she rolled over. She strained to make out his face, but he was nothing more than shadows and soft sounds, tantalizing caresses of hands whose strength she could only imagine from the exquisite restraint of his touch. She tried to reach out to him, but her arms lay heavy at her sides, her fingers pressing into the sheet.

Blunt nails raked down one leg. "Lenore . . . Lenore. Come." His sensual torture tracked up the other leg. Softening, he sought the tender skin on the inside of her thigh, exploring in widening circles, close, but never quite close enough, teasing her with promises of fulfillment that ended just short of fruition.

"Please . . . please," she whimpered as she instinctively lifted her knees, letting her legs fall apart in response to his knowing invasion. "Jon . . . touch me! I need you."

"Yes," he murmured, one finger sliding in, parting the wet, swollen folds that protected her entrance. "I need you, too. But . . . come to me."

Lenore shuddered as he withdrew and backed away from her, fading into the night, leaving only a beckoning hand for her gaze to follow and then that, too, was gone.

"No!" she cried, snapping to a sitting position, managing now to lift her weighted arms and reach for him.

She awoke from the dream. Clammy sweat beaded her face and trickled between her breasts, chilling her despite the thick flannel gown she wore. Her chest pumped up and down frantically, too hard, with the force of her breathing, and her heart hammered uncomfortably, audible in the silent, empty bedroom.

Empty? Of course. Finally, with difficulty, she brought herself back from the edge. "Stop it, stop it," she said to her crazed libido. "It was only a dream. It wasn't real."

She switched on the light, just to be sure she was alone. The patchwork quilt lay in an untidy heap where she had pushed it near the foot of the white-painted iron bed. A bentwood rocker held a worn teddy bear. The dresser and highboy both wore white crocheted scarves made by some distant ancestor of her friend Caroline. This room, where she and Caroline had slept as girls on vacation from boarding school, had, even then, been like a museum display entitled "Late-Twentieth-Century Girl's Room." Now, even though the bunk beds they'd shared had been replaced by a double bed, the room still looked so innocent and virginal that she felt momentarily ashamed of her eroticism.

She poured a glass of water from the carafe on the nightstand and gulped it down before pouring another and sipping. Her hands shook. The glass rattled for a moment against her teeth. Quickly, she set it down.

She stared at her reflection in the dressing table mirror, seeing a perfectly ordinary female face on which the residue of distress and frustration mingled with bewildered hurt. She carefully composed her features, reminding herself that the dream had been no more real than any of the others that had plagued her over the past three years. It—and those during the previous two nights—had simply been different manifestations of the same problem: She wanted a baby.

Tucking a strand of unruly hair behind her ear, she tried to render same order to her dark brown locks that possessed—if one were being kind—"body", certainly not "curl." It was cut in a short, practical style that needed a salon only once every six to eight weeks for a trim. With a frown, Lenore recalled how, in the

11

dream, the man had teased her breasts with her own long, curling tresses.

"Good Lord!" she groaned, leaning forward, grasping the covers and dragging them back up over her. A reminiscent shudder of need coursed through her. She lay down, legs and arms rigid. "You're depraved, Lenore Henning!"

I am not! another side of her argued. She was a mature, sensible woman; an accountant who knew that two plus two always made four—not four and a half, not three and a bit, but an indisputable four.

There were immutable truths in this world, and she accepted them gladly; they kept life in balance.

Tides rose. Tides fell. Seasons came, seasons went. People were born, they matured, grew old, and died. It always had been so. It always would be so. And she'd do well to stick to the truths that had governed her so far. There was no place in her life for chimeras that came out of the night to disturb her rest with images like something out of the *Kama Sutra*.

Snaking one arm out from beneath the covers, she switched off the light, hoping sleep would come again.

Hoping for the dream?

Oh, yes . . . No!

Yet . . . She rolled restlessly to one side. What if, she thought with an anticipatory shudder, what if this time the dream goes all the way?

Oh, hell! If it did, she wouldn't survive it, that's what. She'd die right here in the front upstairs bedroom of the old, two-story log house she and Caroline owned. She could imagine her friend arriving eventually to discover her skeletal remains under the covers. The autopsy couldn't possibly show that she'd died due to an overdose of lustful pleasure. But she had to laugh as she imagined her skull grinning from ear to ear.

"Fool," she muttered. "You're not just depraved, you're deprived. Go on back to Frank. That should take care of the problem."

Frank? Hah! Fat chance. Breaking with him after a four-year relationship had been a relief. There'd been no spark left, no real connection, if indeed there ever had been one. Whatever. There'd certainly never been any *Kama Sutra*–like imagery. Not like there was with . . . Jon.

Jon? She sighed and flopped to her back again, linking her hands behind her head. So now he was Jon. Not "John," but "Jon," as if it were short for Jonathon. And how could she know that? She couldn't, except . . . she did. She knew it as well as she knew two plus two equaled four. Strange, though, the night before and the one before that, her phantom hadn't had a name. It was only tonight she had called him Jon and had known the rightness of the name. Jon . . . She drew a deep, tremulous breath that shuddered out on the whispered sound of his name. "Jon . . ."

Her need was as real as he was illusory.

She'd have taken a cold shower, but she knew it would be no more effective than it had been on either of the two previous nights. Besides, early May in the high Canadian Rockies was no time to be taking a cold shower in a barely heated house, and she was wide awake without it anyway. She was too aware of her body, of every tortured nerve ending, for her not to be fully awake. Lord above! She imagined she could still smell the man's scent on the pillow beside hers, though it remained as pristine and undented as when she had gone to sleep in the double bed.

This whole damned phenomenon must be part and

parcel of the burnout syndrome, she decided. Though it was not one of the side effects the doctor had suggested she might encounter. Tears, depression, anger, bizarre behavior—such as breaking up with Frank (at least that was how Frank had chosen to view it)—sleeplessness, and unexpected bursts of manic energy followed by the kind of exhaustion that had sent Lenore to her doctor in the first place. Those symptoms, the doctor had said, Lenore could continue to expect with greater frequency unless she took a serious break from mental stress.

The physician had ordered two months of rest minimum, adding that she recommended something physical and mindless, such as chopping wood if Lenore was strong enough. She'd also suggested one of the back-to-basics communes that had sprung up in the fifty years since the millennium. Lenore, though, was too much of a loner to want that. Besides, here in this old house, she was about as back to basic as she could get. The place wasn't even powered by a household Ballard Cell, for heaven's sake!

Stacking the pillows behind her, Lenore hitched herself up and leaned back. "Is enjoying wild sex with a stranger a back-to-basic requirement?" she muttered, then wondered whether talking aloud to herself came under the heading "bizarre behavior." Likely.

And he was a stranger. Even dead asleep, she knew she was begging a man she'd never met to continue his erotic seduction. In her dreams, though, it didn't feel like bizarre behavior. Then, it felt damn good, better than any real-life encounter she'd experienced in all of her thirty-seven years. That being the case, how could her imagination conjure something like what she'd been experiencing?

14

It simply made no sense.

But neither did lolling around staring at a ceiling now tinged with pale shafts of light showing themselves through the tops and sides of the chaste white eyelet curtains over the dormer window.

Tucked up against the western slopes of the Rockies, the log house received dawn later than the valley floor below where the Fraser River ran. Daylight entering her west-facing room meant it was long past the time she normally arose.

It was definitely time to get up.

And chop wood?

She just might do it. If physical exhaustion would eradicate the symptoms of mental exhaustion, it would be worth it.

Stepping off the rag rug and crossing the cold floor, Lenore whipped back the curtains and leaned on the sill, gazing out over the land and idly picking at chipped paint.

The sight before her dispelled the last vestiges of the dream.

Golden light sparked the snowcaps of the Cariboo Range that formed a wall on the western side of the valley, gilded the dark tips of evergreens and spread like melted butter down the slopes toward the river. Smoke, blue-gray and lazy, arose from chimneys in the town along the riverbanks. Didn't anyone use fuel-cells up here, even now? When they were young, she and Caroline had called this place and everything in it "The Time-Warp," though both had loved their summers here with Caroline's grandparents, Grandma and Grandpa Francis. It had been a welcome relief from the relentless regimentation of boarding school.

The sense of being in a time warp increased when a

woman emerged from a house and began pinning clothing to a line where it would dry in the breeze. Now there was a back-to-basic woman if there ever had been one. A convoy of three transport trucks took turns passing each other on a long, straight stretch of highway; then a car and a pickup zipped past those, northward bound. She smiled, empathizing with the pleasure she knew the drivers would be taking in the freedom and individualism of controlling the speed and behavior of their vehicles, far from the dictates of the traffic-controlling glideways of more populated zones.

The river, also northward bound, shimmered as it moved. It swept up the valley until it turned in a vast arc far beyond, where the Cariboo Range parted conveniently to let it slip through. There it turned west and south, to continue its journey to the Pacific, fed by snow-melt from mountain range after mountain range along its way.

A week ago when she'd arrived, patches of melting snow had lain along the sides of roads where plows had stacked it throughout the winter just past. Now, even that was gone, though behind the cabin, a thick bank of white fluff remained in deep tree-shade. Clear, cold water trickled slowly from the snowdrift as it melted to form a tiny rivulet.

That rill ran to the year-round stream from which the house drew its water supply. In turn, the stream emptied into an even brisker creek that bubbled and danced, jumping in exuberant spurts in its rock-strewn bed beside the narrow, twisting track leading down from the constricted beach where the cabin stood. Eventually, it spilled into the Fraser and in time, joined the spreading fan of mud and silt reaching far out into the Strait of Georgia, five hundred klicks away near the northern end of the Cascadia Corridor. There, it evaporated and rose in the form of clouds that condensed and fell as rain and snow, to melt and trickle into the rivulet, which ran to the stream that became the creek that added to the river and evaporated, again and again and again.

Always, that thought had pleased her when she and Caroline had set little bark boats afloat in the creek and watched them bob away—to the ocean, the girls had been sure. There was a pleasing, satisfactory continuity in it she had recognized even as a child, a child with few roots and those tenuously planted.

That sense of continuity was what she'd come here for, not unsettling dreams that could never be fulfilled. What she needed was that beautiful, peaceful sense of nature's cycles spinning eternally, like the very earth on which she lived.

This was a good place to be, and she was grateful to the Francis family for their generosity.

She swung the window wide and sucked in a breath of the thin, crisp mountain air. Maybe that was half her problem right there—the thin air. Oxygen starvation did weird things to people. She'd adapt in a few more days. All she had to do was concentrate on the normalcy of life as it really was and not let herself dwell on ridiculous fantasies.

A tractor on the valley floor worked a field with a plow. Gulls and crows followed it in a wheeling cloud as if a celestial hand sprinkled salt and pepper over the land. In scattered clumps among the fields, along the roadsides, and around the ranch houses, deciduous trees stood almost quivering with eagerness, flaunting the new yellow-green of quickening life.

Possibly, that was the other half of her problem. Spring. Her biological clock—which ticked louder and

17

louder each year—had come too damned close to trapping her in a relationship that had utterly no meaning to her. Its alarm rang more and more sharply in her soul each spring. Though never like this.

Lenore sighed and shoved herself back from the window. It was time to put her erotic dreams of the night behind her and get on with the practical pursuits of the day. What was needed here was a serious dose of the pragmatism that had served her all her life. Dreams were for the weak of mind. Fantasies, for fools. And she was neither.

First thing after breakfast, she'd scrub the kitchen floor. Then she'd sit down with a good book and immerse herself in someone else's life.

Later, she'd spend an hour—at least an hour—working on the afghan she'd started crocheting years ago. She'd bake bread. She thought she remembered how, and if she didn't, downstairs was a collection of museum-quality cookbooks. She might even turn on her compad, which she hadn't done once since her arrival. If the doctor had had her way, Lenore wouldn't have even brought it. Leaving it behind, though, would have meant cutting herself off much too thoroughly.

With plenty to occupy her, she would not spend even one minute thinking of a bronze-skinned stranger named Jon, with golden hair and grass-green eyes, and broad, muscular shoulders.

What?

Bronze skin? Golden hair? Green eyes? Dammit, it had been dark in the night! He had been nothing more than a shadowy shape, a soft whisper, sure hands, and hot breath. He'd had no form, no color, no substance beyond those hands—and those lips. She felt a rush of heat color her face as the skin he'd kissed tingled at just the memory of his touch.

From the top dresser drawer, she selected a good firm bra for her full breasts, cotton panties that came right up to her waist, and thick socks. Not the garments of a fanciful woman. Not the garments of erotica. They were her clothes, the kind she always wore, good quality, practical, long lasting. They provided value for her money.

And that, she decided, stomping down the stairs to make herself a good, practical breakfast of warm oatmeal, was what was important in life. Getting good value. Nobody ever got that from a dream.

Burning . . . Pain. Swirling dark, welcoming, warming . . .

No. Must hold focus, concentrate. Bones to knit, blood to staunch, wounds to heal—too large, too deep, too big for one alone. . . . Help me. Help me. Where are you? I ask so little. A small, warm point of light. Return, return!

No one. Nothing. Sleep and heal and let the swirling dark glide in. . . . I must not die! Kahniya, *seek help. Seek . . .* Zenna!

Jonallo! Zenna clutched mentally at the *Kahniya* encircling her neck as, for an instant, one brief, heart-wrenching moment during a risky translation, her brother Jonallo's presence swept through her senses, stunning her. It was so strong, she nearly lost her focus, came perilously close to sliding out of the already unsteady link she had maintained, aided by her amplifier, with the criminal B'tar.

Then, agonizingly, the fleeting connection with Jon

was no more. Had it, even for that split second, truly been?

On the ground again outside the house she shared unwillingly with her captors, Rankin and B'tar, she resumed her corporeal form. In that first instant of full, Earthly awareness, she saw her three-year-old daughter, Glesta, running toward her, tawny hair streaming behind her, stubby legs pumping, a glad smile on her face. Zenna caught a relieved sob in her throat as the only reason she obeyed Rankin and B'tar's dictates flew into her arms.

Chapter Two

"Damn, that hurts!" Lenore slammed the heavy axe into the chopping block, tugged off the oversized and stiff leather gloves—all she'd been able to find—and sucked on a blistered palm. Crunching numbers for a living did not lead to tough hands.

The blisters, popping up on the pads at the base of her fingers, had developed over the past hour. And in the last few minutes it had begun to break open, which effectively put an end to her wood-chopping and made stacking the logs a task for another day. But at least she was tired, she thought, kicking off her boots at the back door, then bending to stand them neatly on the mat in the corner. Maybe tired enough to sleep the night through without dreaming.

Placing both blistered palms against the small of her back, she stood erect, groaning. She unbuttoned her heavy flannel shirt, shrugged out of it, working her shoulders to try to relieve the stiffness and pain between them. The unaccustomed labors of the day had definitely taken their toll.

In the kitchen, she took three loaves of fully risen bread dough and slid them into the hot oven before adding two logs of wood to the fire. She smiled, recalling the astounded expression on Nancy Worth's face when she had asked for yeast in the small, community store where she picked up supplies.

"You'd better get out of this valley, and fast," Nancy had said. "You're turning into another Jane McQuarrie!" As if Jane was the only person in the valley who baked bread. But, on reflection, Lenore realized Jane might well be.

The kitchen stove had been burning all day, so there would be plenty of water heating the coils running behind the firebox for a nice long soak in the century-old claw-footed tub. Maybe fuel-cells weren't necessary. After all, weren't chunks of wood, in their own way, fuel-cells of a sort?

Bubbles, she thought, heading for the bathroom. Lots and lots of bubbles. Even a hard-working, practical woman deserved the solace of a bubble bath now and then.

The hot water stung her hands, and it would take more than one bath to ease the twin aches in lower back and between her shoulder blades, but she had to start somewhere. She relaxed against the warm slope at the end of the tub, stretching her toes out to keep herself from sliding right under the water. She closed her eyes, drawing in the scent of the perfumed bubbles, mingled with the aroma of slowly baking bread.

Ah . . . Heaven.

She had no idea how long she lay there before the

water began to cool, but she knew she should stir herself and get out of the tub. She tried, against the weight of lethargy, to sit up, but it took too much effort. Besides, what was the hurry? There was no one to want the bathroom, no one to make any demands of her, no insistent compad chime, no doorbell, no traffic sounds to disturb her.

Bathe it, soothe it, cloak it in calm. Strength ebbing . . . no, focus, tighten, aim and . . . there! It's done. Rest now. Breathe. And . . . reach again. Cloak, surround, ease. Good. Once more . . . cannot. But must. She, the strongest essence, must be well, whole, to help. Tighten, reach, touch and . . . done. Ahh, to drift . . . the swirling, welcome dark beckons. . . .

As the aches in her back floated away, the smarting of Lenore's hands turned to a delicious warmth that soaked up her arms, into her shoulders, down her spine and through her legs, softening her muscles, leaving her totally relaxed. She entered a state of perfect peace filled with the faint popping of bubbles in the warm water, the scent of baking bread, the scent of the forest moss, the soughing of the trees and the distant crackle of the fire glowing, sending dancing light against the cavern walls. . . .

Cavern? Her eyelids fluttered as she tried to open them, but their heaviness daunted her, and she let herself drift, wanting to know only the warmth of the water, the comfort of the tub. Peace.

Just a few more minutes, she thought dreamily. Another five, anyway. The water, oddly, seemed warmer now, as hot as when she'd first run it. How strange . . .

She sensed his presence—his energy and promise—

even before hard lips covered her startled cry. His kiss, unlike any kiss she had ever experienced, filled her with heat. A hard body slid intimately between her legs, slippery with soap and warm water. A hard hand pressed against the back of her head, keeping her face above water, and a hard, determined tongue dipped into her mouth. She sighed, accepting the stroke of that tongue against hers. She sucked on it, tasted it, and found it to her liking. Her heart rate climbed. He demanded her tongue, received it, toyed with it, treasured it, then returned it to her safekeeping. Her hands, cupped over warm, taut skin covering muscular shoulders, trembled.

"Yes," he whispered, lifting his golden head. "Come to me."

Lenore shifted her legs, drawing him deeper into the cradle of her thighs, seeking his heat, his hardness, opening for him. "I'm here, I'm here," she said, her voice ragged. "Please, don't make me wait."

"Come," he said again. "Hurry. I need you."

She arched her back, her hands gliding over his sleek, bronze skin, nails digging into his tight buttocks. "Now!" she gasped. "Now, Jon!"

"Now!" he whispered, and then he was gone.

Lenore gasped and sat up, water spilling down over her full, aching breasts. She looked at her nipples, touched them, feeling their hardness. Her body pulsed with unfulfilled need. Her legs trembled. Reaching down, she pulled the plug to let out the water, cold now, bubbles just a memory in scum. How long had she been caught in the fantasy that time? She had not— she was certain she had not—been asleep.

It was as if she had been . . . She frowned, disliking the connotations of the word that came to mind. *Possessed.*

She shivered. Was that what was happening to her? Was there an unfriendly—or perhaps an overly friendly—spirit trapped with her in the cabin? Her sensible, pragmatic side wanted very badly to pooh-pooh the notion, but the image had been so strong, the physical sense of touch so real, a hitherto unknown side of her shook with fear of the supernatural.

She struggled to regain control of her senses. Supernatural be damned! "There's no such thing as ghosts," she said, standing up so fast she sent water slopping everywhere.

Isn't there?

The question seemed to come from deep in her mind, but still, she snorted with disgust. She glanced at herself in the mirror. Dammit, she did not believe in ghosts. Nor did she believe in hauntings. There was nothing wrong with the cabin; ergo, the fault lay within herself.

"So leave," she muttered. "Doctors aren't infallible. Clearly, mine doesn't know what she's talking about."

Burnout or no burnout, what she needed was to get back to her own home, her job, her responsibilities. Those, surely, would keep her mind off weird, erotic fantasies.

However, would returning home permit the other dreams to recur, the ones in which a small child came to her, seeking companionship and love and . . . connection? Or the one in which she experienced being the mother of the child, afraid, not so much for herself, but for her daughter, who she felt was threatened in some way.

Each time she awoke from one of the mother dreams, she felt sick and disoriented, her head reeling and her heart aching. Worse, though, was the dream when the little girl herself came into Lenore's mind, demanding attention. From that dream, she awoke feeling bereaved, yearning to go back into it and find the child, to cuddle her close and accept the loving trust that was offered with such joyful expectation of having the feelings returned.

In addition, images of the little girl—much as she disliked admitting it even to herself—had come when she knew she was wide awake. She might be sitting at work in her office in the Crompton Building located in the center of Sector Seattle, or in her car locked onto the glideway across Puget Strait, or walking in the park near her home. The little kid with her curious questions, her bright observations and her strange insistence that Lenore come and play visited often.

It was, of course, the child she ached to have and never would. Hence the intense feelings of loss and privation when the vision ended.

Opening her eyes, she shook off the memories of those dreams and figments of her weird imagination. Deliberately, seeking normalcy, she looked at the pale peach bathroom walls, at the electric baseboard heater—another relic of times past—powered by the turbine in the stream above the cabin. The stack of towels on the vanity, her cosmetics placed neatly on a glass shelf under the mirror—she attempted to comfort herself by cataloging these prosaic items. The toilet, complete with fuzzy lid and tank covers, remnants of the tenure of Caroline's long-dead grandmother, had no place in a fantasy, she thought as she stepped from the tub, grabbed a towel and rubbed her skin briskly.

She folded the towels she had used, hung them squarely on the rail over the baseboard heater, slipped into her flannel nightgown and a terrycloth robe, and went to the kitchen to check on her bread.

It wasn't until she had shoved her hands into oven mitts to remove the loaves, beautifully golden-brown, the exact shade of Jon's hair, that she realized something else was terribly, eerily awry.

She set the last loaf down on the cooling racks she'd laid out, took off the oven mitts and stared at the palms of her hands.

"What the hell?" she said, sinking down onto a hard wooden chair, suppressing the scream that rose tight in her throat. "What in all the flames of hell is going on?"

Lenore struggled to shake off debilitating terror as she stared at the undeniable but inexplicable. Not so much as a trace of a blister showed on the palm of either hand. She prodded the resilient pads of flesh at the base of her fingers. There was no tenderness, no torn skin where blisters had broken. No angry red flesh beneath. No slow seeping of fluid. Nothing. Her hands were as they had been before she began chopping wood.

Standing again, though her knees felt weak and almost numb, she bent and touched her toes. Her back didn't hurt, either. Not a twinge. She swung her arms. Her shoulders didn't ache; they were strong and limber.

"That," she said loudly, finding some courage in the sound of her own voice, despite the tremor of apprehension she wished were not present, "is some great bubble bath!" She wanted, very badly, to believe what she said, to find in the bathroom some magic elixir that she might have poured by mistake.

It was, however, the exact same brand she always bought, the exact same bottle she had brought with her. She had not accidentally used something her globe-trotting friend might have left behind on a previous visit, something exotic from one of Caroline's Asian treks.

There were no toiletries in the bathroom besides the ones Lenore had carried up the mountain with her.

She had known that, of course. She just hadn't wanted to admit it. She sighed and sat down on the faux-fur cover of the toilet lid. "What is going on?" she said again. "What in the hell is happening to me?"

Shaking, Lenore pulled her robe tighter, feeling an unexpected chill in the warm bathroom.

"Food," she said. "You're lightheaded from lack of food."

She was also, she thought, incredibly thirsty. Something, the altitude, maybe, or the dry climate, had made her crave liquids terribly the past few days. The thirst was greatest when she awoke from one of her dreams, she realized, wondering if there could be a connection.

Her stomach growled. Hunger, like thirst, had been her constant companion for the past few days—almost since her arrival. That must indicate the doctor's prescription of rest and relaxation was working. Ordinarily, when she was depressed or stressed, food was the last thing on her mind. Loss of appetite was simply one more of the symptoms that had driven her to seek professional advice.

Her stomach growled again, and a vision of a thick, juicy steak accompanied by a mound of mashed potatoes and gravy floated before her eyes. Lord, if she started to eat like that, she'd weigh a ton before she left. The McQuarries had stocked the cabin for her with a wide variety of real meat from their private stock—pork, beef, chicken, ham. If she ate even a quarter of that bounty she might have to take on the entire woodpile, she thought, slamming the bathroom door behind her.

In the kitchen, she ladled out a bowl of stew from the pot she'd left simmering all day on the back of the stove. It did contain meat, though not in great quantities. She cut into a hot, steamy loaf of the freshly baked bread, knowing it was much too soon to do so—it would turn doughy at the touch of the knife—but unable to resist. As a treat she even slathered butter on the slices.

She ate hungrily, draining two glasses of milk with her meal, telling herself that ghosts did not exist, therefore, she hadn't experienced that episode in the tub, where she had actually felt the man's physical body, run her hands over his back, dug her nails into his buttocks. It was no more real than the little girl's voice in her head, or the worries of the frantic mother. All had been hallucinations.

Likely, she thought, shoving her empty dish away, she'd hallucinated the wood-chopping, as well. And the blisters, she decided, checking her hands again.

Sure. That was it. She really had fallen asleep in the tub—it was another manifestation of that extreme lethargy she'd complained about to the doctor. And sleeping, she'd dreamed of the wood-splitting, dreamed another encounter with the bronze-skinned man.

There would, of course, be ample proof that she hadn't chopped wood. All she had to do was go outside and assure herself that the neatly stacked cords of dry poplar remained intact in their round, unsplit state. The axe would still be where the last wood-splitter—likely Angus McQuarrie—had hung it on the wall of the shed. She probably hadn't even ridden Mystery to town and back today. She would find the horse neatly tucked away in his stall, not wandering between the cabin and the forest where she had imagined leaving him earlier, so that he could nibble at the sparse grass.

Although she had convinced herself of what she

would find outside, she was still reluctant to go out and prove it to herself.

Slowly, she walked to the back door where she stuffed her feet into her boots and dragged a jacket on over her robe. Outside, she wrapped her arms around herself as she stared at the shed. The axe was stuck into the chopping block. A freshly split pile of wood lay in an untidy heap beside it, off to one side of an incomplete cord of sawed logs, which had, earlier in the day, been intact.

With a sick feeling, she remembered she had planned to restack the split wood in a few days when her hands healed.

She paced to the small barn and found it empty. She turned when Mystery trotted up, whickering in the pale light of the newly risen moon. She backed him into his stall, as he playfully tossed his head and nuzzled her pockets in hopes of finding a treat.

It felt normal, tending the horse. He felt real, he smelled real, he sounded real. This, she hoped, was not another delusion, but it was getting to the point where she couldn't tell. Maybe, she thought, filling Mystery's feed box with the mixture Angus had prepared, maybe none of this is real and I'm safely locked away in a padded cell somewhere.

She stood and stroked the horse's neck while he munched. "I don't know, Mystery," she said. "I just don't know."

One thing she did know, though, was that she didn't want to spend another night in the house. She'd leave this minute, except she knew negotiating that track down the mountainside in the dark wouldn't be a sensible move, and she prided herself on being sensible at all times.

"At first light," she told the horse, "as soon as it's safe to ride, we're out of here."

This night, sensible or otherwise, she planned to sleep not one wink at all.

And when she heard, felt, sensed, a voice saying, "Come! I need you!" she fought it off with every erg of effort she could muster and strode back inside, locking the door firmly behind her.

Angus McQuarrie, lying beside his comfortably plump wife in his big, comfortable bed, in the warm, comfortable ranch house on the flat valley floor below Lenore's cabin heard the plea, too. He stirred, woke, and sat erect.

He stumbled from the bed, grabbed his pants and struggled into them. Reaching for his sweater, he knocked over a statue of Elvis standing on the dresser. It fell to the floor and bounced, waking Jane, who rolled over and waved her hand in front of the light, turning it on.

"What are you doing?"

"Got to go out. I know where it is. I know, this time. I know!"

She picked up the glasses she had affected the day their first grandchild was born, declaring that she wanted to "look like a proper granny," even though everyone, even in this old-fashioned little backwater, had corrective surgery each time their sight deteriorated in the slightest. He'd been lasered years before! Glasses got in the way. Through the thick lenses, Jane peered at the readout in the base of the lamp. "Angus, it's after midnight. You're not going anywhere. Come back to bed."

His compulsion was too strong to withstand. "I can't.

31

I saw it." He shook off her hand and tugged on his socks. "I saw the place. We'll be rich, Jane. Rich, I tell you."

"Oh, Angus, you've had that dream again, haven't you?" Sounding weary and disturbed, she followed him into the kitchen, her voluminous nightgown flapping around her ankles. He shouldn't have told her about the dreams of the last few nights. She believed it was nothing more than his crazy, life-long belief that there was gold just waiting for him up in the mountains, if only he could figure out where to look. "There is no mother lode," she insisted, "no gold. You've tapped on every chunk of rock in a hundred-klick radius. You've panned every stream for the past forty years. There is no gold in or around this valley."

"There is. It's there. There's a cave of some sort. I have to go there. I'll find the gold where I find the cave. Now let me go, Jane."

He fought for possession of his hand so he could zip on his high-topped boots. "Jane!"

"All right, all right." Now, she sounded resigned. "But have something warm to drink first. You need your strength if you're going prospecting in the middle of the night. And let me pack you something more to supplement your emergency rations. If I know you, you could be gone for days." It was true. He had taken other prospecting trips and stayed away longer than he intended. And he knew Jane was right when she gave a puffing, annoyed sigh. "But don't you realize it's spring, now, with plowing and planting to do?"

Momentarily, he resented her disapproval. "Not this time, Jane! This time, I know where it is." Angus closed his eyes for a second, swaying, seeing the vision growing sharper, clearer, until Jane clamped his hand to the back of a chair, steadying him. He looked into her worried, tired eyes, magnified by the lenses of her spectacles and softened. "Jane . . . when I bring it home to you, you'll see what a waste of time trying to wrest a subsistence from the soil of this valley has been. No more plowing. No more planting. No more working ourselves into our graves."

"Come on, now," she argued gently, as if he were sick. "It hasn't been such a bad life, farming here, has it? Just sit down for ten minutes. The gold will wait, and you need food and drink."

At the thought of food and drink and the strength it would impart, he felt the terrible pressure to move abating, easing just enough that he gave himself permission to sit, to watch her make a big pot of tea. "Yes," he said. "Food. Drink."

She set a mug of tea before him, and when he picked it up and sipped, he found it strong and sweet and creamy, just the way he liked it. He slurped. She served him a big wedge of homemade chocolate cake and handed him a fork.

"You eat that; then if you still feel like going for a hike, I'll cook you a proper breakfast and make some sandwiches to take along. Is your emergency pack up to date?"

Angus nodded and ate, then started gulping his second cup of tea as the scent of frying ham filled the kitchen.

Nancy Worth's eyes popped open so fast she thought her lids might suffer whiplash. "What?" she said, peering into the dim light shining through the bedroom door from the bathroom. She always kept a light on at night—a habit left over from when her mother lay sick and often needed her help. She realized she was sitting erect, her heart thundering. Not a great one for self-analysis, she wasn't quite sure whether it was fear or excitement that had brought her so thoroughly awake.

I . . . need! I . . . need! The words somehow impressed themselves on her consciousness. What did she need? Not to go to the bathroom. Not to see Peter. Not food but . . . a drink of water.

She tossed back her light throw and stumbled from her bed, bare feet slapping on the warm floor as she headed for the light beaming from the bathroom across the hall. There, not even bothering with a glass, she put her mouth under the faucet and gulped greedily. At last, standing, she wiped her wet face with the end of a towel, gripping the front of the sink with both hands, almost gasping for breath.

Come. Come to me. It seemed that a voice implored her from . . . somewhere. Where, she didn't know, couldn't know, but in that voice there was a hint of some kind of promise. She swayed, eyes squeezed tightly shut, struggling to understand what that promise might bring her. The unknown offering made her heart pound with excitement, excitement mingled with not a little fear.

For one brief instant, she flashed on a scene she had envisioned before, a cruise ship on a sea so blue it hurt the eyes to gaze upon it, on islands she suspected were Grecian, though she had never been to Greece. She had never been anywhere, but if she obeyed the dictates of that voice imploring her to seek, to find, she would behold the wonders of Greece. She would know the magic of seeing her dreams come true.

She opened her eyes and turned, strode from the bathroom of the safe, boring home she had shared for so long with her parents, but now shared with no one and nothing but her fantasies. Leaving it behind, she stepped outside into the night, following, following, following . . . she knew not what, but knew with as great a conviction as she knew her own name that she had no choice.

Chapter Three

"Come to me!" The cry was urgent. It echoed through the empty room. Lenore started, dropped her crochet hook atop her work and stared at the familiar room, walls she had known and on occasion helped scrub, helped paint, helped hang pictures on.

"Lenore! Come!"

This time, there were no sensual overtones. There was no physical touching, no heart-stopping seduction. And this time, it was no fantasy; she was fully awake, fully aware of who she was, where she was.

She was also terrified.

All the hairs on the back of her neck stood erect. Every follicle on her arms and legs prickled. Her gaze darted frantically around the room, at the chintz sofa and chairs, at the pot-bellied heater where flames licked behind the glass door. She strained her eyes, looking for shadows on the walls, shadows that did not match the shapes of the old, comfortable furniture, shadows she did not cast herself.

There was nothing that did not belong, besides the voice, still echoing.

In her ears? Or in her head?

"Who are you?" she demanded, shooting to her feet, her fists clenched at her sides. "Where are you? What do you want from me?" *Oh, God, what am I doing? I don't believe in ghosts!*

"Jon. I am Jon," came the reply.

Again, her eyes shifting rapidly, nervously, she sought substance to put behind that voice, tried to determine the direction from which it might have come, something, anything, on which to focus.

"Do not be afraid. I am Jon," the voice came again, soothingly this time, deep, resonant, vitally masculine. "You know me."

Once more, she wondered if the words had been spoken aloud, or had they simply sounded in her mind?

Wherever the voice came from, whatever its means of transmission, with it, with the latest utterance of his name, came an odd lessening of her fear, and then, as suddenly as her anxiety had arisen, it was gone.

She smiled. A sense of serenity flooded her. Yes. He was Jon. She knew Jon. She trusted him. His name held the promise of union—and more. It offered love—love in the purest, most spiritual sense, love in the most carnal sense, love in every way that love could be offered, and she yearned for it, all of it, every aspect, every nuance, with him.

The very air, holding the sound of his name, offered a pledge of what their joining could bring. She smiled dreamily as she cupped her hands over her lower belly as if to cradle, to hold safe, the treasure that was not yet granted but would be, but only if she—

"I need you," he said again, his words whispers on the wind. "You must come. We have great need of each other."

"Yes," she said aloud, taking a step toward the door. "I must come to you."

Her voice in the stillness of the room shocked her. She fought, suddenly, to dispel the aura of rectitude and strength and potency that had surrounded her, the sense that if she were with him, all would be well.

"No!" she cried.

She violently rejected the notion that all the love, all the goodness, all the fulfillment she had ever wanted could be had if she would only reach out and take it. Reach out to Jon. It was never that easy. All was *not* well. All would not *be* well. All of this was crazy, and she was determined not to be a crazy woman.

She was Lenore Henning, CPA, daughter of Winston Henning, who owned so many lucrative businesses she had lost count. She was . . .

Empty . . . barren . . . loveless. She ached with the pain those words evoked.

Had she uttered them? Had he?

"Go away!" she shouted. "You're driving me insane! You—" she broke off with a sob that was half-laugh. Dammit to hell and back! Sane people did not have conversations with phantoms! Nor did they want ghosts to . . . to mate with them. Love them. Impregnate them.

"Go away!" she cried again, pressing her hands to her ears so hard she heard the blood rushing through her veins.

"I cannot." The words came over the sound of rushing blood. In her head. Around her. Outside her and inside her, tugging at her, drawing her away from safety, security, sanity. "Please. You must come to me. Much is at stake."

Impossible. This entire scene was unbelievable. It couldn't be happening. She was wide awake and hearing voices. Still, something compelled her to ask, "Where are you?"

Into her mind flooded a picture, an image half-forgotten, of a day when she and Caroline, teenagers hiking and exploring, had been caught by an unexpected summer storm sweeping down the flank of the mountain. They had taken shelter in a cave as the rain became hail, then sleet, and rain once again before the storm ended.

A cave where a bronze-skinned man with tawny, dark gold hair had lain naked on a low shelf of rock. She shook her head, confused. Jon's face floated before her, green eyes overflowing with incomparable love, compassion, and assurance. And the promise . . . oh Lord! The promise in that look . . .

"No," she whispered and shook her head again, trying to dispel the apparition. As his image faded, it was replaced by the sensation of a hand on her back, gently urging her forward.

"Stop," she said, stumbling across the braided oval of rug, tripping on her half-completed afghan. She looked down at the heap of orange, cream, and brown material, at the gray metal crochet hook lying in the middle of the fabric. Seeking to center herself in reality, she clutched the side of a china cabinet in one hand, the frame of the doorway in the other. Inside the cabinet, cut crystal wineglasses rattled in time with her trembling. Bone china cups quivered before the.. upright saucers. On the floor, the zig-zag pattern of the afghan danced before her eyes, but the cave, and the man, were superimposed upon them like a bad holo image.

Energy flooded her, along with a sense of rightness, a conviction that she must go to this man. Why did she hesitate, even bother to resist? It was foolishness, an exercise in futility that was almost laughable. She wanted him. No, it went deeper than that. She needed him; her very existence depended on him. He was her mate, the other side of her soul. She could taste the desire in the back of her mouth, feel it deep in her bones. It hammered in her blood, throbbed in her womb.

Still, with the part of her she could control, she fought his power. "The cave was empty that day," she said, tasting tears and knowing they were her own. "You were not there. No one was there! I can't be dreaming you because you were not there."

"I am . . . now. You know I am. You are not dreaming. You know you must come. Your needs and mine must be met. It is the way of life. Otherwise, there can be only . . . death."

The picture flickered like a poorly received satellite signal then solidified, became real, almost tangible, clearer than even the most flawless hologram. He appeared to be sleeping. His bare chest, hairless, firmly muscled, rose and fell slowly. Too slowly? Alarm flared within her. A seep of reddish brown fluid spread on the rock below his left side. His hair, she saw as he feverishly tossed his head, was also caked with blood. One leg, obviously broken, hung half off the ledge, his foot twisted at an odd angle. Around his neck he wore a band of some gleaming substance she couldn't identify. It appeared to be beads of . . . light?

With supreme effort, she shoved the vision away, and it vanished again.

A sense of terrible, soul-destroying loneliness overcame her, sending her back to her chair with a sob of
anguish. She had rejected him, turned her back, and he
would die. Love would die. Her child would never be.
Life . . . what promised to be life, would drain away,
leaving an open, empty shell from which poured an
unending stream of grief as black as night, as red as
blood, as foul as bile.

"Must I die, then?" the voice said, a mere whisper of
tones. Resignation tinged its emotional content. Regret.
A deep sense of failure. Unendurable loss. "Must we all
die? Must *Zenna?*"

His torment was her torment. It flooded her, choked
her. It was more than pain, more than fear, and then
suddenly, resignation was overridden by another surge
of urgency, mingled with a feeling of deep concern
for . . . someone? Zenna . . . his . . . sister? And responsibility. Determination that he would make her understand. That she know the cost should he be left to die,
know it and feel it as intimately as he did.

"In death, I will be unable to reassemble my . . ."

Reassemble what? Was it a word? If so, it was not
one she could immediately identify, not one whose
sense she could fully comprehend, but it was important,
no, more than important, vital that someone . . . something . . . a situation be rectified. The burden lay heavy
on her heart.

"Help me, or I will die. The . . . she/they/it will die."
This time, she got a sense of eight individuals connected
as one, like a sixteen-point snowflake. They were not
physically linked, though. Their confederation of eight
went much deeper than that. But how? And why? And
who? "Come to me. Come to me, and you will understand all. Lenore, I beg your assistance."

41

So intense was the plea that Lenore found herself back on her feet, walking toward the back door. Her hand lifted, turned the knob, pulled the door open, and she stepped out into the frosty night.

The cold ground against her bare soles brought her back to her senses.

"No," she said and fought the strong tugging, the powerful insistence that she move forward despite herself. One foot lifted. It planted itself another step away from the house, away from safety, away from warmth. The other followed.

Again, she resisted. "No. I must dress. I will freeze if—"

The wrenching need to move onward, into the blackness of the forest, to go to the cave, continued to assault her mind, to power her body. But she fought it with all her strength, while the outer compulsion battled back.

Swaying, she remembered what he could give her, what he had promised, and knew that his pledge was true. She had only to keep walking, to go to him, and he would release her from the terrible need she had suffered for so long.

But . . . a small part of her that remained her own knew that if she did it now, in this way, they would both die. They would . . . *all?* die.

"I will come to you. I will," she vowed, weeping in her effort to resist the influence of his need, of her own. "But let me go, first. I need . . . things."

"You will come," he said. It wasn't a question, but a conviction, and she felt his relief, his satisfaction and gratitude and joy. It danced in the air around her, vibrated on her nerves like a bow on violin strings tightened to near-breaking point. The very air seemed to shiver with his emotion. "You will!"

"I will," she said as she let acquiescence flow through her, out of her, and into him. There was no point in fighting it any longer. He needed her. And she—Oh, how she needed him! What he had, what he could give. What he would give.

The mental force eased its grip on her. She turned, rushing back into the house.

"But hurry," the faint voice whispered in her mind. "Hurry . . . Help me."

Time seemed to slow for Angus McQuarrie as he sipped his hot tea and listened to the sizzle of ham in the pan and the sharp cracking sounds of breaking eggs. As Jane punched the toaster into action, the urgency to find that cave, to discover the gold Angus knew would be in it, dwindled but did not disappear completely, leaving him feeling confused and unsettled, as if he were being torn by forces he couldn't understand.

He picked up a fork and attacked the meal Jane set before him. The desire to seek gold grew less and less compelling with each bite. And with its passing, the strong conviction that this time he knew, also faded.

Knew? Knew what? He scratched his head, looked down at the plate before him showing smears of bright yellow egg yolk, a few bits of rich pink ham, brown crumbs of toast, and crusty hash browns. He glanced at the big clock on the wall over the stove. Twelve-fifty-four? The window outside showed him it was dark. Nighttime. He gave his head a rapid shake.

"What are we doing?" he asked Jane. "Why did you cook me breakfast at this time of day?"

"You wanted to go out," she said. "You had one of those dreams again. I didn't want you to leave without food in your belly."

His tone was heavy. "The gold." It wasn't a question.

She nodded. He thought that, through her thick glasses, he could read wariness along with resignation. "I'll get your pack."

"Yeah." The gold. It was up there . . . somewhere. He thought he had known. In the dream, it had been so clear, like a vision. But now, it was fading the way dreams do when one tries too hard to remember them. There'd been a cave. That he knew. And in it, he'd seen the gleam of gold. It had called him. It had called him strongly, almost as if a voice had spoken in his mind.

He shivered, staring out the wide window wall that faced his fields, with the dark bulk of the Rockies soaring straight up beyond, blocking the stars. What was it out there that called him? And where was it?

"Now, who could that be?" Jane asked, drawing Angus's attention to a flickering light well beyond the window wall of the kitchen. Someone stumbled along the side of the east pasture. The light paused, dipped, and he knew the person had parted the strands of wire that kept the stock from the hayfield. The light wove uncertainly onward, cutting a slow but steady path across the freshly plowed and planted field.

Once, it bobbed out of existence as if it had been shut off, but as Jane damped the lights in the kitchen, offering a better view of the outdoor scene, he saw that whoever staggered across the ground had fallen. That person now recovered the lightcell and reeled on, traveling in an ever-more erratic pattern as if unsure of the right direction.

One moment, the light bobbed toward the Johannsen ranch house close by but unseen in the dark. The next, it angled back toward the McQuarrie place, as if whoever was lost out there might have been drawn by the lights and was now confused because they'd been shut off.

"I'd better check this out," Angus said, "since I'm already up and dressed." He tugged on his jacket and fumbled with the fastener. "Looks like someone's in trouble," he added as the person fell again, getting up more slowly this time.

"Heading toward Johannsen's ranch, by the look of it." Jane commented. "Maybe Pete's had too much to drink."

"Hmmph." Angus wouldn't have been surprised. Pete Johannsen was not a happy man, what with his on-again, off-again relationship with Nancy Worth. But who could he have been boozing with until this time of the night? Most everyone hereabouts got up with the chickens and went to bed not long after them, too.

Just before the fence that separated his east hayfield from the highway, he intercepted the carrier of the light-cell and came to a stunned halt. "Nancy? Nancy Worth?"

He stared at her. She wore only a short, moth-gray nightshirt, no shoes, not even slippers, despite the crispness of the frost on the grassy verge here. Her eyes held a dazed expression, quickly hidden by her squint as he beamed his lightcell right in her face.

"What the hell are you doing out here?"

She blinked and he turned his light off her face. "Angus. Oh. Why are you here?"

"Why are you in my field in the middle of the night?"

"I . . . I don't know. I had to go . . . somewhere. To be . . . with someone."

"Be with who? Peter? Did he call you? Is he sick? Why didn't you drive? What are you doing on foot and with no clothes on?"

She shook her head, looking confused. "Not . . . him, not Peter. Someone else. I . . . think. I don't know who. It's like I did know, but now I can't remember. This is crazy, isn't it, Angus? God, I'm cold." She wrapped her arms around herself and looked down at her feet. "I don't have any shoes on!"

"I know." Angus was concerned about the woman, not only her physical state, but her mental condition as well. "Come on, let's get you inside and warmed up. Jane has tea on."

Nancy hesitated for a moment, then gestured at the steep mountainside to the east. "But . . . up there . . ."

Angus wrapped his jacket around Nancy's shaking body. "Up there . . . what?" he asked steering her toward the house, only half a klick away, where the outdoor floodlights Jane had switched on spilled across the new grass of the yard, turning it an electric green. He followed the direction of Nancy's wistful stare.

"Someone . . . Something . . ." She frowned. "I don't know. Don't remember, exactly. But I had to get there. Up there, somewhere. A ship?"

"Right," he said, hurrying her along now, feeling the cold himself without his jacket. She was obviously hypothermic, irrational. *A ship? On the mountain? Sure!*

"Up there"—he pointed to the west—"is one hell of a big black cloud that's going to dump a few tons of rain on us any minute now." Even while he spoke, the stars began to disappear as if being swallowed by a monster.

They had just reached the shelter of the porch when the load of rain let loose.

In no time, Jane had Nancy bundled in a quilt, her hands wrapped around a large steaming mug of sweet tea. A pair of Angus's own heavy gray wool socks came almost to her knees, but despite that, her teeth chattered against the china as she sipped.

A thunderous hammering on the door sent all three whirling around as it was flung open, and Peter Johannsen strode through.

"What's wrong?" he demanded. "I saw you and Nan out there in the middle of the field. What's going on here, anyway?" He crouched before Nancy, took the cup from her, and smothered her hands in his. "What were you doing, honey? Were you trying to come to me?"

Nancy looked at him, and her face crumpled as she rocked forward against his shoulder. "Peter . . . I'm so glad you're here. You'll keep me safe."

"Sure I will. Come on. I'll take you home with me and get you warm."

Jane tapped Peter on the shoulder. "Jacquie's room's all made up and ready. How about you get Nancy tucked in there, and tuck yourself right in beside her? Best way I know to warm up a cold body is with a warm one, and she shouldn't be going outside again tonight."

She gave Angus's arm a tug when he would have stayed there to stare at the sight of Peter Johannsen lifting Nancy Worth from the chair, quilt and all, gray socks dangling, and carrying her down the hall. "Come on," she said. "We need to get back to bed, too."

Wearily, he let Jane lead him back to their own room. In a way, he was glad. He was much too old to be clambering up mountainsides in the dead of night.

Lenore's shoulders ached under the weight of the earth-quake kit kept at the ready by every sensible person in the entire Cascadia Corridor, following the devastation of '21. Her thighs, unused to climbing steep hills, burned with exertion. Her lungs strained deprived of oxygen at this high altitude. She clutched the trunk of a tree, holding on, aiming the beam of her lightcell along the faint track through the forest. She rested for only seconds before dragging in a deep breath breath that failed to satisfy her body and forcing herself away from the tree.

She plodded onward. She knew with the same instinctive knowledge that draws a salmon to its home river from the vastness of the ocean that she would put no foot wrong. She skirted trees felled by winter storms, leapt streams in her path and recognized that no matter how convoluted the track, she would find Jon at the end of it.

Suddenly, without conscious thought, she turned right and found herself on more level ground, a benchland that led back toward the next steep incline as it curved around the flank of the mountain. The evergreens grew more sparsely here, admitting fitful shafts of moonlight that rose and faded as black and silver clouds scudded across the sky, giving glimpses of a million more stars than ever shone over the Cascadian metropolitan area.

Lenore cast wary glances upward wherever the trees were thin enough. Despite the moon and stars, she didn't like the look of the sky. There were far more clouds now than when she had started out. They boiled up from behind the mountain range to the west, across the valley, rising in a towering column of darkness that broke into wind-tossed bits playing tag with the moon.

She hurried, worried about the coming storm.

The rocky soil, slippery in spots, crumbled under the soles of her hiking boots, but she made better time now that the ground was more level. She walked on faster, her heart beating heavily, her mouth dry.

She longed for water, but stopped for nothing. She

jumped the width of a rushing creek and followed its banks to where it bubbled out of a crevice between two rocks. She stopped, tilted her head back, and looked up the sheer wall of granite, swinging her light in an exploratory arc.

There! Ten feet over, a few feet up a natural staircase, she could see a blackness the beam could not dispel. The cave. She had arrived, and safely. Now all she had to do was get in there and get the man out. Get Jon.

She hitched her pack higher. With one hand clutching the lightcell, she struggled to gain the first of those steps, thinking that they had not seemed so far apart when she was sixteen.

Edging sideways, trailing the pack behind her, she pushed through the narrow cave entrance, recalling how she and Caroline had entered it, seeking only to get out of the rain, and discovered that five feet in, it widened to a chamber large enough to wander around in, intriguing enough to encourage exploration.

Then, though, they had hesitated at the end of the slit, peering into darkness lit only fitfully by the lighter Caroline had always carried in those days. They had wondered aloud about bears, cougars, and armed survivalists who might inhabit the cavern. They had giggled, promising each other that bears and cougars would have left tell-tale signs, and survivalists would have had sentries posted. Besides, if there were any of the latter, maybe they'd be male, and worth visiting.

Both had been glad to be out of the pounding hail and whipping wind; it made them feel invincible enough to take on any wild animal they might encounter—including survivalists.

Now, all alone, Lenore was filled with a different kind of trepidation. She sensed no other presence. She felt sick. Had the whole episode been nothing more than an indication of her near-breakdown state?

Or . . . was it merely that she was too late?

"Is anybody here?" she said, emerging fully into the main gallery, a cavern some twenty feet across at its widest, ten feet high at the front, with several shelves and ledges along its sides, which sloped sharply to the floor at the rear.

"Hello!" Her seeking light beam encountered only bare walls, dusty ledges, and boulders that had tumbled down. A deep sense of loss flooded her. To have come this far to find nothing, after being so sure, seemed a cruel punishment.

"Where are you?" she asked, sending the light in erratic, swinging searches. Maybe an earthquake during the twenty years since her last visit had opened another room where Jon might be hiding. This was no limestone cavern, hollowed out by water, but one left in the formation of the mountain itself, like a bubble in folded cake batter. Earth tremors often shook loose enough of the crumbling, shaley mountain substance to create leads into new caves.

She and Caroline had explored the place thoroughly, having returned later with proper lights. They had, bravely they thought, spent the odd night in the cavern that summer and the next. This had been the only chamber then and appeared still to be. There was a narrow chimney near the center of the back wall, but neither of them would have fit through it, not even at the slim, lithe age of sixteen. Therefore, a man the size of Jon would not have fit, either.

Despite the clearly empty state of the cave, she called his name. "Jon!"

There was no reply. She laughed softly, bitterly.

Of course there was no reply. He didn't exist. He never had. What was she doing, standing in a cave in the middle of the night, with a storm brewing outside, calling out to a specter created by her strange, ungovernable needs?

As if in reply to her foolish question, thunder rumbled ominously outside. Great! The threatening clouds were about to let loose. The only thing to do was wait it out. It made no sense to try to outrun a mountain storm.

Lenore sank down onto a ledge, the same one where she and Caroline had sat out the earlier storm. She turned off the light. Though it did have a solar-power cell, she had no idea how long it might last without recharging. Through the narrow slot of the opening, she saw a patch of moonglow slide into blackness. Moments later, heavy rain hissed onto the cold ground. The full fledged downpour arrived as rapidly as if someone had turned on a hose.

And there she sat, trapped in a cave where she'd come searching for a man, or a ghost, who had never for one minute really existed.

She felt like a fool, waiting there in darkness thick enough to choke on. She turned on the light again. She wanted to pretend to herself that the events of the past three nights—four, this one included—had never happened, which, of course, they had not, except in her distressed mind.

She was definitely a mental case. Fit only to be locked up. The best thing she could do for herself was wait for the storm to blow itself out then hike back down to the cabin and ride Mystery to the Quarries' ranch where she'd trade horse and fantasies for car and reality.

Then, she would hold herself together long enough to drive out of the mountains to where she could lock on to the nearest east-west glideway that would connect her vehicle with the westernmost north-south one, and go home. Then, she would visit her doctor again, and this time demand to be admitted to a psychiatric institute for her own safety.

She was clearly insane.

But . . . if you thought you were crazy, could you be? Probably not. She could take some comfort in that.

"All right," she said aloud, "let's sort out the dreams then and find a satisfactory explanation for them, if being nuts isn't it."

She'd known for a while that she wanted a long, secure, satisfying relationship and ultimately, a child, maybe more than one. That could account for the fantasies, for their graphic eroticism. She simply had needs that weren't being met, especially in the months since she'd broken up with Frank. No, for much longer than that, which was why she had broken up with him. Making love for five or ten minutes every Thursday evening after watching a holo Frank claimed would get him "in the mood" simply hadn't been adequate for her. She wanted more. Much more.

She blew out a long breath. Frank had not been the right one for her and she doubted, deep inside where most doubts lie, that the right man had ever been born. For that reason, her mind had created him. She smiled wryly, wondering whether she would end up with a phantom pregnancy she and the man ever actually made love during one of those dreams.

She'd once known a woman whose poodle had suffered from the delusion that it was pregnant. It showed all the signs and symptoms, got fat and waddled, but never produced a litter.

It was time she faced the undeniable facts that her

dreams had about as much chance of being met, given her age, as that poodle's did, given its owner's vigilance. Besides, who in her right mind ever really wanted to get fat and waddle?

Weary from her day's exertion, from the long, hard hike, still fighting a disturbing sense of loss, Lenore pulled out her floatpad, unrolled it, and stretched out on it. It maintained her body temperature, conformed to her shape, and kept her a comfortable few inches off the rock. She set her pack behind her and leaned her head and shoulders on it to rest for the trek down the mountain. She slumped farther down, extended her aching legs, turned off the light, and laid it close at hand in case she needed it. She let weariness overcome her and closed her eyes.

Closed her eyes, sensed his presence, opened them again and he was . . . there. There . . . and yet not there, more like one of the imperfect holo-images projected by a toy one of her friends had owned during their childhood before such things had been perfected.

Except . . . she saw his dry, cracked lips move, she heard as if he had spoken, a glad, echoing cry: *Minton!*

Chapter Four

Minton dragged himself through the field in which he had materialized. His skin burned from the coarse vegetation scraping his belly and limbs. He cast out a beam, searching for Wend, much more to him than just the Octad's healer, but his own birth-mate. He needed her, the solace and belonging he would find with her, or, in a lesser way, with one of the others. But there was no one.

Then, for a startling instant, he sensed Jon! He tried to focus, but the ephemeral touch was already gone. He knew it had been real. His *Kahniya* told him it had, exulted with him the hope that the Octad's leader lived, however precariously.

He crawled on as moonlight flooded the field around him. He knew not where he was going, nor really where he was, except half-buried in vegetation that scarcely struck him as edible. He was hungry, thirsty, and his

Kahniya provided just barely enough warmth to keep him alive. That he was naked suggested he had completed the translation alone. But . . . translation from where? To where? He had only vague memories of other places, of day, of night, of day again, and now, here he was in another night with dawn again approaching. He recalled other times of being naked and alone, of translating again and again in the ever-fainter hope of finding someone of his own on the vastness of this alien planet, Earth.

How could this, his first venture into joining an Octad, have gone so terribly wrong? Was it his lack of training? Was it because he'd been too anxious, too eager, too hopeful of finding Zenna, his bond-mate? Had his been the faulty concentration that had broken the connection with the others, sending them all whirling away into a black abyss? If only he had dared use the second version of the amplifier he and Zenna had invented! But he had not. He knew it was too unstable, for the same reasons the prototype had been, which was why he was certain, had always been certain, Zenna wasn't using it willingly to translate with Rankin. Those who knew and loved her, but especially himself and Jon, her birth-mate, were sure of her innocence, and feared for her.

Jon! He sent forth another probe into the night, felt it shoot away and dissipate into nothingness, meeting no other mind, no other soul, nothing to catch it, hold it, enhance and return it to him. He was blind, helpless, alone but for his *Kahniya*.

It subtly directed him to turn to his right, to keep crawling. Head down, he obeyed and was stopped suddenly when his skull connected with something solid. Looking up, he saw what he at first thought was a man towering over him, but on second look proved to be a doll of some sort. A very large one made of cloth, he realized, struggling to his feet to examine it more closely. It wasn't large as he had thought, merely high, held off the ground a distance equal to its height by the pole his head had bumped into. Its feet, had it been so equipped, would have rested at about his shoulder level. It wore one-piece garment from which some ragged, pale-colored material protruded at both arm and leg openings. It had a hat, but no shoes, and its arms and legs flapped in the chill breeze.

Nevertheless, clothing was clothing, and since this . . . creature was not a human, but a parody of one, he felt no compunction in knocking it to the ground. He tore it apart, watching the hat, a gray thing with a wide brim, roll away in the wind. He lacked the strength to chase it. He struggled to tug out the stuffing that formed the creature's body within the garment, then struggled even harder to get the clothing onto himself. Once pulled up, the outfit covered his legs only to his shins. The back of it strained as he shoved his arms into the sleeves and adjusted it to fit over his shoulders. It was far too tight, but he was grateful nonetheless for the covering it provided. He could zip it only halfway up his chest.

The effort of dressing had exhausted him. He lay back down in the dry vegetation he had pulled from the doll, letting his *Kahniya* replenish him as best it could. Light would help, and heat. To generate the latter, he crawled on.

But soon he stopped again to lie still and absorb light and faint warmth from a rising sun.

The land under him vibrated. A humming sound filled his ears. He struggled to sit, fighting the weakness that still held sway over his limbs. The act of sitting sent his brain swirling away into darkness again for long, unbearable moments where all he was aware of was being lost, being alone, being one, not part of a community of souls, not even part of the all important Octad. Falling back into the greenery, he shook his head, rose up more slowly, and sat, peering through the stalks of the plants at a large orange machine. It bore down on him, creating large tremors in the ground, indicative of its weight and power—and danger.

He fought to collect himself, to translate out of its way, but he didn't have enough strength left.

Forcing his battered body and bewildered mind to action, he staggered to his feet, reeled sideways, and stumbled out of the path of the machine. Before he fell again, he heard a shout. The noise of the machine changed. Then the mechanical beast came to a halt and the soil stopped quaking.

A man leapt down from a high perch atop the vehicle, strode through the vegetation, and stopped before him, looking up at Minton from under the brim of a hat.

"Well, hell!" He planted large, work-worn hands on his hips. "What have we here? What are you, some kind of nut? Trying to make crop circles or something in my winter rye? Gotta tell you, buddy, it works better when the stuff is ripe, like grain in the fall. Gotta tell you, too, it's crazy to do it barefoot here in northern Minnesota, even in May. There was ice on the pond this morning and—hey, are those my old coveralls from the scarecrow I left out last fall?"

The man waited for a moment, then tapped Minton on the chest, between the sides of the garment that failed to cover him. "Hey! You listening to me?"

"I am . . . listening."

"Yeah, but are you understanding? What are you doing out here, anyway, dressed only in my scarecrow's suit and your diamonds, Susie?"

Minton tried to make sense of the man's words. *Scarecrow?* "Diamondsusie?" he said aloud.

"This." The man reached for Minton's *Kahniya*, and Minton stepped back, clapping a hand to his necklace as he finally developed enough presence of mind to know he must not tell this man the truth. Desperately, weakly, he sought answers from within the man himself, chosing one of the wild speculations spilling out in an unending, uncontrolled stream from the stranger's brain.

"I picked up a hitchhiker. He knocked me out, hijacked my . . . rig, stripped me, and dumped me at the side of the road."

The man shook his head in disgust. "Too much of that happening nowadays. Used your chip to key your rig to his own, I suppose."

Not quite certain of how to answer, Minton shrugged noncommittally.

"So here you are, two full sections away from the road. Whyn't you stay where he put you? Better chance of getting help out there than in here. When'd this all take place, anyway?"

Minton was unsure of the concept of time as it might be seen here. "Long . . . time."

"Like last night? This morning? Yesterday some time?"

"Uh . . . last night, I think. Maybe the night before." How long would it take a man to find help in this part of Earth if he'd been dumped on the side of the road? He knew he couldn't tell this man about the other solo translations he vaguely recalled having made, or how long he suspected it had been since his Octad had broken contact. "Maybe . . . longer," he said.

Another chilly gust pushed against Minton. He wrapped his arms around himself, as closely as the too-tight garment across his shoulders would permit.

The man gave his head a hard shake and reached up onto the machine, bringing down a jacket similar to the one he wore, but heavier and longer. "Better put this on," he said, tossing it to Minton. "Then climb on up there." He stepped on a metal stair that lifted him easily aloft. He took his seat behind the controls, and the step sank back down. Minton clutched the side of the machine as he swayed with sudden weakness.

"Hey! You gonna pass out on me?" The man looked sharply at Minton. "You sick? Hurt?"

Minton steadied himself. "Hungry," he said.

"Well, come on," the man said with an impatient bark of laughter. "That's something that can be dealt with easy enough, but I haven't got all day. Get on up here. I'll take you back to the house. My wife will feed you." He grinned. "And she won't even debit your chip."

Chip . . . that was something he should know about, but what exactly escaped Minton at the moment.

"We can call the cops and get a line on your rig. What was it, anyway?" the man asked, as Minton allowed the step to lift him to the operator's platform. There was only one seat, so he stood, clinging to the clear shield in front.

"What was . . . what?" he asked, pulling the man's jacket more tightly around him. Its warmth was welcome. Already he felt stronger, but only slightly less confused.

"What kind of rig you drive?"

Again he grabbed at a stray thought. "A . . . reefer. Taking Alberta beef to New York."

"Yeah. That's what I figured. Price of beef nowadays,

it's worth anybody's while to hijack a rig. Anybody ever tell you picking up a hitchhiker's not smart? You shoulda just stayed on the main glideway all the way across the country."

He gave Minton a piercing look. "How come you left it in the first place? Got friends or family hereabouts?"

Minton shook his head. "No. I just wanted to see some of the countryside." That much, at least, was true. This being his first trip off Aazonia, he longed to observe everything. It was also what he was supposed to say in such situations.

The man laughed. "Not a hell of a lot to see, is there? Just fields and sky. Lots of that." He pulled up between two large buildings, one of which had a series of windows sweeping across its facade and a long stage, about shoulder height, accessed by stairs. On that, visible through a clear barrier beneath a railing, Minton saw chairs and a table, both of which he recognized from the images experienced Earth visitors had fed him, specifically Jon, and the others during the few hours leading up to the abortive translation. People on Earth ate sitting on chairs with their bowls on tables before them, not, as was the custom on Aazonia, reclining comfortably and sharing in a civilized manner.

Much good all that information had done him. He was as lost as he would have been without the bits of useless knowledge he had garnered.

He knew that he was going to have to come up with a better, more believable explanation for being found in the man's field before the authorities were called. What his rescuer believed would not satisfy anyone who probed deeper into the event. Jon and the other law-enforcement officers who had helped train him for this mission had impressed upon him the need for adequate "identification" in this society where there was no mental communication and hence no instant knowledge of each person encountered.

The chip! It was coming back to him now as warmth and a small sense of security assisted his *Kahniya* in healing him. The identification used on Earth in this time consisted of a chip implanted in the wrist bone of every individual at birth. It credited and debited its owner's accounts, activated all manner of devices keyed to that person—and identified its wearer to proper authorities.

He did not have one. Nor did any of the others. The unexpectedness of the window to here and now had prompted such swift action that there had not been time to counterfeit and imbed such a device in the wrists of the Octad.

"You're a big fella, I have to say that about you." The man interrupted Minton's flying thoughts as they descended from the vehicle. "Name's Harry Jenkins," he added, shoving a hand out in front of Minton.

Almost at once, Minton remembered this was a greeting, one that needed to be returned in kind. He extended his own hand and the man gripped it, gave it one quick shake, then released it, looking quizzically at Minton. "And you are?" Harry Jenkins prompted.

"Oh! Minton. Minton, uh, Ames," he said, remembering the man had offered two names for himself. "Ames" he took right out of Harry Jenkins's mind because when he'd commented on Minton's size, he'd thought about a family who'd once lived nearby, all big men, by the name of Ames, and wondered if Minton was related to them.

"Well, Mint, come along in then, and we'll get some breakfast into you."

Minton agreed and followed the man inside, where he met Harry's wife, Trinity, who served both men a huge meal. A meal Minton enjoyed far more than anything since Zenna's disappearance.

"Now," Trinity said, setting down her coffee mug, "I guess we'd better get the law informed so our guest can lay his complaint. Shouldn't be too hard to track down the rig with a satellite search for its chip, but the meat—" She looked at Minton and shook her head sorrowfully. "You know that'll be long gone, don't you?"

Minton sought for some sense of what she was talking about. Theft. Theft of foodstuffs. Was there so little to go around that such theft was a frequent occurrence? He dared not ask, so only nodded as if he understood.

"Okay, hon," Harry said. "You take care of that, and of Mint, will you? I'm back to plowing under that rye. One of my fallow fields," he said to Minton, as if that would explain everything. It explained nothing because Minton was too focused on what the woman was doing to give Harry much attention. The door slammed as Trinity waved the back of her hand in front of a small, infrared dot on the edge of a table.

At once, a holographic image leapt into being, a man with dark hair over the lower half of his face, as if to replace that which he did not have on top of his head. He held his fists linked before him on some kind of structure behind which he sat.

"Jerry, this guy is Minton Ames. He's got a tale of woe to tell you. Minton? Click your chip in right here, will you?"

Knowing he could do no such thing, Minton gathered himself, narrowed his focus . . . and left.

As Minton translated out of the sure danger of being found out by the local authorities, he heard distinctly and felt strongly Jon's unmistakable signature behind the ragged sound of his own name: *Minton!* He fixed his focus on it and tried to home in, but it had come too quickly, broken off almost before he was fully aware of it.

Where? He demanded of the ether. *Jon! Again!*

But the only mind his met was one that, at the moment, carried far greater power than Jon's weak and uncertain signature—and one that was infinitely more dangerous.

Rankin! Minton reeled and fell from his translation.

Rankin's rage slammed into Zenna at the same instant as she responded instinctively to the unexpected surge of a cherished, familiar signature. Her psychic cry of *Minton!* was lost in the fury of being snatched from where she stood, snatched from her child, snatched into blackness that seemed never to end until she awoke to the warmth, safety, and security of being five years old.

Without opening her eyes, she knew she sat curled on her grandfather's lap, listening to the story he told while the scent of spicy nut bread fresh from her grandmother's oven wafted to her on the breeze. She snuggled closer into her grandfather's cushiony warmth, reveling in the resonance of his voice taking on the character of each animal in his story. When his rumbled *grumpion* voice changed to a falsetto, mimicking the sounds of a terrified *welligan*'s squeak, she giggled, opened her eyes, and smiled up at him. "Say it again, Grandfather."

Sunlight, filtered through the leaves of a *belgrina* tree, played across his face. The wicker chair creaked as he rocked. She wanted nothing more than to stay there, to be safe, hidden in a place where nothing bad could ever happen. But slowly, agonizingly, adulthood returned and the knowledge that Rankin's anger could kill . . . someone? something? if she remained hidden in safety. At first, she knew not who Rankin was—only that he was an entity to fear, a presence to guard against. She didn't know why he was angry. Nor was she fully aware of whom he might kill if she failed to respond to his insistent probings, only that she must return to his where/when if she were to protect . . . someone.

Her body lifted and slammed onto a hard surface, jolting the last of the safe image from her mind, leaving her gasping with pain as the toe of a hard boot kicked her side.

"Open your eyes, woman!"

It was Rankin. Of course it was. And she knew he was the enemy. He had once been an assistant to herself and Minton, but now he was a captor, a traitor, an adversary. She opened her eyes to prevent being lifted and slammed against the floor again. He bent over her, one hand fastened in the front of her clothing, his black eyes glittering with malice, face drawn taut. In his other fist, he clutched a small, silver device she recognized, if only vaguely. Amplifier . . .

"Where is he?" he demanded.

Who?

Breath knocked from her lungs, she was unable to vocalize, as he had—and she loathed knowing she had let Rankin into her mind without so much as an attempt at shielding. Luckily, his anger had kept him seeking only one thing from her. He had not probed deeper.

"Speak, woman. You know who. You heard him. I heard him. Where is he?"

Zenna pulled in a difficult breath and, clutching at a wooden pillar of some sort, drew herself to a sitting position. She tasted blood in her mouth, on her lips, and knew Rankin had struck her face. One tooth rocked loosely as she tested it with her tongue. Swiftly, she called on her *Kahniya* to heal it, but the healing was already underway, curing not only her mouth, but the pain in her ribs as well. Her *Kahniya* was undamaged, which meant Rankin had no intention of killing her. Yet. Had he ripped it from her neck, though . . .

She struggled to her feet, realized she had climbed up with the assistance of a table leg, and leaned on its top, steadying herself as her vision swirled. The cold air, the low level of oxygen, and the view through the open door told her Rankin had translated the two of them to one of his other camps, this one high in the Andes. She sensed nothing of B'tar. Nothing of Glesta. And once more, as it had been for so very long but for that one, unbelievable instant, nothing of Minton.

Upright, she felt better, more able to face the man she hated, but still she refused to speak and kept her thoughts firmly cloaked from him. The amplifier, she knew, would be of little use to him for several more hours. She was surprised he had managed to translate them so far; the amplifier held so little energy after powering the recent trip from Aazonia to Earth. Only his rage and undoubted terror had permitted such an effort. She fixed him with a contemptuous stare. The only way to handle Rankin was to show no fear, to remain stronger than he. He held her daughter hostage, but despite that, she knew he needed her expertise to continue with his illegal practices. Without her to keep it tuned, the amplifier could fail at any moment. It could anyway, but so far, she had been able to keep it working.

Rankin glared at her. Finally, as she had known he would do, he broke the silence.

"I refer, of course, to Minton, your devoted mate. He is here on Earth. Near where we were."

She laughed. "He is not."

"You sensed him. I sensed him. He was searching, not for you, but for your brother." He set the amplifier in the broad beam of sunlight slicing low through the door, where it would gather power. "Both must be here. On Earth." His dark gaze narrowed. "I will find them, Zenna. And when I do, they will die. Unless you send them back."

She kept her tone cool, amused. "Unless my brother finds us first. At which time, he will kill both you and B'tar, and me, too."

She perched one hip on the edge of the table, hoping Rankin would fail to notice her shadow lying across the amplifier's absorption cells. It wouldn't stop the regeneration, but it would retard it. Full-strength sunlight was by far the best. The angle of the rays told her darkness would fall soon—and suddenly—as it did in these latitudes. The longer regeneration took, the more chance Jon would have to contact Minton, or Minton to contact Jon, without Rankin's enhanced senses detecting them.

"Really, Rankin, your naiveté amuses me. What we heard was nothing more than an echo. You will recall, we translated through the trailing edge of a solar storm. If you had put your moderate intelligence to more legitimate and less criminal usage in your youth, you would know, as do most people who study even elementary science, that such storms bounce signals through both space and time. Perhaps my former bondmate was calling to my brother from elsewhere . . . or elsewhen, and because I am, naturally, receptive to both their signatures, I heard them. With the aid of the amplifier, so did you.

"But," she continued, leaning toward him to keep her shadow over the receptors, "to assume that they are on Earth is to show your great ignorance of the facts. Not, of course, that I should expect better of you." Her scathing tone tightened his face. In reality, Rankin had an average—but badly misused—intelligence. It pleased her, though, to keep him angry with her by denigrating it whenever a chance arose. Angry, he tended not to think as clearly as he might otherwise.

"Let me explain in terms you might be capable of comprehending, *patán.*" She spat the last word at him, leaving no doubt that she meant it not affectionately, but as a slur on his intellectual abilities. His mouth tightened and his fists clenched, but she ignored those symptoms of his rage. Here and now, with the amplifier out of commission, he was helpless.

"When an Octad is translating—as my brother's must—without the mechanism you force me to employ, much energy is concentrated by those eight minds. When that energy is caught in a vortex, it is swirled around and can be cast out in many directions, not merely the direction it is aimed. Translation is not an exact science. That is why it takes a full Octad to translate between the links of space and time to achieve a certain objective—such as a window to Earth, in this time frame.

"The window through which we translated is narrow and ragged. No one of any sense would attempt to translate through it without the amplifier. Not if they expected to live."

Rankin's small eyes narrowed even further in suspicion. "What prevents your mate from reconstructing your experiments? He may have an amplifier now."

She laughed. "No, Rankin. Your own fears render you

paranoid as well as foolish. Minton knows as well as I do how unsuccessful my experiments were. He recognized before I did the instability of the invention. That is the reason he and I parted on such poor terms. I chose to believe in the validity of my own work. He chose not to."

She narrowed her eyes and twisted her lips in a show of scornful ire toward her husband. "He also chose to report what he saw—rightly, it turns out—as my failure, in order to stop me taking what he considered unacceptable risks. Yet, despite its having been a failure, at least scientifically, I cannot, will not, forgive Minton for what he did. Thanks to him, my permission to continue my studies was withdrawn before I had a chance to perfect the device."

She shrugged as if none of this was of great importance to her now. "Nor will he forgive me for refusing to believe him. We may have been bond-mated, but we were also competitors in our field. Bitter competitors, it turned out. Our espousal was terminated the moment he saw fit to denounce me. So if you think he'll come searching for me, you are wrong."

She drew a deep breath and let it out slowly. "My brother, of course, is a different matter. Trust me on this. When there is a window adequate for him to bring an Octad through to Earth, he will do so, and his purpose will be our deaths. Mine. B'tar's. Yours."

"There won't be another of those for ten years," Rankin said, clearly gloating. "So you rattle nothing more than empty threats, woman."

She smiled. "The Federation does not forget criminal activity, *patán*, nor does it forgive, so what I tell you is not a threat, but a promise. And I will do nothing to try to prevent or forestall that death. I would rather be dead than continue to assist you in your efforts to maim other civilizations with your poison."

"If you die, your child will die. I, personally, will see to that."

"You will not have a chance to do that," she said evenly.

"Oh?" He sneered. "You plan to do it yourself? If that were the case, you would have done it long since."

Zenna held her tongue still and her thoughts severely cloaked. Somehow, she would, through sheer strength of will, send Glesta to The Other before the moment of her own death came. The Other ... whom she had found by accident while carefully seeking another Aazoni mind. *Any* other Aazoni mind. It was a weak presence and untrained, but receptive both to her and to Glesta. The Other, Zenna knew, longed for a child, and she ruthlessly used that longing to create in The Other the perfect foster-mother for her daughter should one become necessary.

She shivered. With Jon on Earth, however unexpectedly, however impossible it might seem, that time could be much sooner than she had anticipated.

Chapter Five

Lenore. She wasn't sure whether it was a spoken word or an echo of something from her memory, another whisper on the wind.

Lenore! It came again and she turned her head, gasping at the sight of Jon. He was there! Really there. Beside her. As in the dream, bronzed and lying in a golden glow that emanated from him or maybe from his strange necklace. He lay naked, injured. And large. He was larger than life, larger than she'd dreamed. He must have been six and a half feet tall. His shoulders, sleek and exquisitely muscled, were the broadest she'd seen. And his legs . . .

She drew a deep breath, held it, bit her lip, felt the sting of her teeth penetrating the skin, and tasted the coppery taint of blood.

Which was the dream? Which was reality? What she saw now? Or the empty cave?

Tentatively, she stretched out a hand to touch him. Her fingers met with a hard-muscled shoulder. His skin was resilient, the form it sheathed solid. He was real enough.

But cold, terribly cold. She slipped off her floatpad and rose up on her knees over him. Oh, lord, was he dead?

No. His chest still slowly moved up and down as he breathed. As if in response to her touch, he rolled his head toward her, revealing a scalp gash crusted with blood. He moaned. His bent leg was even more swollen than it had been in her dream, the skin hard and shiny from ankle to knee except where the unnatural whiteness of a broken bone protruded through an ugly wound halfway up his calf. His foot still stuck out at an unnatural angle.

Lenore stared at him. Where in the hell had he come from? What's more, where in hell had he been? Or was there something wrong with her eyes, as well as her head? She blinked them, squeezed them shut, then opened them again. He was still there.

She slid forward and stepped off the ledge, circling in front of him. With gentle fingers, she touched his leg just above the ankle and felt, in contrast to the clammy cold of the rest of his flesh, a terrible heat of infection pulsating from it. He winced and emitted a soft moan. He must be real if he could feel pain.

She flicked a glance at his face. His lashes, long and dark with tips of gold, fluttered on the taut skin under his eyes, but did not open. She remembered the blood that she'd seen in the dream seeping from under his side. It was still there, a dark stain but dry, she realized, touching it, glad not to have to risk rolling him over to examine the injury from which it had issued.

A wisp of wind laden with the scent of evergreens wafted in, chilling the sudden beads of sweat on her face.

Goose bumps dotted the man's skin. He needed treatment, and he needed it fast. But there was no way, no way on earth she could move someone of his mass. Still, she had to do something for him. He must be near the point of hypothermia, if not already in its clutches, in the cool, dry air of the cave. Hypothermia. Shock. She tried to review what she'd learned of outdoor survival with the various hiking groups she'd belonged to over the years. None of it seemed adequate now.

She fumbled with the Velcro at the base of her pack, dragged her sleeping bag out of its case, opened it, and gently spread it over him, careful not to let it touch his injured leg. She considered trying to move him onto her floatpad, but knew it wasn't feasible. Still, the warmth of the bag should help. She turned its control to high.

He murmured something, tried again to open his eyes and then sank back into what appeared to be unconsciousness. She pulled a small stove from her pack, activated its cell, and set it on the floor of the cave just below their ledge, hoping the heat would rise and envelop him.

With shaking hands, she opened her first-aid kit and withdrew a packet containing a pad saturated with antiseptic. She cleaned her hands with the first one, opened another and bent toward his head.

He stirred and shifted, moaned as the wet cleansing tissue touched the open wound. "Shh," she said, carefully flicking out flakes of grit. "Lie still. Let me help you."

She finished cleaning his injury and the thick hair surrounding it, considered wrapping a bandage around his head, but decided against it. Better to let the gash air, though it must be kept clean. After stuffing a heavy sweatshirt into her sleeping bag case, she carefully slid one hand beneath his head. As she lifted him, she felt the silky thickness of his hair against her palm, flowing over her wrist. She slipped the makeshift pillow under his head, smoothing it on the rock before lowering him onto it.

Her first-aid kit was only a basic one, with no inflatable splints, which meant she would need to cut sticks to immobilize his leg before she lifted it onto the ledge. But in the meantime, as long as he remained unconscious, he wasn't moving it. It could wait until daylight, she decided, as would her trip out for help.

Suddenly, he made another sound, and her gaze flew back to his face. He parted his lips, his tongue came out as if to moisten them, then his head lolled to one side again. Of course, he must be thirsty. How long could the human body last without water? Could she wake him long enough to get him to drink some?

How long had he been in the cave? she wondered as she rummaged to the bottom of her pack, finding a stack of small, light cooking pots. She took the largest one, scrambled outside, and filled it from the bubbling spring. She'd had the first dream four nights earlier, she reasoned, entering the hideaway again, so if he had been responsible for what was happening in her head, he had been here at least that long.

After clipping on its detachable handle, she set the pot on top of her heater, not wanting to further shock his system with the glacial cold water.

She gazed at his face. It was probably the most perfect, the most beautiful male face she had ever seen and . . . she stared, leaned closer, looking harder. If he had been here for four days, where was his beard? He was certainly old enough to have one. Twenty-five, she thought, maybe as much as twenty-seven. At the very least a full decade younger than she.

Disappointment tasted bitter on the back of her tongue as she recognized the difference in their ages. Whatever promise she might have imagined, he was not for her. He would never be for her.

Young men wanted younger women. Men her age wanted younger women, too. Hell, let's face it, a man twice her age would prefer a woman half of it.

Some elemental part of her railed against such injustice. He was hers. She had found him. Didn't that give her some rights?

No. Of course not.

Besides, he could . . . She looked at him again. Hell, he could have any woman he wanted, any time, anywhere, and for a certainty, what he wanted wouldn't be a half-dried up accountant pushing thirty-eight. Not even one with a rich father, and it wouldn't take a genius to figure out pretty quickly that her rich father was too mean and ornery to die any time soon, so any expectations of her ever inheriting his wealth were damn slim.

His jaw was square, his brows, straight but for a slight lift in the center, were a shade or two darker than his hair. His nose sculpted a strong line down the center of his face, and his chin held a jut of determination even in his sleep. He emanated power, a presence that would fill any room, any house. His male potency was unmistakable despite the delicacy of the strange necklace he wore.

But it was his skin that fascinated her. It glowed that wonderful, bronze tone she had dreamed about. Clenching her lip between her teeth, she ventured to touch his shoulder, sliding the thin silver sleeping bag down several inches to expose more muscles and flat, dark nipples. Running an exploring hand over him, she told herself, recognizing the lie, that she was only checking his temperature. He was appreciably warmer now.

As was the water, she learned when she jerked away from the strong temptation to further explore his skin. He was unconscious, for heaven's sake! There was a name for people who did things like that.

She stirred the water with one finger, then soaked the corner of a bandage from the first-aid kit and held it against his lips, squeezing gently. To her gratification, his mouth opened and she managed to trickle several more drops onto his tongue.

She dipped and squeezed and dripped, watching his throat work as he swallowed. She gave him more, and this time, he sucked greedily on the cloth. He had consumed perhaps a quarter of a cup before she remembered that if he had internal injuries, giving him water might have been the worst thing to do.

It was not.

She stared at him. Had he spoken? Had he said that? No. He slept on, or remained unconscious.

Telepathy. The word popped into her head, as loud and clear as the denial she'd just heard. On its tail, hung fear. She squared her shoulders, trying to calm her whirling thoughts. She did not believe in telepathy any more than she believed in ghosts. Every pore of her being rejected the notion. It just wasn't possible!

Dammit, who was he? she asked herself. Where had he come from? Why was he here? Even more to the point, how, exactly, had he gotten here?

The questions whirled through her mind, answers, each more bizarre, tumbling in after them. Trying to keep them at bay, she went back outside to gather fire-wood, knowing she had to get more heat into the cave before she left him and hiked out for assistance.

What if he was a skydiver whose chute hadn't opened fully, letting him fall to the ground through the trees? she speculated as she broke brittle, dead limbs off tree trunks. His clothing could have been destroyed in the fall, couldn't it? He could, she supposed, have crawled into the cave.

With a compound fracture in his leg? Up those high, stacked slabs of rock that formed the three irregular stairs? No. Not a chance. Besides, assuming he had fallen through the trees, they wouldn't have totally de-stroyed even the cheapest jumpsuit on the market. There would have been tatters on him. If nothing else, today's fabrics—even so-called disposables—were tough, which was why environmentalists hated them. They didn't degrade for decades.

With a large armload of firewood gleaned from the forest, she made her way back. Maybe there was a se-cret nudist colony somewhere in the mountains and he'd wandered away, fallen, hurt himself and . . . right, crawled into the cave trailing his broken leg all the way up the rocky path. Sure he had.

She crouched beside the spot she and Caroline had discovered, on subsequent visits to the cave, made the best place for a campfire, and set down her bundle of sticks.

There had to be a better explanation for his naked presence. Hadn't she read somewhere recently about a photographer who inveigled his friends into stripping off their clothing, donning climbing gear and striking poses on sheer rock faces? The photographs were then turned into postcards, which reportedly sold faster than they could be printed. Tourists, it seemed, loved them for reasons perhaps best understood by a mind on vacation.

Was Jon one of those weird exhibitionists who volunteered to strip down and climb rocks, she wondered, glancing at his sleeping-bag shrouded form. She broke tiny twigs into little bits, laid them on top of a pad of dried moss and grass, and struck a sparker. If so, where was the photographer? And where was Jon's climbing gear? The article she'd read had carried pictures of groups of men and women incongruously looped with ropes around their bare middles, coils dangling from their naked shoulders, some with rope slings bisecting their buttocks like hefty G-strings.

She blew gently on the tiny flame as it licked up through the tufts of brown grass, catching in the twiglets, snapping and crackling. Carefully, she set larger branches around the small fire, watching them catch, grimacing at the rapidity with which they were consumed. She'd soon have to go out for more wood. She thought longingly of the poplar she'd split and left in an untidy heap by the chopping block. What she wouldn't do to have a big pile of that right next to the ledge. It would warm the cave nicely and burning it would be a lot more fun than stacking it when she got home again.

She glanced at the man on the ledge. If he'd fallen and hurt himself, and they'd put him there while they went for help, surely they'd have dressed him first, or at the very least, covered him! And they would have, if they'd had any sense at all, done just what she'd done, collected wood and tinder and started a fire to keep him warm.

Even assuming he'd had friends to do just that, the only trace of a fire was what she and Caroline had left.

The vent at the back of the cave sucked air in from the front, carrying away wisps of smoke with it. Lenore set a few more larger sticks on the small blaze, speculating on the possibility that the vent was wider than it appeared, back there in the darker end of the shelter. Could a man, falling from a great height, have plunged through it, breaking his leg and lacerating his scalp? Could he then, have managed to climb onto the ledge before passing out? But why would he have done that? The ledge certainly provided no better bed than the floor of the cave.

No, that plot line leaked like an old skiff, as a writer friend of hers was wont to say. There were too many holes in it. Notably, the narrowness of the crevice, which she and Caroline had examined, and the man's largely undamaged skin. He was also, she noted, very, very clean, which he would not have been had he somehow squeezed down that rock chimney.

So . . . what if he'd escaped from jail? Biting the inside of her cheek, she glanced at him again. Wasn't there a prison work camp somewhere along a side road off the highway to the south? She was sure she'd seen signs to that effect, and warnings not to pick up hitchhikers. Had he ditched his prison garb?

She frowned at her now briskly burning fire and shut off the stove to conserve its fuel since it was doing little to heat the cave anyway.

His being an escaped prisoner seemed an unlikely idea. Surely he wouldn't have dumped his clothes until he'd managed to snag a different outfit. She remembered the line full of clothing she'd seen being hung out in the sun and wind to dry. Yes, clothing was available.

And there was always the possibility that he was an escapee from a mental hospital. That, more than any explanation, appealed to her. Except the next most obvious one—that she was the fugitive from the booby hatch and he wasn't there now any more than he had been when she first arrived at the cave.

No, she decided, sitting on the ledge beside him again, resting back against her pack, as far as plot lines went, she liked best the one in which he'd been a nude mountain climber, showing off for a photographer who sold his wares to tourists. Maybe the rock chimney was a little wider than she'd thought. Maybe he could have slipped through it. Maybe . . .

Thunder crashed right overhead. Lenore jumped, waking from the doze she'd slipped into, her head and shoulders falling off the bag she'd propped herself on. Her inadvertent movement knocked the lightcell to the rocks below. Sliding down to the floor, she crawled along the ground, moving her hands carefully, searching for it in the fitful flickering of the dying fire and the faint glow that came through the entrance of the cave, suggestive not of moonlight now, but of a gray, misty dawn. The rain continued to hiss down in a steady stream.

Oh, damn! Damn! How long had she slept, dreaming that she was with Jon, caring for him, helping him? How strange. In the dream, there had been no need for artificial light in the cave. It was as if the two of them had been surrounded by an illumination that came from everywhere all at once. It had followed her outside, she recalled, making it easy to select the dry, breakable limbs that protruded low on the trunks of mountain hemlock trees. Then, there had been no thunder, no rain, as if a giant umbrella had covered the territory around the entrance to the cave. She'd had no difficulty finding dry clumps of grass or the brittle beards of moss she'd used for tinder.

Yet now, it was dark in the cave. Now, it rained out-side.

Her left hand encountered the lightcell and she scooped it up, switched it on, grateful for the reassuring beam that it issued.

Dammit, if she had been lying there with her head on her pack, sleeping again, how had she gathered wood, lit the fire? She touched her jacket. It was dry. Clenching her teeth, she did what she had, until this moment, not dared to do.

She swung the beam of her light, and her reluctant gaze, toward Jon.

He wasn't there. Her sleeping bag lay flat on the rock, one corner hanging down toward her. She grabbed it, jerked, and it slithered down, leaving nothing exposed but the makeshift pillow she'd fashioned and her half-empty pack. That . . . and a brownish stain that might have been blood. Or the residue of something she or Caroline had spilled during a picnic twenty years before.

"No!" She heard the tight whisper emerge from her throat, squeezed her eyes shut, hoping, and saw nothing but star-shot dark, tinged red, and opened them again.

"Clap your hands if you believe in fairies," she said, and clenched her fists at her sides lest she do something so inane as clap her hands.

The pot of water stood on the little cellstove. She touched it. It was cold. Her mouth was dry. She felt weak, more exhausted than at any time in the weeks before she'd forced herself to seek medical help. It was as if her very substance had been drained away by these recurring dreams. She lifted the pot, sipped from it, slaking her terrible thirst, set it back down carefully and hunkered by the stove, closing her eyes again, gently this time, waiting, waiting, waiting.

She let her mind go blank, left it open, tried to let it float free, suspending disbelief, but no apparition appeared, injured or otherwise when she opened them again. No bronze-skinned, golden-haired man spread his superb body over the rock shelf at her knee level.

To remind her exactly how pedestrian her life was, always had been, always would be, her stomach growled, calling forth a memory of the stew she'd packed into two tight-lidded plastic containers the night before. And the loaf of bread she'd brought to supplement the emergency rations of dried food in her pack.

She quickly rebuilt the fire, stacking a good supply of freshly split, dry poplar around and over the twigs and limbs, watching it catch and snap, flames leaping high to illuminate the cave. Using the last of the water in the pot, she washed her hands, opened one container of stew and put it in the saucepan before turning on the stove again. Setting the now unnecessary light on the ledge above her, she held the loaf on her knee, sliced off two thick slabs of bread, spread butter on them with the same knife and laid one aside. She sank her teeth into the other and enjoyed it while the rest of her meal heated. Hunkered by the stove, warmed by the blazing fire beside her, she stirred the stew, sniffing the good, meaty aroma that began to rise.

She added more wood to the fire, feeling its warmth begin to penetrate throughout the cave and then sat on the corner of her sleeping bag to eat the stew. As its sustenance filled her, the feeling of weakness diminished. She sopped up the last of the gravy and swallowed the last crust of bread. Taking the pot outside, she rinsed it, filled it again, drank from it and carried it back inside.

"Now why," she asked herself, standing erect in the

cave and staring at the water, "did I do that?"

"Because I'm thirsty," Jon's voice said and her skin prickled as the hair tried to rise off her scalp.

Lenore dared not turn and look at the ledge. She watched circles ripple across the surface of the water as her hands began to shake. "Go away," she said. "My eyes are wide open. I'm awake. You do not exist. I cannot hear you."

"Your food smells good. Will you share it with me as you shared the water, before?"

"Phantoms do not eat." They shouldn't be able to swallow water, either, she knew, nor suck it greedily from a wet cloth.

"But mountain climbers do."

She flicked a quick, sideways glance at the ledge, through the heat shimmer of the fire, and saw a leg dangling, a foot twisted awkwardly, tight, shiny skin, more blue than red now, rising toward a bent knee. The broken bone had disappeared, the wound through which it had protruded scarcely existed. She closed her eyes, opened them, then looked again.

Lifting her head, she saw the rest of him, his head up now, his upper body lifted as he half-rose onto his elbows. His eyes shone green, his hair gleamed. His teeth, when he smiled at her, flashed pure, beautiful white making her feel guilty for having missed her last dental appointment. He was lifeguard gorgeous and awake, infinitely more of a potent presence than he'd been unconscious. Inside, she trembled.

"I am very hungry."

She knew he was. She felt his hunger as intensely as she had felt her own, knew intimately the degree of his thirst and again the word telepathy clanged an alarm bell inside her.

No, no, no! The thought brought revulsion as well as renewed fear. She did not want, could not bear the idea of someone messing with her head, getting inside her private thoughts, reading them, knowing her innermost being. Dammit, there were places in there even she refused to go!

She wanted to scream, wanted to run, wanted to hide. Which was insane, because telepathy was not possible. He was not dipping into her thought stream and ladling out what he wanted. He could not be; therefore he was not.

Shivering, despite the warmth now reaching well beyond the fire, she stepped around the flaming wood—and stared, becoming fully aware that, exactly as she had wished, she now had a big stack of the split poplar from the pile behind her cabin. She didn't have the faintest idea how she'd gotten it there.

She couldn't think about that now. She spilled the water from the large pot into the two smaller pots, emptied the second tub of stew into the largest one and turned on the cellstove again.

She risked another glance at the ledge. She frowned at his recumbent, naked form and quickly covered him with the sleeping bag.

"Thank you," he said. "It takes a great deal of . . . energy, trying to keep warm. Especially when one is healing. That is why I required . . . drink—and required you to drink—before I could wake up. My energy stores had been quite . . . depleted, first, by healing the break in my leg, and also by bringing the firewood you wanted. Either should have been an easy task. Both were difficult, but necessary. You required warmth as much as I if you were to have strength to share with me."

"Yes," she said, as if she knew what he was talking

about, which, in a way, she supposed she did, however little sense it made. The fact remained, the firewood was there, and she didn't recall trekking all the way back to the cabin for it. That would have taken at least ten trips back up that steep mountain track with a filled wheelbarrow, and surely she'd know—her muscles would know—if she'd done something so utterly ridiculous. Unless it, too, was a fantasy.

The fire it made felt good and warm, though.

Lenore crouched beside Jon, this time holding the vessel of water to his lips while he drank. Then, backing away, she sliced bread, buttered it, laid it aside.

She poured a portion of the stew into the plastic container and stuck a spoon into it. Setting it on the ledge beside him, she helped him sit more erect and gave him her pack to lean on. "Can you manage it yourself?" she asked, handing him the food. "Or would you like me to feed you?"

He smiled again. "You may feed me." It was, she thought, as if he were bestowing a favor.

She fed him.

Chapter Six

As she broke a bit off one slice of bread and put a morsel into his mouth, the term "break bread together" popped into her mind.

"Breaking bread is an old tradition," he said, startling her, making her jerk her fingers back from the soft brush of his lips. "It makes us friends." His words, had a strange ring to them, as if they had been rehearsed, but not well, a certain hesitancy, as if he were forced to translate each one before speaking it.

Many people had accents, and even if English wasn't his first language, he could have heard the phrase. It was a thought that could occur to anyone who performed or watched the act of breaking, rather than cutting bread. The term probably came into being before the widespread use of knives as table implements.

The logic of her reasoning reassured her. He was not

reading her mind. She shoveled a heaping spoonful of stew into him.

"The tradition," she said, aware of sounding pedantic, "is that people who have 'broken bread' together, that is shared a meal, should not be enemies. I don't believe it's ever been said that eating from the same loaf automatically makes people friends."

He merely looked at her and opened his mouth for more stew. When he had eaten all that she'd put into the plastic container, she offered him more, which he took hungrily, along with great, insatiable gulps of water and three more slices of bread.

"You said you're a mountain climber," she said when he appeared to be replete. "What is your name? I'm sure someone has reported you missing. I'll have to go and get help, and let the authorities know that you've been found."

"Help?" he asked, cocking his head to one side. "Why do you need help?"

Lenore had to laugh at his inane question. "I don't need help," she said. "You need it!"

"Why?" he asked again. "We are together now." It occured to Lenore that he said it as if together they could do anything.

"Together, we can do anything," he said, and she backed away from him quickly.

"Stop that!" she said sharply. "Stop reading my mind!" Then she edged away another foot or two, conjuring up a weak laugh. "I mean, I wish you didn't act as if you can read my mind. I know, of course, you really can't. It just . . . seems that way, sometimes. It makes me . . . uncomfortable."

He looked dismayed and almost comically guilty, like a small child caught in a shameful act. "I will not probe your mind again. You let me in, therefore I assumed you to be willing. I apologize for my error. From now on, I will only read those thoughts that you project to me." He did not look as if the words lay easy on his tongue. She wondered whether he had ever apologized to anyone else before. A man as beautiful as he was had probably sailed through life getting away with murder.

She shivered again, remembering her speculations about his origins. Ted Bundy, a twentieth-century mass murderer whom she had studied in an online psychology course, had been an extraordinarily handsome man, too. A fact that had probably led his victims to like him, to trust him, to fail to be suspicious of him and his motives.

"It is not my way to intrude," he continued. "But, impaired as I am, and with you expressing no objections in the beginning, I thought it was acceptable for me to borrow from your strength and health." He reached down and slid a hand over his injured leg before covering it with the sleeping bag. She gasped, expecting him to pass out again at the pain he must have caused himself, but apart from a slight wince he appeared unaffected.

"You are . . . still bothered by something," he said, then added quickly, "I can see it in your face. I was not entering your mind. I will not. I have promised."

Lenore stood from her seat on the ledge and stepped down, facing him from several feet away, meeting his puzzled green gaze. "Damn right I'm bothered by something," she said, refusing to be taken in by his guileless look, his crazy promise. Of course he wouldn't read her mind "again." He had never done so in the first place.

There was no way he could, and she didn't need any promise of his to be certain of that.

"I'm bothered by a whole lot of stuff here, buster. Suppose you just quit being coy and tell me who you are, what you're doing here, and where your climbing companions are."

Now pain showed in his eyes, in the curved lines that bracketed his mouth. In that moment, he looked older than the twenty-seven years, max, she had given him. "I do not know where my . . . companions are," he said, and she understood somehow that to him emotional pain was worse, by far, than any physical discomfort his broken leg might cause. "That is why I require your help. To find them. They need me. I am their leader. I am responsible and I . . . lost them."

"Who are they?"

"My Octad."

His words, so simply spoken, forced her in some odd manner to recapture the desolate, lonely feeling she had experienced shortly before leaving the cabin. As if an echo had rung out in the cavern, she realized that "Octad" was the word she had been unable to understand, that she had in her dream believed meant a combination of she, them, and it. Octad. The eight. Odd, how she understood it now. Or . . . did she? Once more, she experienced the image of hand-linked skydivers, but also had the sense it meant much more. Maybe she had come up with the word Octad, requiring something her mind could accept.

She had the odd feeling it could mean "family," but the perception of a much deeper relationship remained. Or was it simply that she lacked the customary concept of family, having never really had one? She strongly wished for a means to understand this entire event, to understand him, who he was, why he was here, and why he had called her to him.

Without knowing quite how she had gotten there, she found herself standing beside him as he reclined on the ledge. She reached out, unable to prevent herself from giving in to the curiosity that drew her, and touched just one glowing bead on his necklace.

It was as if a small electric current zipped up her finger, through her hand, her arm, and snapped her lids closed over her eyes. In that instant, she saw a garden—no, she was in a garden—lush and rich and flower-filled. She smelled incredible scents from blossoms growing in thickly planted beds, rioting across lawns, hanging—dripping—from delicately limbed trees and shrubs. The predominant colors, pink and yellow and green, glowed under a sky of turquoise blue. A placid stream meandered past. Fish jumped, silver in the sunlight. Birds with exotic plumage and sweet calls flitted from tree to tree. It was a Maxfield Parrish setting, and she yearned to wander through it, to accept the peace engendered by the landscape. It reflected . . . no, projected, a sense of homecoming, a recognition of perfect harmony, a knowledge that here was sanctuary from all that could ever bring harm or discord. She longed to follow that stream, to discover where it led, to circle past the trees that blocked further view, knowing somehow there would be other incomparable vistas revealed with each step she took.

She staggered slightly from the impact of the vision, and the movement unlocked her fingertip from the golden bead of light, breaking contact. She remembered to breathe as she stared at Jon, watching him watching her.

She clenched her teeth, resisting with all her might

the desire to touch that bead again, to return to the warmth of that unreal garden.

The desire eased enough for her to step away from the ledge, away from Jon, away from temptation, and suddenly she was assailed by the memory an earlier sensation, one of desperate need, of incomparable loss, of being forsaken, or of having forsaken someone—no, not one, others—of great value. It echoed too closely the feelings engendered by her dream of the mother seeking a haven for her endangered child.

"You must help me . . . collect my Octad," Jon added, his green eyes fixed squarely on her, and she experienced a tug of emotion so strong it nearly drew her back to his side. "You must help me take them home."

A flicker of the Maxfield Parrish–like landscape flashed before her, but she battled it down.

"I don't 'must' do anything," she retorted, glaring at him, and felt the pull subside. "Not even stay in this damned cave."

"No!" His voice was sharp, his facial expression one of disbelieving hurt. Clearly, he thought her capable of abandoning him there, which of course, her hasty words had suggested. "You must not leave me."

"I will, of course, get help for you," she said. "But you have to be willing to help yourself, too, by answering my questions. In case you aren't aware of it, you have a badly broken leg and a head wound that should have been stitched. As it is, it's probably too late for that, and you'll end up with a scar. It's a good thing your hair is thick."

"Why?" he asked, his head tilted in curiosity. "For all its thickness, my hair did not protect my head from injury."

She frowned at him. "It's good that it's thick because it will hide the scar."

He sat silently for a moment, studying her. "What is a 'scar'?"

"What is a scar?" she echoed, and he nodded. She closed her eyes for a moment as sadness filled her. Was that the answer, then?

The poor soul was mentally incompetent! She'd seen other simple people who had great physical beauty, serene faces, unlined regardless of age, because they had no cares, no worries to mark them. It explained much, she thought, then reeled under the barrage of new questions her conclusion raised.

Maybe he seemed intelligent at times, but there were idiots savant, weren't there, who could play beautiful music, but not be trusted to walk across the street alone? There were those who could add massive columns of figures in their heads, but were unable to master the complexities of putting on their own socks. Maybe this man had something going for him, but a good vocabulary wasn't part of it. *What is a scar, indeed.*

"I need to know who you are," she said gently, ignoring his question about the scar. It was unlikely he'd remember having asked it, or care about the reply if he did. "You have to tell me how you got here." She managed what she hoped was a reassuring smile. "Someone must be worried about you."

Again, he looked at her sadly. "My entire Octad will be concerned, disturbed by my absence—assuming they still live." His throat worked as he swallowed. "I have no sense of them! Not even of Fricka, who maintains our surround. Only of you . . . and some dim points of light and strength where assistance might have been

91

found had you not come. But you did, so I released them."

"You . . . released them," she echoed. "I'm sure they appreciated it." Not that she believed him for a minute, but . . . the fact remained she was here in this cave, and she had the creepy suspicion that he had actually caused her to make the hike up the mountain. The "how" of it all was another matter. One she chose not to dwell on too long.

Moving closer, she touched his hand gently. His skin was nicely warmed now. It felt good to touch him. She wanted to wrap her fingers around his wrist and slide them up over his arm, to feel the crispness of the hair that lay so neatly, almost invisible, over his skin. She wanted to crowd closer, press her cheek against his bare chest. She wanted to put her arms around his torso and rock him tenderly, cradle him, nurture him, feel him nurturing her. She wanted to touch that necklace again! She wanted that quite desperately, wanted to . . . know!

What is it you wish to know? his voice asked inside her head. She was sure it was inside her head. She had heard him, yet his lips had not moved. They still did not as he added, *You need only ask. Touch my* Kahniya *again and it will share my life with you.*

Quickly, Lenore edged back again. "Who are you?" she demanded, surprised by the hoarseness of her voice. What she had really wanted to ask was *What* are you? The realization that she was actually unsure of what he was, terrified her.

"I am Jon," he said. He smiled, a smile that beguiled her, drew her to him as strongly as had the warmth of his skin. "Yes, it could be short for Jonathon," he added, though she had not said that name aloud. "Do you like it?"

92

She stared at him.

He nodded. "You do. It is a good name. You may call me that if you wish, though I am more accustomed to Jonallo, or simply Jon."

"Jonallo?" The emphasis was on the middle syllable. It sounded like . . . like some kind of skin preparation to take care of itching.

"That is correct. My parents, Attana and Ling named me so. It means Bold One. And you are Lenore."

Had she told him so? Had she called him by his name since arriving in the cave? Obviously, she must have, but she didn't remember. A vague memory surfaced, of the voice in her living room using her name. She shoved it away.

"All right, Jon," she said, refusing to buy into the Jonallo name he wanted her to believe, or the names of his supposed parents. What kinds of names were those, anyway? Ling? He certainly lacked any visible connection to the Chinese race. He was going to great lengths to confuse her, and she recognized a snow job when she saw one. He reminded her of the many people she had met who pretended to be so open and aboveboard that no one, not even the IRS could possibly doubt the veracity of their tax returns. She'd learned to watch out for them—they could be dangerous to her professional integrity. They were the kinds of people she insisted reveal every detail of their taxable transactions. Luckily, in her profession, she was allowed a reader that could delve more than just superficially into any client's chip. If any refused to cooperate with her, she refused to work for them. Too bad she didn't have it with her in this cave. Or even in the log house down the mountain.

She'd simply have to rely on her own instincts.

"Now, let's have the truth," she said. "Let's start with

the basics. What are you doing in this cave, without your clothes?"

"I am a mountain climber," he said. "I was climbing in the nude for a photographer who sells the pictures to a . . . company that makes postcards. People from foreign . . ." He pursed his lips before going on, as if searching for an unfamiliar word again. "Foreign . . . nations buy them."

Lenore put even greater distance between them. She stared at him through the heat shimmer as she crouched to lay another few chunks of poplar on the fire. Had she been talking aloud during her speculations? It wouldn't surprise her. She'd been babbling to herself all week.

"I see," she said. "And where is the photographer?"

"I do not know."

"Where is your climbing gear?"

He blinked, looked thoughtful, and then shrugged those magnificent shoulders. His abdomen rippled above the silver fabric of the sleeping bag. "Perhaps . . . up there," he said.

He glanced at the cleft in the rocks where the smoke wafted away.

"I was up there and fell, uh, through." His tone was bright, as was his smile. His expression was one of pride. "I slid down that chimney and crawled to where I now lie."

"Yes," she said, narrowing her gaze at his handsome, ingenuous face. "Where you now 'lie.' Lie, as in 'tell untruths.' "

Again, he looked so guilty she wanted, inanely, to laugh. "I have no wish to tell you untruths, but . . ."

She glared at him in irritation, paced back to stand at the bottom of the ledge, her eyes on a level with his as he sat leaning on her pack. "But what? That story about the climbing, about the photographer, it's too pat, Jon," she said. "Too much an almost verbatim repetition of what you must have heard me saying while you pretended to be unconscious, and I don't accept it now any more than I did then. I was merely speculating in the absence of any concrete evidence."

He looked perplexed, charmingly so, much too charmingly so. "I did come through that chimney. Or perhaps just . . . near it."

"No damn way!"

Snatching up the lightcell, she rushed to the back of the cave, crouched, narrowed the beam and directed it upward. She turned back to him triumphantly. "As I thought. It hasn't enlarged itself miraculously over the past twenty years. You'd need to have as little substance as the smoke from the fire to have come through that cleft. Now, I strongly suggest, mister, that the next few things you tell me had better be true, or I'll walk out of this cave and forget I ever met you."

He looked at her for a long moment as if assessing the depths of her intentions, then said, "I had much less substance than the smoke when I came through that crevice, or perhaps through the—the very stone itself— of these cavern walls. But because I was weak, because I was lost and alone, I could not control my descent. I lacked the strength and cohesion provided by my Octad."

"So how did you get, here, then?" she all but shouted, entirely losing her patience.

"My—" Again, there was a word that sounded almost like a song, so alien to her that she could only guess at which language it might have its root in, but he touched his necklace—"was able to give me guidance. It found shelter for me in this cave. But even it, due to electronic interference from the solar storm, could not prevent my materializing before time."

Lenore sank down onto a stack of rock slabs near the fire. "Materializing," she said. Her voice sounded hollow to her own ears. Sickly, she recalled the times when he had not been in the cave with her—or had not seemed to be. Had he been "dematerialized" then?

Feeling like Alice, she asked him.

He nodded. "I was dematerialized. But now I am fully corporeal." He thumped his very solid chest with hard knuckles. "I will remain in my corporeal state. As you are, so you can see me. So you can touch me. I enjoy having you touch me. Will you do it again?"

Lenore had serious doubts as to her own state, corporeal and mental, but held back from expressing them. "Not on your Nelly, pal!"

His face took on a half-questioning look, head tilted slightly to one side. "I cannot access the word 'nellypal.' Will you explain it for me?"

"I'll explain nothing to you until you tell me what the hell you're doing here, where you were when you weren't here, and when you expect to disappear again." She glared at him. "I hope it's soon!"

Jon recognized the fear in her tone, and wished she would allow him to properly alleviate it. Since she would not, he would have to do his best without the required soothing mind-touch. "I will not disappear again," he said. "I did it only because it was very difficult for me in my weakened condition to maintain control over my form. The food, water, and warmth you brought me will allow me to remain as I am now, and to heal."

"Another lie," she accused, her gaze following his fingertips as he lifted a hand to his head.

"Oh, no. It is the truth."

"Jon . . . if your name is Jon, you are beginning to annoy me mightily! Get on with it. Tell me your story!"

"If I must, to please you, then I will, but you know it yourself, if you would but admit it. I have given you all the information you need. More, you took from my *Aleea-Kahniya.*"

"Ah-lee-yah-ka—what?"

"Ah-lee-yah-kah-nye-ah," he said slowly. Again, he touched his necklace and for an instant, he knew how deeply she longed to do the same.

Her entire being reverberated as she projected the desire to revisit his home. Through the brief glimpse she expelled, he knew she would always think of it as a beautiful, magical garden filled with sweet scents, warm breezes, dazzling birdsong, and that incredible sense of peace. As her throat ached with the need to return there, so did his; he wanted to help her return, if just for a moment. He admired the courage and determination she evinced as she forced her mind away from the temptation to touch his *Kahniya*, or even the single *Aleea* she had stroked.

"*Aleea-Kahniya*," she repeated, then frowned, her mouth twisting to one side as if in disgust. He sensed she was disappointed in the way the words came out flat and unmusical in her voice. Without her knowledge that she was once more projecting, he heard her mind say the syllables over, and over, striving for the proper lilt. He knew she had heard it. He knew, too, that soon she would be able to replicate it. She had an amazingly quick and agile mind. She needed only train her vocal processes.

"We seldom use the full word, though," he continued. "Just *Kahniya*. Each of us has one. Our parents create it for us at birth, with only two small *Aleeas*. As a child grows and learns, he adds more *Aleeas* to his *Kahniya*."

"What does it do for you?" she asked, then spun away angrily. Of course. She hadn't wanted to ask because she didn't want to give him or his story any credence at all. The fact that she had blurted out the question gave him hope.

"It is my center," he explained. "It holds all my memories and those of my family for whenever I choose to access them. Because in my employment I must do much traveling, I often choose to use it in this way. I need only to touch it to be where I want to be, with those whom I love, in places where I feel safe and happy. The *Aleea* you touched took us to my grandparents' estate on the Isle of Nokori. It is a beautiful place, is it not?"

She didn't answer, but half turned back, watching him warily.

"My *Kahniya* also guides me through difficulties," he went on. "It keeps me as safe as it can. It is my pathfinder through danger, seeking shelter for me when I am injured or ill and unable to find it for myself. It helps me heal myself.

"Though this is my first visit here, I am not entirely unfamiliar with Earth," he went on. "But I do know that you of this world do not have *Kahniyas* in which to store your *Aleeas*." He smiled. "Would you like me to help you create one as a reward for assisting me, for coming to me when I called you?"

She shook her head rapidly. "You did not call me! I had a dream. Maybe one so compelling I acted like a fool and hiked up the mountain in the night. I knew of this cave, so of course that's where I came when the weather became threatening. That I found you here was pure luck. Your luck, buddy, not mine."

"I would be pleased to teach you to create your own *Kahniya*," he said, completely ignoring her diatribe. "But to do so, I would need to enter into your earliest memories. I could not, of course, recover them all, but many of them will still be present."

Lenore wanted to scream and rail against his quiet assurance that he could do what he said. It was insane! As if one of those golden beads—that looked more like light than anything of substance—could possibly hold the image she had seen of the tropical garden. The tropical garden he now claimed belonged to his grandparents.

The bead she'd touched, though, had been warm, almost alive, and had given off a palpable but pleasant current.

"What possible need would I have of a *Kahniya?*" she demanded in frustration. As she repeated the three syllables again they fell short of sounding as liquidly musical as when he spoke them, but she thought, oddly pleased despite her failure, she was improving. He didn't comment, but his smile told her he appreciated her attempt.

"To access your memories," he said.

"I have access to all the memories I want," she assured him loftily. "Anything I have forgotten, I've likely done so because remembering it would not be beneficial to my mental health."

Hell! Talking with him was not beneficial to her mental health, which had been precarious enough for her to have conjured him up.

"Your mental health is excellent," he said as if he were positive. "You concern yourself for no reason. Seeing me, hearing me, doing as I asked you to, is not evidence of madness, merely evidence of your being receptive to my needs. Even before I came, I believe you must have had some knowledge, whether you are aware of it or not, of me and my kind."

"I have knowledge of numbers, of facts, of reality," she insisted. "But certainly no knowledge of voices that whisper on the night winds and disturb my dreams." Even to her, the denial sounded as hollow as it was.

"You must have," he said, "or your talents would not be so well-honed. You may be developing a latent ability. I have been told that such exist on Earth, though rarely. Your race is not as evolved as some, but it's happening. Slowly, as most evolutionary changes do. You could be a harbinger of things to come. But without entering your mind, which I will not do again without your permission, I cannot tell. I know only that your mind is receptive to that of an—"

She didn't understand the word. "A what?"

"Ah-zone-ee," he said slowly. "I am from Aazonia." When he repeated it in normal-time, it emerged as mellifluous and rhythmic as the word *Aleea-Kahniya*, she thought, like the name of a Southwest native tribe or a Polynesian group, though he didn't look either—except for that bronze skin.

Oh, for heaven's sake, he hadn't said "Aazonia." He'd said "Estonia." His accent was strange. But did it sound . . . Russian? No. But . . . Maybe people from Estonia didn't speak Russian. "Estonia's near Russia, isn't it?"

Jon sat watching her solemnly, his much-less swollen leg still hanging over the edge, her sleeping bag piled on his lap. He looked strangely vague for several seconds before he nodded and said, "Yes. Estonia is near Russia."

She stood and kicked the toe of one hiking boot against a chunk of wood that had rolled out of the fire and watched curls of smoke rise and dissipate as twig ends caught the heat and ignited. "I've heard that Russian scientists have been doing some sophisticated experiments with mind control." Let's see how he reacted to that.

He said nothing, but continued to watch her. She took several steps toward the entrance to the cave. If she ducked and scrambled out, could he catch her? Could he force her, through imposing his will on hers, to stay? Had he truly, in that way, compelled her to come to him? If so, why? Were the Russians, or Estonians, or the Latvians for that matter, any kind of threat to her way of life? No. Not after all these years of relative peace. But why else was he sitting there naked, other than to prevent his place of origin being traced through his clothing? Surely, though, if his people were advanced enough to have perfected ESP, they'd have been able to fabricate a suit of supposedly local clothing and proper identification for their agent.

Oh, damn! She'd obviously read too many international espionage novels from the old books Grandma and Grandpa Francis had left behind.

She paced, stopped, one hand on the rock face, trying not to let him know how hard she was shaking. "Did you—" She swallowed hard. "Did you really compel me to come to the cave to help you? Did you get into my head somehow and make me want to come to you?"

He looked faintly wary she thought. "Yes. I did do that."

"Why?" Again, all she could manage was a taut little whisper.

"Because I needed help. My strength was all but gone. I was near death, and you were my best resource. Without water, without food, I was unsure I could even begin to heal myself, even with the assistance of my *Kahniya*. But I did not 'force' you to come. I offered you what you needed in return for what I needed."

"What *I* needed?" Lenore reeled away another step or two, remembering what he had offered her, remembering how willing she had been to accept it from him. "How could you possibly know what I need?"

"It was all there. It was easy for me to see. And easy for me to allow you to see it. I thought you would be happy. I truly did not know it would cause you pain, my opening your inner spirit to your conscious mind. And I did need you to come to me. But I would never expect you to give me what I require without offering you something of value in return. It is not the Aazoni way."

"Aazoni." All right. She gave in. He had said "Aazoni," not "Estoni." She knew that. Her head spun. Dry air and open-mouthed breathing sucked moisture from her throat, leaving her scarcely able to swallow. She looked at him, sitting there so calm, so serene, so . . . oblivious, or maybe simply uncaring, of the violation he had perpetrated on her. Fury erupted through her body, boiled up, and spewed out as powerful, as sudden, and as violent as last night's storm.

Chapter Seven

"You arrogant, inhuman son of a bitch!" she said. "You got into my mind! You dipped into my private, most secret places! You intruded where you had no right to intrude! You used me, used my deepest emotions, my most basic human needs and pretended to offer me all I had ever wanted, simply so I'd bring you a drink of water?

"All right, you bastard! I'm getting out of here right this minute! One of us is crazy, and I prefer it not to be me. It shouldn't be hard for the FBI to locate a Greek god in his birthday suit, so good luck, sucker. I'm turning you in!"

She dove for her pack, intending not to leave him so much as a crumb of comfort. If he'd gotten himself here in the nude, he could get himself out in the nude. He could teleport himself right back to Estonia for all she cared, but she wasn't assisting him anymore. Whatever his purpose, she wanted no part of it. She snatched her sleeping bag off him.

"Lenore."

His voice, soft and mellow, stopped her as she tried to stuff the bag into its case. She refused to meet his gaze. If he could do all the things she suspected, could he also kill with a glance?

"You are right. I can be arrogant, and I am guilty of using your needs to draw you to me. You are also right to call me inhuman. But one point," he said, and now she lifted her head, looking up at him. "You are wrong on one point." He moved off the ledge, took his weight gingerly on his broken leg with its crooked foot, then took another limping step. He was very close to her. Very tall. Very broad. And very, very naked. She was not a short woman. Had always considered herself ungainly. But now . . . she forced her eyes upward to meet his.

"I was not," he said, so softly she had to strain to hear him, "pretending. No Aazoni can pretend feelings such as those I shared with you. Whatever happens from this moment on, I wish you to know my feelings when I reached out to you were genuine. As genuine as yours."

Something in his eyes spoke to her with as much eloquence as his words—possibly more, and told her he spoke the truth. The truth, at least, as he saw it.

Her anger collapsed as swiftly as it had risen.

"All right, 'Aazoni,' where do you come from, then?" she said, fighting to maintain her equilibrium, to prevent his sensing how desperately she wanted to know everything about him. She tried to inject deep suspicion extreme doubt into her tone. "Where is this 'Aazonia' of yours?" All she managed was frightened sarcasm.

"A time and space not . . . here. Not . . . now."

She reared back. "Hold on! Are you seriously telling me you're an alien? From another planet? Or another time? Another dimension, maybe? I don't believe you."

"You do, Lenore," he said, his tone gently chiding, his hands resting lightly on her shoulders. "But it frightens you to believe it, so you deny it. You cannot deny, though, that when I called you, you responded."

"I . . ." She shook her head in confusion. Oh, brother! Had she ever responded! It should have made her blush to remember, but it didn't. It only made her ache again with the kind of longing that just wouldn't go away. She backed away from him, and his hands fell to his sides.

"I was weak, near death," he said, "after my Octad broke apart. In those extremes, yours was the spark of warmth that drew me. I was trying to reach you, but I could not complete the translation to your exact location. The best I could do was bring you to me when I fell short and was injured, unable to translate again."

Her head careened with the effort of trying to understand, trying to accept the unacceptable, believe the unbelievable. He was tiring visibly now and returned to the shelf of rock where he lay back without his makeshift pillow, which now lay at her feet along with her sleeping bag. "I had need of your strength. I called you, and you came."

"Close, but no cigar," she muttered. "You kept backing out on me just before the crucial moment." He only gazed at her quizzically as if he hadn't the faintest idea what she was getting at. Okay, so he probably didn't. "Come" had several meanings, and he might not be familiar with the idiom as she used it. That he didn't pick up on it and smirk, told her better than anything that he probably was as good as his word about not poking his mental feelers into her mind. And possibly even alien . . . A human male of his apparent age, unless he were a particularly sheltered priest, would surely have caught her innuendo at once.

"Now," he continued, "thanks to you, I can hold my corporeal form with less trouble, and can heal myself and provide warmth and light for us both."

She gazed at him from near the front of the cave, aware again of the glow filling the space, light that appeared to have no source. And the pleasant warmth surrounding them—why hadn't she realized it before?—could not possibly be produced by her now almost extinguished campfire. Despite the balmy temperature, chills trickled over her skin.

"You're dreaming again, Lenore," she said.

"You liked the dreaming." He smiled. "I gave you pleasures, did I not?"

"Pleasures!" She'd die before admitting that. "Frustrations, maybe, fears, horrors and heebie-jeebies, yes, but not pleasures!" Her denial held as much substance as his body had an hour before.

"It might not be the best choice of word, but you have forbidden me to share your thoughts. I must therefore take my words from. . . . others."

She felt dizzy. She felt sick to her stomach. Had he been sharing his phantom visits with her around the community, asking what he should call her responses? Had all of Rocky Point been made privy to her erotic dreams? Would they all gawk at her when she next showed up in the community? Would Nancy Worth sell the story to one of her favorite tabs? Lenore could just see the lurid headline flashing across the screen of her reader: ACCOUNTANT HAS CLOSE ENCOUNTER. *Stupendous sex with alien in mountain retreat.*

"What . . . others?" she asked, her voice a raspy croaking sound. "What others?"

"There are not many, and the two I can best access are . . . weak . . . distant and scarcely receptive. Like most humans, they lack your . . . special gifts. But they would have sufficed, had you not come to me. One wants gold. With the promise of that, I would have brought him to me." His brow wrinkled. "Why would he want gold?"

"Gold means wealth."

"But he has great wealth already. He has lands, family, friends."

"You said two. What does the other want?"

"Escape. Escape from . . . boredom. I do not fully understand this 'boredom,' but she does not like it. She craves adventure."

"And these other two. If I hadn't come to you, would you have given the man gold, given the woman adventure?" The thought of the 'adventure' he could provide for the other woman gave her a momentary, powerful stab of gratification that *she* had complied with his compulsion. Then she quickly reminded herself that he did not belong to her. And that jealousy was a useless emotion.

"I would have, yes. But first, I would have tried to make each of them see that what they already have is probably better for them than what they secretly desire."

Lenore stared at him, wondering if he would soon begin trying to persuade her that her secret desires were not advisable. That being a single parent was no easy task. As if she didn't already know that! The idea of a thirty-seven-year-old woman yearning for a child to raise on her own was ludicrous. She knew that without him having to tell her.

It was physically possible for women to bear children up into their sixties and seventies, and with a life expectancy of one hundred and fifty years, the practice was not uncommon. But Lenore did not want to raise a child in a single-parent home. After growing up with no mother, she had promised herself she would wait until she had a mate, someone to help her parent a child, before she got pregnant. Her biological clock, however, did not seem to agree with this wisdom.

"So why didn't you work harder on the others? Bring them, instead of me?" *Why did you prey on my most potent desires, if, in the end, you're only going to tell me to suppress them?*

"Before I had strength," Jon said, "there was only you for me to touch, to borrow from. Except," he added, "for one brief moment, Zenna." His voice cracked on the name, and his face twisted with pain. "I touched her. I know I did. Then she was . . . gone."

The heartbreak in his tone echoed deep inside Lenore, an ache she could not negate. "Zenna?"

"My birth-mate. My . . . sister. I touched her."

"Touched her? How?"

"As I touched you."

Lenore felt her eyes widen. That was no way for a man to touch his sister! "That's sick," she said. She heard her voice coming from a long way away. The dying fire swayed and danced and beyond it, Jon's eyes locked with hers.

His expression of amusement told her at once he'd understood. "With my mind, with the memories shared by our *Kahniyas*," he said. "I called to her, not as I called to you, but as I have always signaled her, since we were children. Aazoni families are very close. Almost all are born with a birth-mate."

"What's that?" He'd said sister, but 'mate' could have several meanings.

"Two infants from the same mother at the same time."

"Oh!" Her surge of relief came as an unwelcome surprise. "Twins."

"Yes. A birth-mate is what you would call a twin. But always one of each . . . gender. I know her signature as well as she knows mine. I recognized it, as fleeting as it was, and then it was damped so swiftly I could not find it again, to home in on. I could find only you."

She tried to speak, for a moment, could not, then managed, "What a terrible disappointment for you."

He didn't deny it, but nodded. "I must find Zenna. I am very sorry I was forced to do that to you, sorry I had to . . . to take from you. That I . . . imposed and . . . entered your mind, disturbing you in the process. I did not know you would find it such a terrible . . . iniquity. I had no choice, if I were to live and save the others. I did not at first know you would even sense or understand what was happening. But for me, there was great need. My *Kahniya* needed you, the strength of your healthy body, to heal me."

Again, he touched his wounded head. She stared, staggered closer, looked again, and saw that the skin had knit back together neatly, that the ragged edges showed scarcely a seam. Even as she watched, the hair on his head seemed to shake itself and then rest tidily over where the gash had laid open his scalp.

"Your head . . ."

"It was a small thing." He smiled. "Like your hands."

She started, turned her palms up and gazed upon their unblistered skin.

"They are well?"

She met his steady gaze. Again, she nodded jerkily, then stared at his injured leg. The purple was gone, the taut, shiny skin had taken on the same bronze shade as the rest of him. As she watched, he reached down with both hands, clasped his foot and turned it straight. There was a faint clicking sound, and he smiled. "The leg," he said, "was a little more difficult. It will be several hours before I wish to risk putting my full weight on it. Is there more food?"

She backed away from him, eyes burning as she stared. Great shuddering sobs shook her, but no tears flowed. She wrapped her arms around herself, closed her eyes and prayed for sanity, for strength to withstand the terrible self doubts and mental turmoil that tore at her.

"This isn't happening," she babbled. "You are not real. You are not here. You can't read my mind. You haven't done what I think I just saw you do. You didn't turn into smoke and slide into the cave through a crack in the rock. You aren't—"

"Toor-a-loor-a-loor-a, toor-a-loor-a-lie . . ."

Lenore broke off as the melodious tenor voice flooded the cave with the same kind of melting warmth as the golden glow. Her mouth snapped shut, then fell open again. Her eyes felt as if they might bug out of her head. "What . . . what are you doing?" she croaked.

Jon, sitting upright and naked, legs crossed, arms folded, smiled benignly at her. "I am . . . comforting you," he said. "You are afraid. I do not wish that for you."

He sang again as if she had not interrupted him. "Toor-a-loor-loor-a, hush, now don't you cry . . ."

Oh, yes. Absolutely. There was no longer any doubt. She was stark, staring crazy . . . and sharing a cave with a man who thought he was an alien from another time and space. What was even scarier was that she believed he was, too, however much she might tell herself she didn't. And he was an alien who thought she could be comforted by the ancient words of *an Irish Lullaby*?

Lenore dropped weakly onto the ledge, stared at him as he sang, then threw back her head and laughed.

As abruptly as Lenore had plopped onto the rock, Jon stopped singing. "My song amuses you. That is good." He smiled, the corners of his eyes crinkling charmingly. Lenore's laughter faded to a chortle that sounded to her suspiciously like a sob. She drew in a deep breath, trying to steady herself.

"No," she said. "Your song does not 'amuse' me. Frankly, it scares me even more than I was already scared."

"I am truly sorry. It has never been my intention to frighten you. I hoped to soothe with the song. It is what your mother sang to you when you were an infant."

Lenore shot to her feet. "No!" She turned her back on him, wrapping her arms around herself. "Maybe your mother sang *An Irish Lullaby* to you, but believe me, no one ever sang it for me."

"Yes," he said, sounding so certain that she turned back to face him. It had become hot, too hot, in the cave. She unzipped her jacket. "Your mother sang it to you. It was in your memories. You will sing it to your child one day."

"You can't possibly know that. My mother left me before I was a year old. She joined a commune. My father told me they all committed suicide—killed themselves—several years later, hoping to move to a different . . . plane of existence, I believe. And now I suppose you're going to tell me that she succeeded in her aim?"

"I have no way of knowing. There was nothing of that in your memories of her."

"I have no memories of her! I don't even have pictures of her. My father destroyed them all after she left us."

"You do, Lenore. Memory-pictures. They are there. Before you told me I must not, I saw those memories. Your mother looked much as you do now, but for her longer hair. She had beautiful hair. If yours were longer, it, too, would be beautiful. You see yourself with hair like that. In your dreams."

The memory of a long, silky tress flowing over her breasts flooded into Lenore's mind and to her disgust, she knew that this time, she actually was blushing. Dammit, a woman of her age should be far beyond such juvenile embarrassment.

The biggest problem was that she more than half-believed him about her mother, which didn't say a whole lot about the kind of grip she had on reality. Because when Jon spoke of a woman much like her, but with longer hair, she came close to envisioning her mother, close to regaining a memory she couldn't possibly have. She clenched her teeth until she thought she had control of her voice, then proceeded with her questioning of this weird man, hoping for a brisk kindness that nevertheless told him she meant to be firm, meant to get to the bottom of his ridiculous story and worm the truth out of him one way or another.

"Who are you, really?" she demanded—meant to demand, but her voice came out in a pleading whisper. She cleared her throat. "What are you? Where are you from? And don't give me that Estonia/Aazonia crap, either, Mac. We both know it's simply not possible."

He was suddenly clothed in a dark, outdoor-weight

jumpsuit suit similar to hers, a red ski jacket, laced-up hiking boots, and leather gloves. He hadn't moved. He did move though, to take a black knitted cap from the pocket of his jacket and tug it onto his head, almost obscuring his hair but for a few bits curling around his ears and across his forehead.

"Shall we go?" he asked blandly while she blinked— and blinked again. "Let me help you load your pack."

Before her eyes, the sleeping bag case stood itself upright, and then the bag rolled tightly and slid into it the way a baby kangaroo dove into its mother's pouch, just the way she'd seen on Edu-Holos. She took two stumbling steps back as her pots stacked themselves, their handles unclipping in midair and clattering into the pocket of her pack where she habitually carried them. It was like watching an old rerun of *Bewitched* on the Classics channel.

Then, her pack, plump and readied, its straps adjusted to fit his stature, was on Jon's back, the lightcell snapped neatly into its customary position to recharge from the sky. "Shall we go?" he asked again, just as politely.

Lenore found her voice somewhere. She wasn't certain where. "I thought you didn't want to put your full weight on that leg for a while."

"I won't be doing so," he said, and outside the cleft entrance, Lenore heard Mystery paw the ground and give a plaintive whinny.

She gasped and whirled, distinctly recalling having shut Mystery into his stall for the night to protect him against cougars and other large predators. There was no way he could get out on his own. "You brought my horse here?"

"My strength is not yet fully replenished, and your

113

talents are not yet developed to the point that we could translate together the distance to your home. And I would also like to see some of your world—the way you see it."

Lenore edged toward the slit leading to the outside, never taking her eyes off Jon. "You won't fit through the gap," she said in faint tones. "Not with that pack on your back. Even I have to come in sideways."

"Of course," he said and took her hand. Without having traversed the narrow opening, she—and he, complete with her equipment—were outside. But before she could question her surroundings, inside her mind there grew a picture of a black-eyed, snarling man who emanated hatred and evil and intent to kill.

With a scream, she turned to Jon, saw his face tight with pain, pale with instant anguish. She watched his corporeal form waver as if he were about to disappear again. As she reached out to him, he groaned, "Rankin!" and fell to the ground.

Then, abruptly, the evil was gone and Lenore was tumbling, falling, being churned in a horrifyingly icy deluge of whiteness that came from a vast height, an avalanche of immense proportions that left her gasping for breath, fighting for her life . . . and losing the battle.

From somewhere, a whisper of wind breathed the name *Minton* . . . and she fell deeper into the avalanche that held far greater danger than mere suffocating snow.

With effort dredged from his depths, Minton shielded from the vicious lash of Rankin's mind, but shielded in such a way that he could no longer translate even in atmosphere. He dropped out of translation abruptly, naked, of course, and landed in snow up to his armpits. It frothed around him, filling his nose, his mouth, his eyes, as with a slow rumble, it began to move.

He tumbled over and over, caught in a whirling white-ness in which there was no up, no down, only motion, dizzying and disorienting, intense and and unbelievably cold. He knew he had to translate out of there or risk death, but if he went incorporeal again while Rankin was still alert to his presence, he would surely be found. He knew that, with the amplifier to add to his consid-erable powers, Rankin had the capacity to drag him from his hiding place. Wherever that might be.

At length, Minton realized the tumbling motion had ceased. Now, cold became the sole enemy. Slowly and with great physical difficulty, not fully convinced he was heading upward, but obeying the urgings of his *Kah-niya*, he began scraping with his hands, creating a small air pocket before him.

He struck something solid. Easing his hands along it, he learned it was more or less flat and that it rose before him in large, hard, rounded ridges. Digging more fran-tically, he saw glimmers of what could only be daylight through the thinning cover of snow.

Yes! Air and light flooded in with the next scoop of his hands. He gulped in deep breaths, struggled to keep his frozen body moving, and managed to flail his way out of the snow to lie on top of it. Sunshine, blessedly warm, glowed onto his back, heated his *Kahniya*, and gave him energy.

Standing, he recognized a dwelling of sorts, built of tree trunks laid on their sides, stacked one on top of the other. Poor and primitive, it would nevertheless provide shelter. His protective *Kahniya* must have directed him to it when he was forced to break out of translation. Struggling, often sinking deep into the snow again, he made his halting way around the first corner of the building, seeing no openings as he passed. The next wall afforded him only a narrow slot he knew he'd never fit through in his corporeal state, but the third side, in the lee of the avalanche, was only partially buried. There, a rectangle of different construction from the walls suggested a door. He pressed against it to no avail. Bending, he dug downward, tossing back snow like a *welligan* seeking the tasty nuts that burrowed under a *belgrina* tree after they fell.

Ah . . . there! A device recognizable as a locking mechanism. He mentally probed its interior electronic components, deactivated them, and the door swung inward. He tumbled through and as he did so, lights, heat, and music came on. He turned, and with the last of his strength, he was able to shove the door shut against the weight of the snow that had tumbled down to follow him into the dwelling.

In seconds, the icy white drift in which he stood had melted and been sucked away by some unseen means. Ahh! Perhaps this place was not as primitive as he'd first imagined.

Grateful for the warmth, he stroked his *Kahniya*, searching for the true memories it contained, hoping to ascertain whether he had really heard Jon's call, or only wished it.

All it offered him was a strident warning of Rankin and his depraved, artificially enhanced power. . . .

Did Rankin now have Jon as well as Zenna? Was that the reason Jon's cry was choked off so abruptly?

Despite the warning from his *Kahniya*, he sent out a deliberately wide, sweeping probe, keeping its volume low, hoping Rankin, if he was still seeking, would be doing so on a higher plane.

He had sensed . . . something . . . for scarcely a heart-

beat during his flight from the law in that place called
northern Minnesota. What had it been? A projection of
pain? Of hunger? Of thirst? Of need? Or merely an echo
of those, bounced back to him from some unknown
place and time?

There was no way to tell, for it had been transitory
and weak. But he was still convinced it had been Jon.
As had his *Kahniya*, which had most assuredly sent him
in the direction of the Octad leader. Rankin's interference had, unfortunately, snatched him out of his solo
translation short of his objective.

The best he could do now, he reasoned, was search
this dwelling for clothing, to provide warmth until he
was strong enough to collect it for himself from the
atmosphere; for food, to give him that strength; and for
something that would tell him where on Earth he might
be. Snow, and the avalanche he'd experienced, in addition to the steepness of the terrain, suggested mountains. But . . . which mountains? Which continent? He
suspected it was the same one Jon had ended up on;
at least he hoped it was. The closer they were to each
other the better. He'd much prefer to find Jon without
having to translate again. These solo translations in a
culture where nudity was frowned upon were to be
avoided. He began opening cupboards and drawers in
search of food, eating whatever he found that appeared
edible, until he felt himself growing stronger, feeling
more certain of his ability to survive.

Presently, he began a search for warm clothes, not
only to comply with the dictates of the society he was
inhabiting, but also to help protect himself from the outdoor climate control employed here. The frigid cold certainly did not lend itself to nudity any more than their
strict behavioral codes did. He wished for Zareth's talent

with the art of illusion—or even the much lesser knack Jon could employ when necessary.

Zareth, Ree, Wend, oh, Wend—his own birth-mate. Wouldn't he sense her total absence if she had failed to survive? Would he not have heard her death-tone, however far she might have been swept from him? Even here, in this alien place, wouldn't he know? He longed for her soothing mental touch.

Wend, their healer . . . Would she have enough strength left to heal herself if she were injured? He longed for her, for Jon, his bond-mate's brother. In despair, he longed for all the others, too, but dared not send out probes to seek them.

Rankin's proximity created such danger! Did Rankin sense Minton's presence, or had he simply been striking out at what he perceived as a threat, some unknown entity that might possibly interfere with his nefarious activities? Perhaps Rankin sent out such killing bursts periodically as a routine precaution.

Minton found many different garments, but selected one of a fabric which, while thin, was insulated enough to keep him warm in the cold environment he'd discovered. Luckily, it had some stretch to it and covered most of him. Atop that, he drew on a jacket of the same fabric, fumbled for a moment with the unfamiliar closing, then mastered it. Stockings, pulled high, covered the gap between the bottoms of the trouser part of the garment and the only foot covering he could find that appeared stout enough to take outdoors. They were extraordinarily hard and open at the back, but they fit—barely.

He slid his feet into the boots and as he stepped down, felt them close around his ankles somehow, tightly, firmly. They allowed his ankles no movement at all, he discovered, clumping awkwardly around the room. What manner of shoes were these? What use were they? He tried to remove them, but they appeared to be stuck fast to him.

He would have to make the best of it. Heading for the door, he spotted a flat image on a wall and suddenly understood. A man in such footwear appeared to be flying through the air over a wide expanse of white. Snow! Exactly like the snow he had dug himself out of, had struggled through to gain entry to this place. And affixed to the man's feet—to the hard, uncompromising footwear—were narrow slats of some unknown composition. He accessed what he could recall of his rushed studies of Earth and finally found an explanation.

The footwear he wore was designed to be attached to those slats. Once they were connected, the wearer could then fly across the snow. He smiled and stomped around the small dwelling until he found a tall cabinet in which were stored several sets of those slats, pointed at one end and curved up. Yes! There was some manner of fastening for the shoes near the center of each slat.

For a moment, he studied the image on the wall, then laid the slats flat on the floor, stepped onto one and felt the footwear attach itself . . . magnetically, he thought. He lifted his free foot and nearly tilted sideways. Luckily, his *Kahniya* caught him, steadied him. He saw poles in the closet and another glance at the image on the wall indicated that these must be used as stabilizers. With one clasped in each hand, their points planted solidly against the floor, he managed to attach his other booted foot to the narrow slat on the left, fully expecting to be lifted from the surface upon which he stood and carried through the air.

It did not happen.

Frowning, he studied the picture further, wishing for a nearby mind to access for current, local knowledge. It seemed he must be the only person within many *westals*. Either that or he had been misinformed, and there were no receptive minds—other than the visiting Aazoni—anywhere on Earth.

Again, loneliness threatened to overcome him. The rest of the Octad ... Where were they? Since he had come through the disastrous translation to Earth's time and space relatively unscathed, and since he was certain Jon still lived—if precariously—he must find the others. Then, and only then, would he have any hope of locating Zenna.

He would not do it huddled here in this small dwelling.

He slid one slat forward. It was not easy. He followed it with the other. Maybe the slats required snow under them before they would permit him to fly. It went against all scientific knowledge he had, but could cold possibly provide lift? He opened the door and stepped awkwardly onto the snow outside, hoping the house would again take care of the flakes that slid inside. With difficulty, he turned, closed the door, and caused the locks to return to their previous position.

Still, the slats did not lift him. He tried to levitate, not one of his major talents, but to no avail. Using the stabilizers to assist him, he shuffled forward, up a small hill, and poised on the brink, waiting for the flight he fully expected. Again, the slats remained stubbornly stuck to the snow.

He gave an experimental push with the poles and was suddenly in motion. Not flying above the surface of the snow, but gliding upon it, going faster and faster. The wind whistled in his ears and chilled his teeth, bared in a grimace. His hair blew back from his brow, and the cold air rushing by stole his breath away. If his *Kahniya* had not controlled his balance, many times he would have fallen and then—oh, then, he did fly!

Aided by his downward speed, the small hill he had just ascended fell out from under his slats, and he was finally airborne. But not for long. As his slats struck the snow again, his *Kahniya* loosened his knees to adjust for the impact and aimed him straight down the hill again. He searched ahead for yet another hillock that would let him fly, and found one, then another and another, always searching for a larger one, taking bigger bites of air with each.

It was wonderful! He laughed aloud with the joy if it, locking the experience into his *Kahniya* so he could share it with his bond-mate when he found her.

Zenna, he projected without caution, so caught up was he in this new experience. *I am coming. I will find you!*

Chapter Eight

Lenore shook her head hard as she realized the avalanche had not happened—at least not to her. She fixed her eyes on Jon's face and saw him blinking as they both regained their feet. He wiped the back of a hand across his forehead and swayed for a moment, clasping his fist into Mystery's mane for support.

"Where?" he said, his voice just above a whisper.

"Where . . . what?" she asked, but she knew. She knew what he needed to know.

"Where would snow tumble from above, sweeping a man off his feet, burying him?" His eyes all but burned into her with urgency. "Where, Lenore? You saw it. I know you did. I was unable to keep from sharing your vision, his vision. You projected it strongly out of your mind. I did not enter. It was just . . . there."

Lenore locked her trembling knees. "Whose vision?"

"Minton's. I know it was he. I know his signature

almost as well as I know Zenna's. They are bond-mated, and for this reason, his *Kahniya* and mine, along with Zenna's, are closely linked."

"Minton is your sister's husband?"

"Yes."

"He . . . he fed us that avalanche experience?"

"Not us. You. You received it when he projected it. He could not help himself any more than you could help yourself projecting it to me. It was the threat of our . . . enemy that tore Minton from his translation. I sensed him, too. He flung out a strong intent to kill. It forced me to shut down any probes I might have sent to locate Minton. But you remained open to him."

Lenore glanced uneasily at the dimness in the trees surrounding them. "I was . . . my mind was . . . open to your enemy?"

"No, no. To Minton. He was searching blindly and found you. You experienced what he did, and you projected it so strongly I entered into it as well. But only because I am near to you. Even standing five feet away, it's unlikely Rankin would have felt your experience. He has not the talent."

"Rankin being the enemy." Heaven help her, she was all too easily accepting this madness. Even being out here with the familiar scent of her horse in her nostrils, the sight of the trees, the sound of the wind in their boughs, the solidity of the rocks and soil underfoot, the familiarity of the visible patches of sky above, as blue and unsullied by flying saucers as always, she couldn't discount what she'd experienced.

"Yes." Jon looked and sounded distracted. "I must learn where Minton is so I can reach him before Rankin does."

"I don't know where he is," she said. "It could be

anywhere there are mountains. I remember digging out of the avalanche, going into a ski chalet. Or . . . I guess I remember him doing it. He could be far, far away."

"No. He is near," Jon said, which she took to be an indication of his knowledge of Earth's geography. "Minton's projection is not as powerful as that of some— Zenna's or mine, for instance. For me to discern him for that instant when he was in your mind, before Rankin gouged him out of translation and I had to remove myself, for me to sense his pain and fear in that instant, he must be within . . . within a hundred *westals*, at the very most."

"Westals?"

His eyes went blank for a second. "A *westal* is approximately half of one of your kilometers."

"So he's not far away." She set her mind to recalling what ski resorts with cabins were in the vicinity. There were several.

"What happens when you find him?"

"With two Aazoni minds, we will be better able to find the others."

"Then, with your stronger . . . powers, why don't you seek him out?"

"Because to do so would be to give away my presence, possibly even my position, to Rankin. And I am not yet hale enough. There is, too, one other problem."

Lenore was quite sure of that. She was certain there was plenty more than just 'one' other problem, and she was afraid she'd have to face each one soon. But not yet. She wasn't ready to fully accept even half of what she suspected simply had to be fact.

"What has this Rankin done?" she asked. "What makes him so dangerous?"

Jon closed his eyes for a moment, an expression of

ineffable sadness crossing his face. "He deals in illegal substances, importing them from other worlds. He sells them to weak people who have become addicted."

Lenore felt her jaw drop and caught it half-way before snapping it shut so quickly her teeth clacked together. "An . . . intergalactic drug smuggler?" Jon nodded and she asked, "Where does he get these drugs?"

"Some of them, some very potent ones, here on Earth. But until the past several years, we were able to keep his activities to a minimum because windows to Earth as well as to other places, are not frequent. Many times I was able to prevent his translating to this space and time. In doing so, we managed to keep his illegal imports to a minimum."

"And then?" she prompted when he did not go on. He looked at her blankly. "You said 'until the past several years.' Obviously, something changed."

Jon's face aged with grief even as she watched. "He stole my sister—and a device she and Minton had developed that allows translations from one world to another without having to use a full Octad. It gives them the ability to translate through narrower, less stable windows, of which there are many—such as the one I brought my Octad through, with such disastrous results. With this device, the amplifier, he has been keeping a steady stream of the essence of an exotic botanical known locally, I believe, as salal going—"

"Salal!" she interrupted with an uncontrollable burst of laughter. "Salal isn't an exotic botanical, for heaven's sake! It's a weed! It has roots that go all the way to China. Anyone who's ever tried to clear land for a garden within fifty klicks of the coast in this part of the world has to battle it constantly. It grows along the edges of clearings, even infiltrates deep into the coastal forests. It fills any open space it can find, sending its roots even into crevices in bare rock. It crowds from the forest edge right out to the high-tide mark. Everywhere it can put down a root, there's another tenacious salal plant! Though thousands of people cut it and sell its leaves to florists to add greenery to their arrangements, they've never made a noticeable dent in its population. Your Rankin is welcome to it."

"To many peoples it is the source of a highly addictive, dangerous drug." His tone held reproof. "Rankin and his ilk have kept a steady, if slow trickle of it flowing into the veins of addicts of several different races. He must be stopped, but if he knows I'm here, he will kill Zenna."

She sucked in a sharp breath. "Kill her?" But of course. Even intergalactic drug lords would have as few morals, as little respect for life as the local ones. Why should it be any different elsewhere? But . . . salal? That was like considering dandelions as a narcotic!

"Yes," Jon replied. "He will not allow her to go free. Unless I—we—rescue her, her death is inevitable. You see, he may kill her anyway, at any time, if she manages to perfect the device which is, in Minton's view, dangerously unstable. Rankin is forcing her somehow to keep it tuned."

He squeezed his eyes tightly shut. His lips compressed. His fists clenched. Then he met her gaze. "Our other great concern is that in simply using the amplifier, translating with it, she might die. It could fail at any time. If my sister dies, half of me is gone, too. These years of being unable to link with her have been . . . torture."

"Jon . . ." As difficult as her life had been at times, she had never been subjected to the knowledge that someone near and dear to her might be in the cross-hairs of some trigger-fingered killer. But then, who, other than Caroline, was really near and dear to her?

He squared his shoulders. "But I will prevail. I am leader of my Octad and it is my task, my profession, to track down and stop wrong-doers."

Now, she shut her eyes. "Oh, my god! First, an intergalactic drug lord, now an intergalactic cop?" She looked at him, wishing desperately he'd just dematerialize again. "What next?"

"Next, with your help, I will gather the others and find Zenna." He stroked the horse's neck. "Mystery, will you carry us to Lenore's home?"

The horse arched his neck and turned his head, looking more alert and intelligent than Lenore had ever thought possible. Mystery had never been a particularly brilliant horse, much more of a nag than anything else. But Caroline liked him. Actually, so did Lenore. To her mystification, the horse appeared to nod as if in response to the question, and Jon patted him again. Mystery bared his long yellow teeth in what could only be a grin. Lenore held her breath, waiting for him to start speaking or singing, or informing the world that his real name was Mr. Ed, and that a "horse was a horse, of course, of course . . ."

Oh, yes, she'd spent far too much of her lonely leisure time with the Fiction Classics. From here on, she'd make a point of avoiding them as she did Nancy Worth's tabloids, and sticking with History holos and vids.

Jon left the horse's side, crouched and leaned over the spring where it bubbled from between two slabs of rock. She thought he intended to drink, but he only tilted his head to one side, offered her a sweet, warming smile, and said, "Your world makes intriguing music. I could hear this when we were in the cavern, but it sounds much more complex now I'm close. I wish I had come to Earth long ago. I had no idea how charming a place it could be. It's almost like Aazonia in its beauty." He shrugged. "Though I was told, I didn't truly believe it."

"Seeing is believing," she muttered. "Not that I believe any of this."

But even as she said it, Lenore suppressed a sigh. Unfortunately, she did believe it. At least, she found herself more than willing to go along with it—with him—when he slipped his right glove off and took her hand in his, holding it warmly, securely, comfortingly. There might be something to be said for madness, after all. Since she had already gotten there, she no longer had to worry about going crazy.

She laughed again.

"Something amuses you?"

"Life amuses me," she said. "I think, for far too long, I've taken it much too seriously."

"That is very likely true," he agreed. "This seriousness of yours has been making you unhappy, has it not?"

At once, she was on the defensive. "What makes you say that?"

"What I saw. What I learned of you. Before."

"Before?"

"Before you forbade me entrance to your thoughts."

"And now?" She couldn't keep the challenge from her tone, almost daring him to reveal more of her deepest secrets—or to admit he hadn't meant his promise to stay out. How could she possibly trust a promise like that? If he could read her mind, he could also make damn good and sure she didn't know he was doing it.

He didn't admit any such thing, or give any indication he knew what she was thinking.

"Now, what?"

"What do you think now?"

"Now, hearing your laughter make the same kind of music as does the water among the stones, I think you are more happy."

Her laughter sounded like a mountain stream? Did he have any idea what a rare compliment he'd just paid her, what a romantic notion he had conveyed? She gave her head a quick shake to settle her brains back into their safe, comfortable rut. "Sure," she said. "Just as happy as if I were in my right mind."

"Lenore, your mind appeared to me to be very right. Merely . . . confused, weary, and deeply, desperately lonely."

She swallowed a sudden wave of distress that threatened to overpower her as strongly as the vision of the avalanche. She fought it as she had fought every other battle in her life—with strength and determination.

Ignoring emotional pain, subduing it, came naturally to her. "All right. Mount up, Alien, and let's get out of these woods before another storm decides to swamp us."

He got on the horse as if he had been riding bareback all his life, which he likely had, she supposed. Or if he hadn't, he'd simply reached into a nearby, unsuspecting mind for instructions. Or . . . had he levitated? It had all happened so fast she couldn't be sure.

To her surprise, since she was not a small, delicate woman, he reached down from his seat and lifted her to sit sideways in front of him.

"Mystery can't carry us both on this rocky trail," she protested, but he leaned around her, patted the horse's neck, and assured her Mystery was happy to do it.

"As happy as if he were in his right mind?"

He chuckled as they moved forward, the horse obeying no command she had seen or felt Jon give. "Wrong minds are not allowed to remain untreated in Aazonia," he told her. "In people or in beasts."

She took that as a direct stab at her own uncertain sanity, despite his having said he thought her mind was sound. "I had treatment!" She turned her head and glared at him. "I saw a doctor. She recommended rest. And look what that got me." Unable to stand the power of his gaze, she quickly faced the front again, sitting stiffly erect, keeping her body from touching his.

He didn't let her keep her distance though, curving an arm around her, pulling her close, his shoulder cradling the side of her face. He felt disturbingly . . . real and even more disturbingly, it felt as if there were no layers of clothing between them. She shivered and lifted her cheek from his shoulder, which her imagination had told her was covered by nothing but warm, bare skin. Her eyes told her otherwise. She wasn't sure which to believe.

"What did it get you?" he asked, his voice a low rumble of amusement in her ear, his breath tickling as he drew her close again.

She glanced at him, feeling helpless against the sexual pull he exerted. "It got me you." Then, in an attempt to focus on something other than the feel of his hard body next to hers—a body that appeared clothed, and yet felt so naked next to her skin—she added, "But I suppose a sexy alien is a slight improvement over a frantic, frightened woman searching for help, crying out into the night for someone, anyone to answer."

Jon reeled with shock. As Lenore had spoken, he'd caught an unexpected glimpse of Zenna's face. "When?" he demanded, clamping his hands on her shoulders, half-turning her toward him. "What woman? Where is she?" He lifted one knee to support her as she almost slid from the horse's back. He saw sudden fear in her eyes, fear as swift and as real as that he'd sensed in the instant he'd captured Lenore's unintentional projection of his sister's image.

Deliberately, he forced himself to relax, so as not to further alarm Lenore. There was so much he had to know, so much that would require her willing cooperation. Had it been Zenna who'd opened Lenore's mind to Aazoni communications?

Could she be near? But if she were, she must sense him. The two of them had been inextricably linked since the moment of conception. Why was she damped? Was it for her own safety? It must be so! Yet the question remained—though Jon hated to ask it, as none of the possible answers set his mind at ease—why did Zenna continue to keep the device operational for Rankin and B'tar?

Minton had evidence that Zenna had translated back to Aazonia, fully cloaked with the assistance of the amplifier, and taken materials from the lab they had shared, materials to keep the device operational. Why, during one of those trips home, had she not sought help? What hold did Rankin have over her? Threats against her family, against Minton? Did she not know how much power the two families, united, could muster? She had to know that! Even with the amplifier in his hands, they could beat Rankin on their home territory if they knew when he would be there. They could set a trap. Here, it might be more difficult, but they would do it.

Unless, Jon speculated, Minton was wrong. It was possible the prototype amplifier that had disappeared with his sister was far more serviceable than suspected, possible it worked without Zenna's assistance. But if that were the case, why did Zenna still live?

Yet if Minton was right, and Zenna was maintaining the invention—and both Jon and Minton believed she would only do so under coercion—then, Jon reasoned, she would not be free to signal any of them. In fact, to protect her life and theirs they should not communicate at all. Even if Zenna sensed them, she would try to remain in apparent ignorance of the presence of a rescue party.

Gently, quietly, dampening his burning need for answers, Jon asked Lenore again, "What of the woman who has been disturbing your dreams? Who is she?"

"No one, really," she said. "My doctor says she's probably just a manifestation of a troubled part of my own psyche, memories of the lost child within me, or the baby I'd like to have."

She stabbed him with a brief, bitter stare. "Not that I have to tell you about that desire."

He longed for the right to ease the mental anguish he had caused by entering her mind uninvited. "No," he replied. "You do not need to tell me about that. I know it intimately." *And I share it with you.*

The last thought, unspoken, startled him. No! He had no desire to procreate. To do so would mean giving up his life as an officer of the law. No, the best way he could repay Lenore for her assistance and, make good his promise to fulfill her desires was to show her that the right bond-mate for her did exist, and that with Aazoni help, she would find him.

"But why," he asked before she could speak again, "do you think your dreams of this woman in some way reflect your need for a child?"

"Because in some of the dreams, there is a child, too,

a little girl. She and the woman do not come together, but somehow they are . . . connected. They are the phantoms who took turns haunting my dreams until you came along and knocked them out of first place."

Jon almost forgot his promise. How hard it was not to dip into the memories she mentioned, dreams, she called them. Why, oh why had he promised her he would not? Why, oh why did the very notion of his entering her mind frighten her so?

Because it was alien to her, completely outside the realm of her experience. He knew that, but it was hard to understand her fear of something that, to him, was a natural function.

In other races he had encountered, most welcomed the enhanced abilities he and his kind were able to provide to those who had the basic, if undeveloped gift for them. In many, of course, there were no such latent talents, and therefore no way for an Aazoni to assist in advancing them. But with Lenore . . . the natural capacity was so strong, so close to the surface, so ready to be exploited, it was all but impossible to keep from slipping inside to learn what he must learn, to teach her what she needed to know to be a whole person. He was sure he could do it without her knowing, especially if he waited until she was asleep. But he had promised. A promise was not something he could break, not and maintain his honor.

Without honor, an Aazoni was nothing.

But . . . that dream woman? He was very close to certain, given the swift image that had escaped Lenore's mind at her first mention of her, the woman must be Zenna. Then what of the child? That, too, must be his sister.

If he could persuade Lenore to open her mind to him

133

again, to trust him, would he find in her subconscious the answers he sought?

Had she been the medium through which he had, for that brief, precious moment during his harrowing descent from the translation gone wrong, contacted the essence that was Zenna? Had Zenna also been probing for Lenore during that instant?

He cast his mind out in a narrow, cautious beam, scanning, but finding nothing that spoke of his sister, nor of Minton attempting again to reach Lenore, no traces, no signatures. If they were there, hunting for her mentation, they were doing so in a manner that she could not feel, was not frightened by, and hence was not projecting. That left him blocked off from any further exploration because of his promise to Lenore.

The others, though . . . they had made no such promise. The thought came to him in a flash as the horse under them splashed through a stream. If he could but find one of them . . . Lenore, he knew, was not unwilling.

She'd become unwilling only when she knew it was he who had been in her mind. Because of the passion their mental joining had generated? The intensity of that connection concerned him, too, but he also welcomed it. It had not been something he'd ever found, though he knew from others that kind of union could exist.

Baloka, it was called. It was, he realized, something he'd like to explore fully, to create from that experience an *Aleea* to keep and return to whenever he felt the natural need of a male for a female. He had such *Aleeas*, of course, from other encounters, but the one with Lenore would be somehow . . . special. Would it be true *baloka?*

Patán! He sneered at his own foolishness. An Aazoni

could not achieve *baloka* with a non-Aazoni. Whatever he felt for Lenore had more to do with gratitude than anything else. But like each of the other memories he carried, it would be . . . unique. He looked at her, at the confused innocence in her eyes. It would be . . . special.

"Tell me of the child in your dreams," he said to distract himself from that line of thinking. "Lenore, I must know."

"Why?"

"Because I suspect, I hope, the child in your dreams might be the child my sister was."

She stared at him in clear disbelief. "Why would I dream about your sister, for heaven's sake? I don't even know her. And especially, why would I dream of her as a child?"

"An endangered Aazoni can retreat to childhood, hide there," he explained. "In childhood is safety, where adult uncertainties, adult dangers cannot be perceived. If that is where Zenna is hiding, back in her secure childhood, peeking out only rarely, and somehow making contact with you, I might be able to reach her there where no one else could. I shared that childhood, know it as well as I know my own."

He stroked his necklace, touching first one bead then another, searching the memories shared by himself and his sister, gliding over them, through them, into them, but finding no hint she might be in them now and near enough to read.

"Lenore, please share with me the substance of your dreams."

Jon could see the refusal in her face before she spoke it aloud. "I'd prefer to leave my dreams to be forgotten. They haven't always been . . . pleasant. And I haven't dreamed of either the woman or the child since I came to the mountains."

"But sometimes your dreams were pleasant?" he coaxed. "Those of the child, for instance?"

She glanced at him. He took her hand and held it, feeling her cool fingers curl around his as if seeking warmth. He gave it to her. Inside him, too, something warmed and strengthened, began to grow—and it was much stronger than the physical passion they had shared and would, he hoped, share again. Once more, he shrugged it off. It was inappropriate, especially under the circumstances.

"The dreams of the little girl are always—fun," she said. "I enjoy the way she laughs and sings and begs me to come and play with her. To dance."

"Do you?"

She sighed. "No. I can't . . . find her. I go out and search—in the dream, of course—but it's as if she's concealing herself deliberately to make me curious enough to chase her. She giggles. She teases. She hides. She tempts me to follow her. And she promises that some day she will let me catch her."

Ah! That sounded so much like the child his sister had been he again suspected it was the hidden Zenna who was contacting Lenore. Who knew how Zenna had been affected by the trauma of being taken from home and safety and love? Perhaps her ability to slide in and out of the childhood memories carried in her *Kahniya*— or even to project from within them had been enhanced. He longed to see for himself, to know!

"Can you tell me more about her? Where is she? What kind of place do you see her in? Is it like the place you saw before when you touched my *Kahniya?* Like my grandparents' home?"

"No, it's nothing like that. I don't think I see her in any particular place. Not an identifiable one, anyway. Though it's always outdoors. There's grass, trees, shrubs—" A swiftly startled expression crossed her face. "There's salal." She frowned. "I see her on Earth, so obviously, Jon, I wasn't dreaming of your sister."

He gripped her arm. "Salal? Tell me! Tell me where!"

137

Chapter Nine

Lenore recoiled from his urgent intensity. "Would you relax?" she said, wrenching her arm free. "Why are my dreams so important to you?"

"Just . . . tell me, Lenore. I beg of you, tell me. It might be very, very important. It might help me find my sister."

Lenore failed to see how, but she closed her eyes for a second, recalling the details of the recurring dream she'd had of the child.

"There's lots of plant growth where she lives—it's likely part of a wilderness reserve so there'd be no one cutting salal, if you're thinking that's where Rankin might be. Cutting anything in such a preserve would be forbidden."

She hesitated, bit her lower lip for a moment while she considered that. Of course, if Rankin was the kind of criminal Jon claimed, he wouldn't care much about the laws on Earth, would he?

"The shrubs," she went on, "salal included, create shady spots where the little girl hides and plays. There are fir and cedar and hemlock and alder trees, ferns, moss, grass, red huckleberry bushes, salmonberry and thimble-berry bushes, blackberry vines, and plenty of spring flowers. The shrubs were all in leaf in the last dream just before I left, and the salmonberry bushes had pink blossoms, but no berries yet. Those don't usually form until June. And I could see the ocean nearby and a gravel beach. Sometimes I could even smell the salt and the kelp. I have very vivid dreams.

"There's a house, a small one, more like a summer cabin than a real home, near the shore."

"People live in these wilderness preserves?"

"Not live . . . not all the time, anyway. Some have cabins they visit for vacations. If they owned them before the preserve was created they're allowed to remain as long as the dwelling stays in the same family. Of course, the property must be kept in good condition, and no harm can come to the surrounding land."

"Do you see a family? Or just the child?"

"There are two men, though never at the same time. One, she fears, the other she simply hides from as she does from me. She doesn't like him, but keeps that to herself."

"Do you ever see the woman you dream of?"

"No. I only feel as if I am her. As if I have a child who is in danger, as if I'm begging someone to come to help, to take the child from whatever peril threatens her."

"When you see the child, do you also sense the woman?"

"No. The two kinds of dreams are always separate, often days, even weeks apart," she said, "and you are beginning to sound like my shrink."

"Shrink?"

"The doctor I went to because of these dreams and other symptoms. But as I was saying, the woman and the girl always come to me separately. Never on the same night. I finally sought professional help because the dreams recurred so often and with such accurate details. They worried me. I felt like I must be going crazy. Especially when the little girl came to me when I knew perfectly well I wasn't asleep. There were times when she was just . . . there."

He steadied her with one arm as the horse almost stumbled due only to Jon's lack of control over its motor senses. "What does she look like?"

"I don't think I really know. She flits from tree to shrub, and in and out of the cabin, just giving me teasing little hints of her whereabouts, ducking around corners just before I can reach her, tempting me to chase and try to catch her. She's ephemeral. So I'd have to say, no, I've never actually seen her." She laughed softly. "Of course, that's because she doesn't exist."

He wanted to remind her that until very recently she had insisted that he didn't exist, either, but held his peace.

The trees thickened beside the rough, narrow switchback trail the horse followed, dropping the level of illumination almost to twilight. Dead twigs and branches crackled under its hooves. Living branches brushed at the horse's flanks, at the riders' faces and hair, and tugged at their clothing. Jon reached out with his mind and gently urged them aside, not wanting to cause harm to the delicate foliage. He was accustomed to shrubbery that knew enough to sweep itself aside to permit other beings passage.

Other beings . . . Need and loneliness flooded through

him, alleviated only by the contact of Lenore's hand with his and the memory of the mental communication they had shared.

But wait!

If her warmth and openness, her natural affinity to the Aazoni mind, had drawn his *Kahniya* toward her, could some or any of the others have been guided along the same path? Was that why Minton had seemed so close? Was he also on his way to Lenore? Once more, he cast forth a beam of energy, keeping it low and narrow, not knowing the whereabouts of Rankin and B'tar, as wary of alerting them to his presence as he was eager to connect with his group.

The horse crossed a small meadow where wildflowers bloomed bright gold and red against the backdrop of dark green forest. Far across a valley below, more mountains rose in the west, gleaming white caps reflecting the sun.

"You said," Lenore reminded him, "that on Aazonia 'wrong' minds were not allowed to stay that way. If that's true, why are police officers required? And why do you have such things as drug dealers who are obviously breaking your laws? Why don't you just fix whatever's wrong with their minds?"

"We try," he said. "Some minds refused to be repaired. Having a criminal mind is a choice some of our people make."

"Who would choose to be a criminal? And why?"

"You do not have criminals here on Earth?" He knew full well they did, but wanted Lenore's views on the subject.

"Of course we do. But they aren't responsible for what they are. They were damaged by circumstances, such as childhood poverty or mental illness, or bad

141

choices made by their parents or teachers or . . . or . . . or a wide variety of factors."

"Would one of those factors be greed?"

"Well, yes. I suppose so. Sure, some criminals do bad things hoping to get rich. Many do. But they're that way only because they were never taught to control their greed. Society has failed them. They have not failed society."

"And what happens when they are apprehended?"

"They're given treatment."

"Even if they do not want it?"

She looked defeated. "I guess not. Often they resist it, or it simply doesn't work on them. And maybe there are those who do choose a criminal lifestyle. I suppose that's why we still have prisons."

"Exactly," he said. "We, too, have those who reject treatment. If they put up strong enough barriers, no one can get into their minds to right the wrongs that exist."

"Then what do you do?"

He looked at her for several moments as the horse carried them from sun to shade to sun again. He consulted with his *Kahniya*, which could give him little guidance in this matter. He opted for the full truth.

"We eliminate them."

Before he could stop her, Lenore slid from the back of the slowly moving horse. She put several meters between them, her back against the trunk of a tree, her eyes wide and accusing. "So you're not just a cop. You're an executioner as well?"

He brought the horse to a stop. "I am many things, Lenore. In my Octad is a healer, Wend. Rankin and B'tar will be given every opportunity to allow her to reform them. If they refuse, we will have no option but to stop them the only way we can. Would you allow someone to go free who causes deliberate harm to many others, purely for his own profit?"

"Maybe not go free, but do you have to kill him? Can't you simply lock him up somewhere?"

Jon laughed as he urged the horse forward again, very slowly, his gaze never leaving Lenore's face. She was no longer retreating. "How?" he asked. "When all he'd need to do is translate out of wherever we locked him up?"

"I . . . Well, yes." She allowed the horse to catch up to her and paced along slowly beside it, looking up at Jon. "Okay. I see where that would be a problem. But what about those who are addicted to the substances this Rankin provides? Why can't you just fix their minds? Where there's no market, there's no profit. That would eliminate the problem, wouldn't it?"

"Where we can, we do just that, but many—most—of Rankin's victims are not Aazoni and have minds that we cannot reach to effect the necessary cure."

She frowned. "Different species? On different worlds?"

"That is right."

"But . . . if they're not even your people, why do you care so much?"

"Because," he said, "the damage is being done by one of ours. It is our duty to control him, to curb his activities. To stop him and those like him." He brought the horse to a halt at her side. "Do you not have other species here on Earth that you work hard to protect?" He knew it was true and wanted her to admit it.

Slowly, she nodded, and he reached down, scooping her up again, placing her on the back of the horse, and looping one arm around her back.

"We do have lesser species that need our help to survive," she said.

"So, you see? We are not so different after all, are we? Who do you protect on Earth?"

"Animals, birds, plants—entire ecosystems. That's why we have preserves. Places where other species can live undisturbed, can flourish without the interference of mankind. We no longer think of humans as being the most important species on our planet. We are simply one of many, all of whom have a right to be here, a right to live their lives as they see fit—as we do, too, of course."

"And how do humans see fit to live their lives?"

"Most of us live in population corridors. Many live and work in agricultural preserves to provide food for others, or park preserves to maintain places for city-dwellers to find temporary peace and recreation. There are forest preserves, where culled trees provide building materials for homes, and mountain preserves, which capture clouds to produce rainfall that fills rivers and lakes and reservoirs. Along the crests of most mountain ranges in the world, where winds are strong, there are windmills that spin turbines to create electricity to supplement the hydrogen cells that run most things."

"It all sounds very orderly."

Lenore laughed. "And sometimes it actually is. A lot of the different preserves have overlapping uses, and conflicts do arise. The majority of people, though, live in the cities that make up the corridors."

"This is a mountain preserve?"

"Yes, in part. It is also a recreation preserve, which is why I came here, for rest and relaxation."

"Have you found those elements?"

"I thought I had. The dreams of the woman and the child stopped. But then . . . you came."

"I," he reminded her, "am not a dream, Lenore. I am real." She made no comment, and in a moment, he went on. "Do you think perhaps the woman—or the child—could also be real?"

Again, she tossed her hair back as she swung her head to look at him. "No," she said. "Of course not. Why should they be?"

"Why should I be?"

The expression on her face reflected mingled confusion, frustration, and anger. "I'm still not convinced you are."

"Then," he said, "I shall have to convince you."

Her eyes glistened, so deep a brown he felt he could almost swim in their depths as he had in a dark mineral pool on Mount Sarrila. She licked her lips. "How?" It was less a word, than a breath.

"You know how," he said, tightening his arm around her as the trail emerged from the forest into full sunlight pouring warm and golden over a grassy meadow that sloped down toward a snug looking dwelling.

Lenore broke free of his hold and again slid from the horse's back, making haste to put distance between them.

"That," she informed him loftily, "is not going to happen."

"Yes it is, Lenore."

Lenore heard the words, but Jon's lips had not moved from the faint smile in which they were set.

Before she could accuse him of breaking his promise and invading her mind, there was a rush of wings and a Stellar's jay alit on the longest branch of a clump of red osier. "Yes it is, Lenore," the bird said again, bouncing slightly on its perch, its beak moving in perfect time with the words. "You can count on it. It's going to happen because you want it to."

Lenore closed her eyes to block the sight of what she knew she really wasn't seeing, the memory of what she really hadn't heard. The damn bird's thoughts had not, absolutely not, penetrated her mind; nor had it been lip-synching something Jon said. On the contrary. The thought the jay had broadcast had come straight from her own mind—and in her own voice.

Had Jon heard it? Did he recognize it as hers? She tried to speak, but could find no words, could only stand there, mouth half agape, staring at Jon, who had dismounted. Jon, who had invaded her most private places, and whom she, for reasons she couldn't quite plumb, had forgiven.

As if her standing there like that was an invitation, Jon cupped the back of her head in one hand and drew her closer with the other. Her eyes popped open, then fell shut again as his mouth took hers in a kiss that left her blood all but sizzling, stole her breath, and finally, fully convinced her mind he was there, this was happening, and there was nothing she could do to change it.

Nor anything she wanted to do to change it.

Under her hands, his warm, bare shoulders felt like steel covered in satin. As her arms encircled his back, her palms smoothed over rippling muscles, her finger-tips bent and pressed, testing the depth and strength she felt there. She glided her touch down his sides, and found not a hint of a scar from the injury that had bled onto the rocks of the cave. His hard buttocks, as they had in her dreams, flexed under her hands, and she moaned softly. Her head rested in the curve of his shoulder, her cheek against the heat of his chest when he finally broke the kiss.

Using two fingers he gently tilted her chin upward and whispered, "Open your eyes, *letise*. Look at me."

She looked, gazed long and deep until she felt herself sliding away to some place she was afraid to go, and swiftly dropped her head. And blinked. She could have sworn that during their kiss he had felt as naked as he'd been in her dreams. She'd stroked her hands over his shoulders, his arms, his back. She'd clenched her fingers into the tautness of his bottom, rubbed her face against the sleekness of his chest and shoulder—and there hadn't been a stitch of fabric between her hands and his body. She knew she had touched his bare skin. And yet . . . there he stood, as fully clothed as she was, complete with knit hat now inexplicably decorated by a brilliant feather from the jay's tail.

His eyes, though, when she risked another confused glance into them, looked as bewildered, as disconcerted as she felt. Before she could stop herself, she cupped his face in both hands, drew him down to her, and initiated another of those indescribable kisses.

Leaning against Mystery's neck for support, Jon assured himself his knees were weak not from the effects of those kisses, but from the trek down the mountainside. Together he and Lenore crossed the meadow and entered the shed where the horse lived. He watched silently as she gave Mystery food and replenished his water. She rubbed the animal's coat, then brushed it, offered it something from a bin that was out of its reach, and patted its nose.

She was a kind woman. She treated lesser beings well. He liked that. His studies of Earth had told him that, as on most worlds, truly good-hearted people did exist in the majority, but there were also those who only pretended to care for others as long as there was personal reward in it for them.

The power of a mental projection caught Jon just as he crossed over the threshold of the dwelling in which he had first seen Lenore.

Zenna! Letise, I will find you!

It was Minton! Jon stumbled and caught at the door-frame. Minton was near, seeking not him, but Zenna. He felt Lenore stagger as the broadcast caught her, too, and sensed her mind fading to black. He flung a protective shield around her mind and drew her close, held her, one hand supporting himself, the other pressing her to his chest as if he could protect her, guard her from harm, though he knew Minton meant none.

Jon cast forth a narrowly focused beam, seeking only Minton. For an instant, something flickered on the edge of his consciousness, but then it was gone.

"Jon? Jon!" He became aware that Lenore had spoken, was pulling on his arm. "Come inside. Sit down. You're still weak. You're shaking. You can hardly stand."

"Yes." He was still weak. Even the effort of trying to buffer Lenore's mind while sending out that small probe had depleted much of what strength he had regained. He needed more rest. More food. More warmth. And he needed something that he did not have—time. This window through which they had risked their translation was small. In another six weeks it would be closed entirely, not to open again for another ten years.

He must succeed in this mission! And to do so he needed his team. And Zenna. To leave any behind was untenable.

Still unsteady, astounded at Lenore's swift ability to

recover from what must have felt like a body-blow to her, he allowed her to assist him across the room. Maybe he had captured Minton's probe before it penetrated too deeply into Lenore's mind. Indeed, he thought as he lowered himself onto a soft, moderately comfortable chair, she seemed completely unaware this time that Minton had once more used her as a conduit.

The chair failed to cradle him and conform to his body, but it was softer than either the rock ledge where he had regained himself, or the back of the horse upon which he had been transported down the mountain. He leaned back and closed his eyes. He had occupied worse seating on other worlds and endured much less captivating company. He liked Lenore's home. It smelled of delicious food, wood-smoke, and forest, all blended with her delicate scent, and he breathed it in, finding strength even in that.

"You're not going to disappear again, are you?" she asked.

He opened his eyes and smiled at her nervous tone. "I am not. I have ample strength to maintain my corporeal form. Thanks to you. I do, however, need food and drink."

"What kind of drink? Tea? Coffee? I have no alcohol."

Carefully, he sought knowledge of those from one of the mildly receptive minds he had sensed before. Alcohol, he knew, was a deadly poison, one he cared not to try. It was as dangerous as the drugs Rankin and B'tar were busily extracting from Earthly plants.

Tea? Coffee? He projected both words out a very small, and he hoped, safe distance. An image came to him of a woman, shorter than Lenore, much the same age, with yellow hair curled all over her head. Yes. The one who had wanted a ship and a blue ocean and a man dressed all in white with shining gold bands on his sleeves and on the brim of his white cap. He probed gently and saw that she was now content with a man named Peter, who wore dark blue clothing and a hat with the words John Deere on it, and was telling her about his new calves.

He placed into her mind the names of the two beverages Lenore had offered him and felt the woman breathe in an aroma while her mind said coffee. She sipped, and her cerebral cortex experienced mild stimulation.

"Coffee," he said to Lenore. "Coffee would be very nice. Thank you." He closed his eyes again as she left the room. As warmth began to penetrate his body, he let the jacket and boots go. He would have preferred to divest himself of all covering, but knew it was best that he disturb Lenore's sensibilities as little as possible.

Moments later, the scent he had lifted from the yellow-haired woman's mind drifted to him in reality. "How do you like it?" Lenore called. "Black, or with sugar and milk?"

Once more, he dipped into the consciousness of the other mind, wishing for the convenience of merely tapping into Lenore's for knowledge of different tastes and sensations. "Black, if you please," he said.

She returned, carrying steaming drinking vessels on a flat rectangle that she set on a low table before him. She lifted one of the vessels, took a seat at a right angle to him, and sipped. He sat watching her, waiting for his turn. It did not come. She tilted her head to one side and looked at him inquiringly. "Please," she said, "drink your coffee before it gets cold."

"You will not feed it to me?" he asked.

"What?"

He knew very well she had heard his words, yet her facial expression told him she had not understood. "Are you really too weak to lift your own coffee cup?"

"No, no, of course not, but . . ." And then he remembered what he would have remembered long before had he not been injured. On Earth, that kind of sharing was uncommon.

With Lenore, though, it was what he wanted. How strange. He never had difficulty adapting to the customs of other worlds, adopting them as his own while he was there, trying to blend in as he investigated a crime. But here, while he was certainly hoping to bring two criminals to justice, there was a deeply personal element to his time on Earth. Maybe that explained his strong desire to have her join him in the ritual of bestowing sustenance, one to the other.

Dropping to his knees before her, he gently took her cup from her hand and, holding it in both of his, tilted it to her lips, showing her how it should be. "Drink," he said.

Her eyes wide, startled, and confused, gazed at him over the rim of the cup, but she drank. He then set the it on the table and waited.

With a frown, she picked up, not her own, for real sharing, but his, as if they were strangers, holding it as he had, in two hands. She lifted it to his lips. The beverage flooded his mouth as contentment flooded his senses. Because he yearned so strongly to share the full emotion of this gracious participation with her and knew he could not unless she agreed, he gently tilted the vessel upright after only one sip. "Thank you," he said. He would make himself be satisfied with even such a small beginning.

No! He negated the thought even as it was born. Not

a beginning. The word suggested there would be a continuation, which there would not be. Could not be. He had six Earth weeks, no longer, and even waiting that long would entail great risk.

"I . . . uh . . . thank you," she repeated and offered him the cup again. Once more, he sipped, then lifted his head. She watched him almost warily, but when he lifted her cup and held it to her lips, she drank. Pleasure filled him. Ah, but she was swift when it came to accepting new habits! Pride in her glowed through him, he beamed it at her with only his eyes.

She blinked, as if even that contact was too powerful for her to sustain and turned her head away from the drink he offered. She jumped to her feet.

"Food," she said. "You told me you needed food. And I forgot. I'm sorry. I'll get you . . . something."

He caught her hand. "You will get us both something," he corrected her. "And we will share. Yes?"

He watched her face pale, then color delicately. Slowly, she nodded. "Yes." It was little more than a whisper. "We will share."

He didn't even have to dip into her subconscious to know all of what she wanted to share with him. He read it in her eyes, saw it in the graphic projection her mind flung outward. It was all he could do to remain there on his knees. Not until she had left the room again did he rise and return to his chair.

Lenore . . . Lenore . . . who are you? Did my Kahniya lead me to you, specifically?

Chapter Ten

Lenore felt hysteria rise in her throat as she stumbled from the living room into the kitchen. What kind of food did a woman serve to an alien? When she had fed him stew, she'd had no idea of what he was. But . . . did she, even now, know for sure? Of course not!

Despite all evidence to the contrary, it was impossible to fully accept Jon as an alien. He looked too human. He felt too human. He kissed too human.

She gripped the edge of the counter and stared into the polished bottom of the antique stainless steel sink. *Wrong, Lenore! The man does not kiss like a human. He kisses like an angel.*

To distract herself, she waved on the kitchen receiver. Responding to her chip, it activated. It was tuned, as it usually was, to a twenty-four-hour newsie, which she picked up in midsentence, scarcely glancing at the holo-image forming in the corner of the room. She wanted only the sound to block out those wild and ever wilder thoughts crowding into her mind like the avalanche.

An avalanche—she had never experienced one, so how could she have known so intensely the suffocating sensation, the cold, the weight, as the snow tumbled her end over end, rolled her from side to side, ricocheted her off tree trunks? Though it had been dark under the depths of snow, she had sensed large boulders narrowly missing her, had the feeling they were being repelled by some force she did not understand. How? How could she know the flood of relief to see daylight when at last her scrambling hands broke through the surface when it had not been her hands at all, but those of someone—something?—in yet another waking dream?

She shivered.

". . . and now on the lighter side of the news," the announcer said, a definite chuckle in his voice. "A pair of otherwise sober Minnesota farmers have reported the strange appearance and then disappearance of a naked man who first showed up in the middle of a field of winter rye. He was picked up, covered in nothing but goosebumps, a ratty pair of coveralls he'd stolen from a scarecrow, and a 'real pretty necklace' according to the couple. He claimed to be a truck operator whose rig had been hijacked.

"When the woman attempted to report the crime to the local authorities, the man simply 'winked out of existence,' she says, leaving behind nothing but that old pair of greasy coveralls. She lamented his not leaving the necklace, saying it would have been better payment for the huge breakfast he packed away than an old scrap of den—"

"Stop!"

Lenore whirled as Jon all but leaped into the kitchen. "Can you make it go back?"

"Back—" She stared at him, then at the bread that had slid out of the toaster. "Make what go back? Back where? Are you talking about the toast? You want it darker?"

He shook his head distractedly as he stared at the image of the broadcaster who had now moved on to the latest announcement from the Weather Control Bureau. "To the man with the necklace. Was there an image?"

"I wasn't looking," she confessed, then suddenly understood. "Do you think it was one of your . . . Octad?"

"Yes. It must have been." There was not so much as a tinge of doubt in his tone. His green eyes, alive with excitement, with hope, glowed.

"Why?"

"Because he translated . . . disappeared from where he was. And left behind the garments he wore." He drew in a deep breath and puffed it out quickly. "We cannot translate solo in the atmosphere," he said, "unless we are naked."

Lenore swayed and clutched the back of a chair, mind flashing on that moment when she had been inside the cave with him, and the next instant when the two of them had been outside, still fully clad, standing beside Mystery, whom he had brought out of his closed stall in some . . . well . . . mysterious manner.

"You translated . . ." She swallowed hard. It was difficult to use the word in that context, but she knew no other for what he had done. "You translated solo out of the cave with your clothes on."

He laid his hand over hers on the back of the chair. "No, Lenore. I did not. We translated. Together. You and

155

I. And I was not wearing clothing. I was wearing the illusion of clothing. As I am now. It is a minor talent of mine, creating illusions. In my Octad, Zareth is the real master of it. An Octad is carefully chosen, each for a special faculty that will enhance those of the others. When we are together, with Fricka to maintain our surround, Zareth can create the illusion that we are not there, though we might be within a crowd of many."

She reached out to touch the shirt sleeve she could see—and her fingers met with skin. She remembered the way his body had felt outside in the meadow when they were embracing, kissing. "Are you telling me you're naked? Right now? That I only think I see you wearing clothes? You're making me think that?"

In less than an eye blink, his clothing was gone.

Her head grew light, and her vision blurred. "Sit down," he said, easing her onto a chair at the table. "I did not enter your mind in order to link with you. The link was already there. Physically. When I moved, you naturally came with me."

She gazed up at him and shook her head, numb and disconcerted, chaotic thoughts flickering here and there and everywhere. Then she pulled herself together.

"Naturally," she echoed. "Oh, yes, of course. This has all just been a perfectly normal, natural four days for any woman who's completely out of her mind."

Jon stroked her hair. "Toor-a-loor-a-loor-a," he sang. "Toor-a-loor-a-lie . . ."

Before Lenore's fist caught him in the solar plexus where she had aimed it, he caught it in his hand. With his other, he tilted her face up and kissed her until she had no thought, sane or otherwise, left in her head. Only feelings, sensations, easily as chaotic as her thoughts had been, circulating through her blood.

She hungered for more. Kissing was not nearly enough. It was, though, all he seemed willing to give her just now. He held her away from him, eyes roving over her face, before he bent and touched the tip of her nose with his lips. "You mentioned food?"

"I'll have soup and sandwiches ready in a few minutes," she said the moment she was able to speak coherently. "When we've eaten, we'll access the newsie-site and get a replay of the item."

He seemed to shake himself, as if deliberately forcing a return of his normal impassivity. "Can we not do it now?" His tone was quiet but insistent, his stare intense.

Shrugging, she complied, seeking a replay, and let him watch it as she buttered the toast, spread it with chicken-flavored nutrient paste, added lettuce, then slapped the sandwiches together. She unzipped two cans of soup and while the heat strips worked, cut the sandwiches, put them on plates, and set one before Jon.

"Nothing," he said, his face bleak. "There was no picture of the man—only the woman who was reporting the incident."

"I'm sorry, Jon." She touched his hand. "You'll find your people. There must be a way. But first, you need to get stronger."

She served the soup in thick bowls. Without being asked or urged by more than the lost expression in his eyes, she picked up his spoon, filled it with soup and held it to his lips. When he had taken the mouthful, instead of using her bowl to feed her, he lifted the spoon she had set beside her soup, dipped it into his own bowl and offered her his food.

Sharing like that, turn and turn about, bite for bite, until his bowl was empty and they began on hers, feeling his lips brush her fingertips when she held out a sandwich for him to sample, tasting the unique flavor of his skin when his finger rubbed against her lips made for the most erotic meal she had ever eaten.

When the meal was finished, he rose, towering over her. "I wish to thank you properly for sharing sustenance with me."

He took her hand in one of his and lifted her to her feet. She rose willingly, too willingly. With his other hand, he tilted her face up and kissed her. She didn't fight it. Kissing Jon was far preferable to thinking anyway. Especially kissing a very warm and extremely naked, and totally aroused Jon.

When the kiss ended, she rocked back on her heels and stumbled toward the counter, her breathing ragged, pulse erratic. Her insides quivered, but she fought for control. She stared at him. He was fully erect, ready for sex. An erection of that nature was not something she thought even an alien male could fake. "You ... I ..." She swallowed hard as she realized that, she, too, wore not a single stitch of clothing. Nor was it visible anywhere in the kitchen.

"What happened to my clothes?" she shouted, taking refuge in fury.

"They are not far away. I merely put them out of our sight."

"Well, you can damn well put them back in our sight! Back on my body!" She wrapped her arms over her breasts, hugging herself tightly to try to remain intact, knowing she was in grave danger of flying away into a million shattered shards of ... of what, she couldn't begin to imagine.

"Please," Jon said. "Do not cover yourself. My *Kahniya* will keep the temperature in a comfortable range.

If you do not find it so, you need only tell me. I like to look at you."

She swallowed hard. Dammit, she liked to look at him, too, and he was right. It was plenty warm in the cabin now, though dusk was creeping in, and the outside temperature had surely dropped.

She made a harsh sound. "Don't bother with idle compliments, Alien. They aren't necessary. I've already said I'll help you. And I'll do it without the expectation of any kind of reward."

"I do not make idle compliments," he said, appearing relaxed and under complete control, though his erection had only partially subsided. "I do enjoy the sight of your body. And its scent—the textures of your skin and hair."

Lenore sighed then dropped her arms from her breasts. "I'm thirty-seven years old, Jon," she said. "I faced reality a long time ago. My body is just that—my body. It's nothing special. And gravity has certainly taken its toll."

"It pleases me." He was suddenly behind her, without her having been aware of his moving, his hands on her shoulders, turning her to face a mirror hanging in the hallway across from the kitchen. "Look at yourself, your body, try to see it as I do. You have straight shoulders, a tapered waist, feminine hips and perfect breasts and—"

"Hair!" she squealed, òne hand flying upward to brush back the long hair that hung down over one of those 'perfect' breasts. "My hair is short. I keep it that way because it's practical and now look at it. How the hell long have we been here, anyway?

"How long were we in that damned cave?" she demanded when he didn't answer. "How could my hair have grown to such a length in what seems only hours to me?"

Jon reached out and drew her against his chest as he rocked her back and forth, sideways, his arms folded across her naked middle. "Toor-a-loor-a-loor-a . . ."

She wrenched herself free, spun, and faced him, hands on her hips. "Dammit, Jon! How long have I been with you?"

"Since the beginning of time," he said, and his expression suggested he actually believed it. His tone made it a truth she came all too close to accepting. She shivered, not with cold, but with something she couldn't quite identify. Less than fear, more than apprehension, much too pleasantly mingled with . . . anticipation.

She forced herself to concentrate on what was immediately important: the collection of information so that when she made a decision, whatever kind of decision that might eventually be, it would have a chance of being a rational one. "When, exactly, did I find you in the cave?"

"By your reckoning, less than forty-eight hours ago."

She lifted her chin high. "And by yours?"

"I do not measure time as you do."

"Fine, but that doesn't explain my hair." She tossed her head and felt the curled locks sweep across her back. She shook her head again, just to be sure. "It would take two or three years for it to reach this length."

"Your hair is the way you want it to be."

"It is not! Change it back."

"I cannot, *letise*. It is your hair. Only you can change it back."

"Arrgh!" With a growl of pure frustration, Lenore glared at him. "That is impossible!"

"Obviously, it is not. If you can make it grow to please

Thrill to the most sensual, adventure-filled Romances on the market today...

FROM 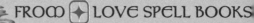 LOVE SPELL BOOKS

As a home subscriber to the Love Spell Romance Book Club, you'll enjoy the best in today's BRAND-NEW Time Travel, Futuristic, Legendary Lovers, Perfect Heroes and other genre romance fiction. For five years, Love Spell has brought you the award-winning, high-quality authors you know and love to read. Each Love Spell romance will sweep you away to a world of high adventure...and intimate romance. Discover for yourself all the passion and excitement millions of readers thrill to each and every month.

Save $5.00 Each Time You Buy!

Every other month, the Love Spell Romance Book Club brings you four brand-new titles from Love Spell Books. EACH PACKAGE WILL SAVE YOU AT LEAST $5.00 FROM THE BOOK-STORE PRICE! And you'll never miss a new title with our convenient home delivery service.

Here's how we do it: Each package will carry a FREE 10-DAY EXAMINATION privilege. At the end of that time, if you decide to keep your books, simply pay the low invoice price of $17.96, no shipping or handling charges added. HOME DELIVERY IS ALWAYS FREE. With today's top romance novels selling for $5.99 and higher, our price SAVES YOU AT LEAST $5.00 with each shipment.

AND YOUR FIRST TWO-BOOK SHIP-MENT IS TOTALLY FREE!

IT'S A BARGAIN YOU CAN'T BEAT! A SUPER $11.48 Value!

Love Spell ✦ A Division of Dorchester Publishing Co., Inc.

GET YOUR 2 FREE BOOKS NOW—AN $11.48 VALUE!

Mail the Free Book Certificate Today!

Free Books Certificate

YES! I want to subscribe to the Love Spell Romance Book Club. Please send me my 2 FREE BOOKS. Then every other month I'll receive the four newest Love Spell selections to Preview FREE for 10 days. If I decide to keep them, I will pay the Special Member's Only discounted price of just $4.49 each, a total of $17.96. This is a SAVINGS of at least $5.00 off the bookstore price. There are no shipping, handling, or other charges. There is no minimum number of books I must buy and I may cancel the program at any time. In any case, the 2 FREE BOOKS are mine to keep—A BIG $11.48 Value!

Offer valid only in the U.S.A.

Name _____

Address _____

City _____

State _____ *Zip* _____

Telephone _____

Signature _____

If under 18, Parent or Guardian must sign. Terms, prices and conditions subject to change. Subscription subject to acceptance. Leisure Books reserves the right to reject any order or cancel any subscription.

A $11.48 VALUE

Get Two Books Totally
FREE—
An $11.48 Value!

▼ Tear Here and Mail Your FREE Book Card Today! ▼

yourself, you can make it short again—if that is what you truly want." He smiled and cupped his hands over her shoulder, pulling her into him for another of those kisses that took her on a wild emotional roller coaster and left her dizzy, incoherent, scarcely able to stand.

"What are you doing to me?" She wanted to scream the words at him, but they emerged as only a faint, plaintive murmur.

"Only what we both want to do."

"No, we both do not!" she denied as she spun from him. As she did so, she felt her hair sweep across her back, caressing between her shoulder blades in a strangely erotic manner. She gasped, reached up, and grabbed two fistfuls of it, dragging it around to the front. One long tress curled around her left nipple. She stared down at it, then whirled and faced him again.

"I cannot believe this!" she cried. "Just look at it! It's positively decadent. This is not like me at all. My father would disapprove very, very strongly. It's . . . not becoming in a professional environment."

"You are not at present in your professional environment," he pointed out so reasonably she wanted to clout him. She didn't need to hear that. Of course she wasn't. What she was—was caught up in another bizarre dream in which she stood naked and long-haired staring at herself in a mirror with a bronze-skinned cross between a Viking and a Greek god posed behind her, his large hands loose on her waist. They made it look impossibly small. Over her shoulder his beads of light winked and twinkled and tempted her to touch them, to follow wherever they—and he—might lead.

"Your hair is very beautiful, Lenore. It is the like of the inside of a *florentia* shell, filled with shimmering lights and secret shades from brown to copper to gold to red that reveal themselves only as you move."

"You're out of your alien mind!" she shouted, raking her hair off her face. "My hair is brown. Unadulterated, plain-Jane brown with no hidden highlights of any description."

"I enjoy looking at it. I see all those things in it." He lifted a handful of tresses and let the strands filter slowly through his fingers to trickle back over her shoulder. "I enjoy even more than touching it, smelling it." His breath warmed her ear, his lips skimmed the sensitive skin just below it.

The memory surfaced of a dream in which he was tangling both his hands in her hair. But . . . was she remembering a dream, or something that had happened only moments before? As if he might do just that again and destroy whatever frail self-restraint she maintained, she edged away from him.

When she was sure she had enough distance between them that he could no longer draw her like a magnet, she rushed into the bathroom and slammed the door behind her. She even locked it, not that she thought for one second it would do any good if Jon really wanted in. Locking herself up would be as effective as Jon's locking up Rankin, should he ever catch him.

Then, leaning with both hands on the sink, she stared long and hard at her hair. Again, she rocked her head slowly from side to side, tilted it back, and felt the fall of it caressing the bare skin of her back. *You can make it short again—if that is what you truly want. . . .*

"All right, hair," she said, "shorten up."

It did nothing. Once more, she willed it to go back the way it had been before that damned alien had messed with it. Of course it did nothing of the sort.

Maybe he could will his—and her—clothing on and off, but she could will nothing, not even her hair to be as she wanted it, and certainly not her body to stop wanting him. Unless he was right, and she really wanted her hair long . . . and curled . . . and sexy, to tickle her nipples and make them pop up into hard, aching beads. . . .

To her utter dismay, she giggled, watching them do just that as she turned her head back and forth, moving her hair over her breasts. Then, she sat down on the fuzzy toilet seat cover, buried her face in her hands and wept. When she was finished, she turned the shower on full force, stepped in and scrubbed her body until it glowed, and shampooed her hair until it squeaked. Then, after wrapping her head in a towel that soon turned soggy—much soggier than if her hair had remained at its normal, practical length—she rubbed herself dry. That done, she grabbed a pair of scissors and hacked her hair off short to the nape of her neck, angled it back and down from her ear lobes, and pinned the front firmly off her face. As far as style went, there was none.

But she felt infinitely more like herself.

Then she snatched up a terry-cloth robe she had left hanging behind the bathroom door, jammed her arms into the sleeves, wrapped it tightly around her middle and defiantly knotted the sash.

"I am my own person, Alien. And the sooner you learn that the better."

Feeling much more in control, Lenore strode from the bathroom. "We have to leave here," she said decisively. "If you want to access the full web and the information we can collect from it, we can do it better from my own home."

Jon glanced at her over his shoulder. He'd been watching a holo on the newsie. He made no comment on seeing her body covered, or her hair short again, just raised one expressive eyebrow, which made her want to smack him, or at least toss a blanket over his magnificent form.

"This is not your home?"

"Not my real home. It's for vacations. I come here to get away."

His face brightened as if he fully understood. "It is one of your safe places."

Lenore had never thought of it in those terms. She nodded slowly. "Something like that, I suppose."

"What makes it safe for you?"

She shrugged. "Well, for one thing, if it hadn't been summer when the Big One hit in '21, I wouldn't likely be here talking to you. Caroline and I would both have been killed when much of the Cascadia Corridor was turned to rubble. Caroline was a day-student in the school where I boarded, but because it happened during summer vacation, we were both here with her grandparents. Her parents weren't so lucky. They died in the quake."

Her voice shook, but she steadied it. "Two-thirds of the Pacific Coast from Northern Mexico to Alaska either changed drastically or simply disappeared. As it was, we got pretty shook up even here in the mountains, and the roaring went on for what seemed like forever."

"You speak of a tectonic action? My studies included the fact that there is geological instability in many sections of Earth."

"Yes. And the luck of your draw landed you in one of those sections. Or close to it. Much of the Coast was in ruins when the Pacific Plate finally slid under the

North America Plate, and dropped the Juan de Fuca Plate about eight feet. It completely changed the coastline. Vancouver Island, which used to be one, is now three separate chunks of land separated by mile-wide channels. Baja California no longer exists except as an archipelago. The Olympic Peninsula is an island. What once was Puget Sound is now Puget Strait, open all the way down to the Columbia River. As I said, we were pretty badly shaken even here, but worst was the fallout from the volcanic ash. Mount Rainier, Mount Baker, and Mount Garibaldi all blew their tops within a thirty-minute period. Mounts Hood and Shasta along with a couple in Alaska acted up a little later, during the aftershocks." She shuddered. "So many people died."

"But not your father? He was here, too?"

She laughed. "Of course not. My father would not lower himself to visit such an out-of-the-way place. He was in Geneva at the time. Naturally, he stayed there until everything was cleaned up and moderately civilized again. Though he did make arrangements for me to attend a boarding school in Europe while that happened."

She drew herself up as if proud. "I chose not to go, but stayed here with Caroline and her grandparents. We were both eight years old and attended the local school for a couple of years. It was a . . . different experience for me, living as part of a family. Grandma and Grandpa Francis were as wonderful to me as if I were their grandchild as much as Caroline was. I'd been in a boarding school since I was five."

"Boarding school?"

"A school where children live and are educated."

He sounded outraged as he asked, "They do not live with their parents?"

"Some do. I didn't. But for those two years, I lived

with Caroline's grandparents and attended the local school. As I said, it was a different experience."

"Your smile tells me it was a happy one."

"Yes. Quite happy. Then, when we were ten, and Grandma and Grandpa thought we were ready for it, they sent us back to the school, both of us boarding at that time. But we returned here after that for holidays and vacations as long as we could."

"Why could you not do so forever?"

"We grew up, Jon. We developed other interests. I took a position of responsibility with my father's firm. Caroline became a roving journalist. Our vacations do not necessarily coincide." And Frank, like her father, had been scathing of her affection for the log cabin perched on a mountainside.

"So you come, but you do so alone."

"Most of the time, yes. When Grandma died, a few years after Grandpa, she left the house and property jointly to Caroline and me. I use it more than she does, though. She's a photo journalist and travels the world looking for oddities and other newsworthy stories—"

She broke off and lunged from the kitchen to the living room where she pressed her wrist against her compad, and began to key in the code that would connect her with Caroline.

"Stop!" Jon's hand on hers somehow broke the connection even before it had a chance to form.

"What? Why, for heaven's sake? Caroline can help you better than I can. It's her job to track down anomalies and—"

"And report them, yes?"

"Well, yes."

"Would you ask your friend to lie for you?"

Lenore looked at him curiously for a moment then

closed the face of her compad. "I see what you're getting at. You expect she would want to report what she might learn on your behalf."

"It is what she does."

"Yes. And you would rather remain undercover."

He clearly didn't immediately comprehend the term. Lenore watched him seek it out, then watched his face clear.

"That is correct. I would rather not have the world at large know my kind and I are here."

"I doubt very many would believe the stories," she said.

"Perhaps not. The difficulty would arise if Rankin and B'tar were to hear them. They, of course, would have no trouble believing. Though I think they are aware of our presence already."

"What if you offered Caroline an exclusive when this was all over?"

He smiled. "I offer it to you, to offer to her. When this is all over. Will she believe you?"

Lenore had to laugh again. "Not in a million years. She'll think my mind has finally snapped. She's a very pragmatic journalist, and doesn't, as her grandfather would have said, 'suffer fools gladly.' " She puffed out a short sigh and muttered, "Damn. Well, like I said, we'll do better with a full-access system such as I have at home. We'll leave first thing in the morning."

"I'm not sure I will have regained enough strength to move us," Jon said.

"I don't intend to 'translate' with you," she retorted. "I have a perfectly good vehicle at Angus McQuarrie's farm."

He looked extremely doubtful. "We will travel in that?"

"Yes. It's a two-seater car. You have some kind of objection?"

After a moment, he met her challenging tone with an uneasy smile. "I have ridden in many different forms of transportation over the years of my career. But not in such a thing as you refer to—a car." His eyes took on that slightly vacant expression she had to be quick to catch, and she knew he was swiping the vision of a car from some unsuspecting mind.

She wanted, suddenly, and with a fierceness that took her aback, to be away from him, not to have to look at him, not to have to wonder what she would learn if she could see into his mind as easily as he could see into those of others. It frustrated her that she could not, and infuriated that she should even want to.

"I'm going to bed. There's another bedroom through that door." She gestured to the far side of the living room. "You'll find linens and blankets in the closet across from the bathroom. Help yourself. Or perhaps you can just create the illusion the bed is made up."

She gave him a long, hard look. "And I do not want my dreams disturbed or invaded in any way at all, Alien. You got that?"

He nodded. Though his face was grave, something about it suggested he was carefully controlling his amusement. She didn't care. Right now, she was still filled with righteous indignation, still on a roll, and she had no intention of letting it go.

She swept a glance over his nude body. "I don't have anything to offer you in the way of pajamas, so I guess you'll also have to create the illusion of some for yourself if you want them."

"I do not require clothing in which to sleep." He regarded her curiously for a moment. "Do you?"

"In this part of the world I certainly do. It gets cold here in the mountains."

"If I maintain a steady, comfortable temperature throughout the house, will you sleep as I do, clad only in your skin?"

She stared at him. "Why would you want me to do that? Didn't I make myself clear? I am sleeping in one of the bedrooms upstairs. You are to occupy the one down here. So what I wear, or don't wear, will be no concern of yours."

"I would like to think of you as sleeping unclad."

Her stomach did a quick, uncomfortable flip-flop. "You can think of me any way you want," she retorted. "So long as I don't have to know about it. Goodnight." She marched up the stairs, trying very hard to ignore the soft laughter she heard rising behind her.

Chapter Eleven

As Lenore buttoned the high neck of her warm, flannel granny-gown, she couldn't help thinking of Jon in the room beneath hers, lying naked and golden, asleep on the bed the Francises had occupied.

She climbed into her own bed, rolled on her side, tucked her knees up to her middle and pulled the covers over her ears. It was a long, long time before she slept.

Jon lay gathering strength and thinking about Lenore, about how fortunate he had been that his *Kahniya* had led him to her—or as near to her as it could get him. She had helped him regain his health. He stretched his muscles. His once-broken leg was fully healed. He wrinkled his scalp. That wound had long since disappeared as had the gash across his lower back. He exercised his mind by letting it drift carefully, quietly, into the minds of the other two he had been able to access, keeping his power very low lest Rankin still be on the alert, though he had no sense of the other man's presence, and his *Kahniya* offered no alarm.

Slowly, carefully, feeling his way, he learned much from the man who had dreamed of the riches gold would bring him, from the woman who thought she wanted adventure. If it were in his power, he would give them both what they really desired—though it would not be what they believed they did. He had done his best already to thank them, showing them how to be content with what they had.

He took from them only what he needed—local knowledge, information about customs he might have missed despite his studying the data gleaned by other explorers of Earth. With so few, and such widely separated windows of opportunity to visit, often information banks had big gaps and much outdated intelligence. He had not been aware of what Lenore called "the Big One," referring to geological activity that sounded, from her description, as having been catastrophic.

Catastrophe came in many different forms, though. He had a difficult and dangerous mission ahead of him and only a limited time in which to succeed. Failure to Jon was not acceptable, so the more data he could gather, the better able he'd be to fulfill his duty.

From Nancy, the woman with yellow hair, he learned that Lenore was a good friend, one who listened and did not judge. Nancy liked Lenore, admired her, envied her, but knew little of value concerning her life away from here. He wished he had been more capable and had delved deeper when he'd had the chance, before he made that promise of privacy to Lenore.

From the man, Angus McQuarrie, he collected knowledge of crops and stock and fatherhood and the warm comfort of a long and fruitful mating with a woman whose mind Jon could perceive only dimly. There was no opening for him to penetrate, just as there was no opening for him in any of the other human entities he knew populated the immediate area. There was, he sensed, no *baloka* between the two, but what existed fully satisfied Angus McQuarrie.

Even more important, from Angus he accessed a firm grasp of geography.

Casting farther, he sought places nearby where avalanches could have occurred, where there would be dwellings similar to this one he was in, but smaller, such as he had sensed from Minton's quick projection. Purposefully, he touched a particular bead on his *Kahniya* and focused on Minton's image, meanwhile casting forth a narrow, laserlike query, sweeping it delicately from side to side, hoping Minton's presence would bounce it back to him, make the needed connection. Instead, he was plunged suddenly, startlingly, into another mind.

Lenore's! He recognized it the minute it captured him, drew him in to a dream she was having where she was lost and alone and frightened. He knew it was wrong to be there and struggled to back out, but her need called to him. He soothed the fears she experienced, replaced them with peaceful thoughts and vivid, happy images until at last she stopped thrashing under her covers and lay quietly, breathing steady, a softness in her heart that made his ache with yearning to touch it.

He did not, but drifted away into a deep slumber, awakening in a few hours fully refreshed.

*　　*　　*

Lenore was amazed to follow the aroma of coffee downstairs in the morning and find Jon had prepared breakfast as well. Ham, hash-browns, toast, eggs fried a perfect over-easy. As he was the last time she'd seen him, he was completely, comfortably naked. She hoped the ham hadn't splattered, but said only, "This is a treat. I didn't know you could cook."

Odd, how her anger and fear had dissipated during the night. She felt . . . wonderful. Rested. Whole. Ready to take on the world. Even a world that included an incredibly appealing alien.

"I . . . borrowed," he admitted. "The man who wanted gold ate a meal like this only minutes ago. His mate prepared it. I followed what he saw her do because she, I cannot read at all."

However he'd come up with the breakfast, it was delicious, and Lenore scraped up every last vestige of it from her plate. After draining her second cup of coffee, she said: "I'd like to get an early start. How long will it take you to get ready to ride down to the valley?"

He stood. "I am ready now."

She remained seated, but arched her brows.

"No kidding! I strongly suggest you clothe yourself before we leave. Angus has a very old-fashioned wife who would never admit to appreciating the vision you present."

Despite herself, she had to grin. "I might, though, just because I like her, take you dressed the way you are now—in skin—to meet Nancy Worth. She'd be very appreciative."

Laughter bubbled up in her throat, escaped. "But then she'd be very appreciative whether you were clothed or not."

Dammit, *she* was appreciative and would just as soon

have stayed in the cabin for several hours . . . days? . . . months? . . . slowly examining every inch of Jon and his beautiful body. And she did not want to share that experience with anyone.

As if he had read the lust in her thoughts—or maybe in her face, since he had promised and she inexplicably believed in that promise—he chuckled and was suddenly dressed again as he had been for the trip down the mountain, complete with hat and hiking boots.

Lenore gaped then clacked her teeth shut. Really, she was going to have to start getting used to this. "You'll roast in those clothes," she warned him. "By the time we hit the valley floor, the temperature will have risen by at least ten degrees. And when we reach the glideway, it'll be up another fifteen or so. And I intend to use my car's climate control to keep myself comfortable in these clothes." She indicated her light jumpsuit and the jacket she had draped over the back of a chair for the ride down the mountain. She intended to shuck it the minute they were in the car.

He looked down his nose at her. "I will compensate as needed." Not only did he look arrogant, he sounded that way. Since she knew he had reason for both, she changed the subject while sliding their dishes into the sterilizer.

"How are we going to get near your sister without alerting this Rankin guy?"

"First, I must reassemble my team. One way to do that is to discover other incidents that have been seen as newsworthy."

He turned and faced the holo image of the newsie in the corner. She stood near him, watching too. It was always wise to know what lay ahead when one meant to travel. Even the glideways weren't one hundred percent accident proof, though they came close.

The holo showed the various patterns chosen by the Weather Control Bureau for the entire Western sector of North America—morning rain over much of the coastal Cascadia Corridor, to keep the evergreen forests at their best, but it would clear by noon to provide a pleasant remainder for the day; heat and sun farther south and in the central dry-belts would boost the fruit and vegetable crops. Southwesterly winds along the spine of the Great Divide would keep the turbines spinning, providing alternative power for the hydrogen separators when cloud rendered solar collectors less effective.

As far as weather went, in places as remote as this mountain preserve, though, they pretty well got what was left over, or what Nature provided. Though urban populations complained bitterly if their civic leaders failed to persuade the Bureau to their way of thinking prior to celebrations, and parades got rained on, the entire system worked well worldwide. With no more hurricanes, tornadoes, droughts and floods, typhoons and monsoons, world population was a good deal safer and more stable. The geologists were still working on earthquake control, so far with little success.

She pulled a skeptical face as the Weather Control advisory faded to be replaced by a panel discussion on the validity of sending yet another ship to Mars for further exploration. She wondered what kind of answer she'd get from Jon if she asked about Mars. Its history. Its potential. Its future . . . as it involved humanity, and decided she didn't want to know—even if he did.

"You'll be looking for such oddities as men disappearing and leaving behind old denim coveralls?"

"Exactly."

Lenore began clearing perishables from the refrigerator and sealing them into protective bags where they would store safely and perfectly in the cupboards until the next time someone came to the cabin and refreshed them.

"Jon . . . one thing you need to understand. A lot of what appears on the newsies, even the so-called 'serious' ones, and in other publications, is pure fiction. There are a great many people who find such fantasies entertaining. And nearly as many who actually believe them. I don't know how we are going to separate fact from tabloid junk."

His perfect brows drew together over his perfect nose. "Can you not tell the difference?"

"I always thought so. But . . . for instance, if I had heard that story about the man wearing the scarecrow clothes and the fancy necklace and disappearing right before the woman's eyes, I'd have put that down to someone's fantasy, reported to titillate those who enjoy such speculation."

"You would not have believed it?"

She shook her head. "Of course not."

"And if you had heard of a woman who had dreams of a man who begged her to come to his assistance and did so, you would not have believed that, either."

She smiled at him over her shoulder. "What makes you so sure I believe it now?"

His chuckle seemed to rumble from his very depths. His green eyes sparkled with amusement. "Your kisses told me you believe in me." He sobered. "And your responses . . . in your dreams . . . told me so much more."

She whirled so fast she nearly fell. "Dammit! I told you to stay the hell out of my dreams!" No wonder she'd felt so . . . fulfilled this morning. A flash of frustration stabbed through her. If she'd had to have them, why couldn't she remember last night's dreams?

"The dreams of before," he said hurriedly. "When I was calling to you for assistance."

"Oh." Feeling slightly ashamed, she stuffed a head of lettuce into a bag and held it until every vestige of air was gone and the seal activated.

"Can you not trust me when I say I will not enter your mind again, Lenore, unless invited? I did not give you dreams last night. You projected fear and grief, however, and I took those from you and replaced them with serenity. But I did not enter."

Some element in his voice compelled her to face him again. He had his hands linked together on the back of a chair, clenching them so tight his knuckles shone white through his skin. "Believe me, please." His earnest face pleaded with her. "It is true, Lenore. I do not lie to you."

"I . . . All right." She closed her eyes for a second to escape the stunning power of his gaze. It didn't help. "I apologize for doubting you. It's just that some of the feelings I have . . . about you, are so different from anything I've ever experienced I'm not sure how to handle them."

His throat worked as he swallowed. "Lenore . . . I truly want to share those feelings with you."

She struggled against disappointment she knew she had no right to feel. "But, of course, you don't share them. There is no way you can. We are, in the very true sense of the words, from different worlds. I understand, Jon. I'm sure you have . . . commitments wherever you come fr—where you live." *Where and when. A place not here, not now.* It was a concept that still gave her great difficulty. "A relationship with someone. I know you were only making empty promises so I would help you. I . . ."

"Lenore!" His hands on her shoulders transmitted urgency even more strongly that his voice. "You misunderstand me. I do not communicate well with only words. If you would but let me show you . . . my way, what I mean, you would know that I am asking you to, uh, sleep with me? That is what you say, is it not, when you mean mate—join minds and bodies? So we can share those feelings."

She had to laugh at the evident confusion in his tone, on his face. "That term—'sleep with'—is a euphemism for having sex, which is a joining of bodies, not minds. You pulled that out of someone else's brain, didn't you?"

He managed to look both haughty and guilty at the same time. "Yes, I did. Nancy Worth enjoys sleeping with the man in the blue hat. I needed a term you would understand."

"Oh, I understand, all right. You want to have sex with me."

He brightened. "May I?"

Again, she laughed. "No!"

Once more, he frowned. "You want the same thing. The same kind of sharing."

She wrapped her fingers around his wrists. "I want a whole lot more than that, Jon, and I don't think that's what you're offering. So, what do you say we leave here, go to my home where I have greater access to information, find your people so you can rescue your sister and translate back to wherever you came from. That strikes me as the most sensible plan."

He looked at her for a long moment, as if assessing her. For an instant she was afraid he might be taking a surreptitious peek inside her mind, that he might know just how badly she wanted to have sex with him. She would greatly prefer that to leaving the cabin and going back to the city. "And you pride yourself on always doing the most sensible thing, don't you?"

She returned his steady gaze.

"Yes, Jon. I do."

Why did admitting it seem so terribly ... dishonest?

At the foot of the trail, Lenore slipped from Mystery's back. "You don't have to," she told Jon, when he followed suit. "It's just that if someone should see us, they'd probably string me up from the nearest cottonwood for overburdening a poor, ancient horse. They'd have no way of knowing you were carrying most of the load."

He tilted his head to one side, lifting his brow. The sun spilled golden light over his head. "Now ... I must ask. Have you been snooping into my mind?" His expression told her clearly he would not be the least bit offended to learn she had done so.

"No. Of course not," she said quickly, trying to hide even from herself the longing to be able to do just that. To know him. "To begin with, I wouldn't know how. For another thing, I'd consider that an enormous invasion of privacy. But ... I know this old horse. He couldn't have carried us both down the mountain without some assistance, and since I sure didn't lend him any of my strength, guess who that leaves as the culprit?"

He nodded. "Helping a poor, elderly horse turns me into a culprit, does it?"

Lenore smiled, enjoying the smile her alien returned to her, admiring the way his teeth flashed white in the bronze of his face, the way small crinkles fanned out from the corners of his eyes, the deeper grooves that creased his cheeks, almost creating dimples. She was glad he didn't have those. It would have been just too perfect. Odd, how clothed and out in the open, fully healthy again, he no longer appeared to be in his mid-twenties. More like her own age, she thought. Possibly even a few years older, though there was no gray that she could see within the dark-honey thickness of his hair. There was just an indefinable sense of maturity about him that she found comforting. And extremely appealing.

Angus's tractor whirred to a stop as they crossed the road toward his fence. He shaded his eyes with one hand as he watched them approach, leading the horse. Lenore waved.

"We're heading out today, Angus," she called. "I'll put Mystery in the barn and stop in to say good-bye to Jane."

"Okay, Lenore." he said from his high perch. "You didn't stay long. Thought you were here for a month or more. Everything all right?" He rested a curious gaze on Jon, taking in every detail, Lenore knew. An expression of mild puzzlement crossed his face.

"Just fine, Angus. This is my friend Jon."

"Jon," he said, looking thoughtful. "I've met you somewhere, haven't I? I sort of associate you with . . . gold. You done some prospecting in the area, maybe?"

"No." Jon's tone was pleasant but firm.

"Jon only arrived . . . uh . . . this morning," Lenore improvised quickly. "A friend dropped him off, and he hiked to the cabin. I had no idea he was coming to visit, but he's much more of a city person than a country person, so I'm taking him back down the Corridor."

"Right. Well, drive carefully till you're locked onto the glideway. The last time I went down that way, I saw how badly Transport's letting things deteriorate up here."

"Yes. I know."

This was one of Angus's hobby-horses and given a chance, he'd ride it to death. He was one of those people who wanted a glideway right to his door, but didn't want the attendant bustle of people it would bring to his peaceful little valley. Of course, this being an agricultural and forest preserve area, the chances of a glideway coming into the Robson Valley were all but nil. Still, Angus liked to complain.

Quickly, to distract him, she said, "Is Jane in?"

"She's gone over to Nancy's store. You'll find her there for the next hour or so. You know how she and Nancy like to chatter. And now that Nancy's agreed, finally, to marry Peter, they have a lot to yak about. Jane's doing stand-in as mother-of-the-bride."

Well! Now, for sure Lenore was going to stop at the store to learn more about this unexpected turn of affairs.

"Your car's all charged up and ready to go," Angus said. "See you soon, I hope."

"I hope so, too." Lenore smiled as Angus set his machine in motion again and glided off in a whir of electric motor, followed by the inevitable cloud of crows.

After putting Mystery safely out to graze on the new grass in the paddock near the house, Lenore led Jon to her car, a snappy little blue two-seater bubble that she realized, as she opened the passenger door, had never been meant for a man well over six feet tall. Though the seat automatically adjusted to his height and weight, dropping down as low as it could and sliding back to its farthest limits, it was still a tight fit for him.

"If you were willing," he said, shifting as if to try to find a comfortable spot for his knees and shoulders, "I could simply take us wherever it is you want to go."

"My car, too?"

He hesitated as she showed the detector panel her wrist-chip, then punched the keypad to activate the fuel cell, setting the car in motion.

"Perhaps not . . . yet. In another day or two, though . . ."

"But the sooner we find your Octad, the sooner you can accomplish your tasks and leave. We will be at my home in less than two hours. But first, I must stop and say goodbye to my friends."

Outside the store, she said, "Come in, and I'll introduce you to Jane and Nancy." Odd, how much pleasure it would give her to do just that. Especially to see the expression on Nancy's face when Lenore walked through the door with a large, golden god to show off. But no. Maybe not, since Nancy had, as Angus said, 'finally' agreed to marry Peter Johannsen. She'd have too many stars in her eyes to focus on Lenore's spectacular find.

"I think not," Jon said. "I'm not certain I will be able to leave this seat while in my corporeal form."

Lenore blew out a puff of air. The man had a point. It absolutely would not do to have him dematerializing inside her car, then materializing again in plain sight. If Nancy saw that, it would be the tabloids for her and Jon for sure.

Chapter Twelve

It took nearly as long to reach the east-west glideway at Kamloops and lock on as it did to complete the rest of the trip. Once on the glideway, with little to worry about beyond punching in the correct coordinates that would switch them through to the north-south system at the right moment, though, it was pleasant to relax and watch the entire metropolitan area of the Cascadia Corridor spread out on either side of them as far as the eye could see.

"This is a very large center of population," Jon observed, surprising her. She'd been thinking he might find her world provincial, if not primitive.

"It is a series of three city sectors," she said. "They extend from Sector Vancouver at the northern end, through Sector Seattle in the center, and terminate at Sector Portland in the south. Once, it was possible to determine where one left off and the other began, but not for many years. Now, the entire region is called the Cascadia Corridor. There are many such population corridors in North America. This is the westernmost one, and one of the smallest."

He looked worried. "Are there no open spaces beyond what I see below?" The entire five-kilometer-wide band under the glideway was a green belt filled with rivers, lakes, parks, and wilderness areas, with frequent off-shoots leading into the urban developed areas.

"Oh, yes. Many. Forest preserves that are allowed to remain as close to their natural state as possible."

"And people do not go there?"

"Of course they do. Where we came from is a mountain preserve. The valley where we left the horse is an agricultural preserve. There are cities, and there are rural areas all over this continent and the others."

"Yes. My studies told me that, but seeing this . . ." He waved a hand at the speed-blurred city-scape on both sides of the glideway, visible right up the slopes of the mountains in the east, crowding right out to the edge of the ocean in the west. "Seeing this, I had to wonder where Rankin might be collecting the herbals he uses to extract his drugs."

"Could be anywhere. Salal grows in great abundance all the way from Alaska to Oregon. If he's collecting it, he could be near, or he could be a thousand klicks away. Though I think most of the commercial—legitimate commercial picking—is done before the flowers and berries form on it in the spring and summer."

Jon glanced, uneasily, she thought, out of the blue bubble that shielded them from the wind of their rapid passage. "I do not wish to find Rankin until I have assembled my people."

She laid her hand over his where it rested on his

thigh. "We will find your people, Jon. Somehow, we will find them."

He turned his hand over and linked their fingers.

"Yes," he said. "We will."

If only she hadn't touched him, Lenore thought, feeling the heat of him circulate through her body, setting her nerve-endings afire. A need for him grew in her, grew to unimaginable proportions, and when she finally left the glideway and guided her car the last few kilometers to the narrow slot where it automatically plugged itself into its recharger, she was trembling with hunger to know what a union with Jon would be like.

When they emerged from the car—Jon managed without dematerializing—he reached for her again at the same moment she reached for him, unwilling, maybe even unable, to give up that physical contact and the promise it offered.

"This is your home?" he murmured.

"Yes." It was difficult to speak.

"Take me into it," he said, and in the request, she heard much, much more.

It seemed only natural, then, for them to continue holding hands as they mounted the escalator that carried them to her second-floor apartment. It seemed just as natural for her to lead him directly through the bright living room and into her dim bedroom. There they stood, facing each other, eyes locked, minds in tune, she thought, each knowing exactly why they were there, both wanting the same thing with the same intensity.

A cool breeze blew suddenly across her back and she realized her clothing had simply . . . gone away. As had Jon's. She glanced at the floor. There were no garments pooled near their feet. Her gaze flew to the chair and found it empty of everything but a tattered toy monkey. She gasped. "What . . . ?"

Then Jon's warm hands were on her waist, drawing her to him. She could not prevent her own hands rising to glide up over the muscles of his forearms, his biceps, his hard shoulders. She quivered as his gaze caught hers, holding her captive. Between her hands, the gleam of his *Kahniya* tempted her. She longed to touch it, to go where it would lead her, back to that place of wonder and beauty and warmth, of birdsong and perfumed flowers and slowly flowing water under a turquoise sky, but . . . which bead had she touched before that had transported her there?

"Lenore . . ." It was the whisper from her dream, the urgency as intense, and the need in the single word as strong, as compelling. She stepped forward and felt his hard warmth against the full length of her body. "Come with me," he whispered. "Come with me to a place you have never been before."

Shivering slightly with anticipation, she nodded. He took her hand, moved her right index finger and connected it to a bead of light and suddenly she was there—wherever "there" was—and so was Jon.

Water danced in silver ripples as far as she could see. Hot sun beamed down. Beneath her feet, soft growth, not grass, not moss, but green and thick with a hint of purple undertones, cushioned her soles. Small white clouds drifted overhead, casting slowly moving pools of shade. While all around seabirds called and flew, blue, green, yellow, bouncing like butterflies through the sweet air, alighting atop the ripples, disappearing beneath them only to pop up again, often with tiny, silver fish in their beaks.

Whispers on the Wind

Small flowers painted the tips of shrubs with bright red, pale yellow, deep lavender, adding their scents to the overall perfume of the air. Ferns from as small as her hand to as large as a redwood waved and whispered in the breezes. Between where Lenore and Jon stood and the rippling bay, a curve of silver sand arced away into the distance on both sides. She turned. Behind her, more trees grew, covered with the palest of green fronds, wafting a sweet scent across the shore area. Beyond those, rising in higher and higher ridges, a rolling, hilly landscape faded from green to purple as it reached toward an impossibly blue sky.

Not another person could be seen. This was their private world, an Eden for a naked Adam and his Eve.

Jon's hand moved from hers, tracked slowly, so very slowly up her arm she could scarcely see it moving, but felt it in every pore of her body. Finally, he captured her breast, held it, his thumb stroking her nipple. She wanted, how dearly she wanted, to hold him close, but she was afraid to break contact with the bead she touched lest the magical place disappear.

His other hand in the center of her back supported her as he lowered her to the resilient growth. An herbal scent, a mingling of thyme, mint, and something she didn't recognize arose around them, and then his mouth was on hers, seeking, demanding, and his hands stroked over her. This time she knew he would not disappear. This time she knew her body would not be left humming and aching with unfulfilled needs.

Her nails raked down his back, and she realized she had lost her connection with his *Kahniya*, but it seemed, now, not to matter. The substance beneath her remained the same, the small, puffy clouds still floated high in the aquamarine sky and the brilliantly colored birds continued to call out in their musical voices.

She gazed into Jon's green eyes, seeing herself reflected there and parted her legs to cradle his body. "I need you," she said.

"As I need you."

"Then come into me," she pleaded.

"Not yet," he whispered. "There is so much more for us to experience together."

The places he took her were like nothing she had ever dreamed. With the touch of a single finger, he could make her gasp. With the nip of gentle teeth, he caused her to cry out and writhe in an agony of pleasure. With the soothing brush of his lips, he eased the intensity down to something she could tolerate. Her body and his were beaded with moisture, whisked away by soft breezes except where their skin, pressed so tightly together, made that impossible.

She arched against him, seeking. She wrapped her legs around his waist urging him to take her. She laughed when one of the red birds landed on his shoulder and said to her, "Look into his mind, Lenore. He is open to you." But she dared not, though she knew it was Jon who had caused the bird to speak. She waved it away and gazed deeply into Jon's eyes.

"Do you want to be in my mind?" she asked.

"I do. But I will not. I want you to see into me, now Lenore. Come with me. I will not violate your privacy. But from you, I have none. I want none. I want your touch everywhere."

"You have it," she whispered, stroking her hands down his back, curling her fingertips into the resilience of his muscular buttocks. She rolled them both over, straddled his thighs, and cradled him in her hands, one cupping and lifting from underneath, the other sliding up his hard shaft, her thumb stroking back and forth, damp from the bead of semen on its tip. He closed his eyes and groaned.

She bent and touched him with her lips, the tip of her tongue, then gently, carefully, her teeth. He bent like a bow, lifting his hips, and she took him into her mouth. He moaned and thrust hard, once, then pulled back from her.

"Do you not want to know how wonderful that feels to me?"

"I do know," she said, lying full-length upon him, her lips against his neck. "You body, your breathing, your voice tells me you like what I do."

"My mind says it better. You make colors in my mind, colors and scents and sensations I have never before experienced. I want to share them with you, Lenore. Please, let me."

She lifted up and looked into his eyes, her own body vibrating with need for release as she moved against him, unable to do otherwise. His plea resounded against something deep inside her, something that longed to give him what he asked, but she shuddered and could not overcome her fears. Instead of opening her mind, or letting him open his to her, she opened her body and took him inside.

He groaned in pleasure, then slowly, lovingly, he began to move inside her. As tension grew in her, as her breathing became labored and her vision blurred, he somehow held her at that point, until she was slick with sweat, crying out faintly, begging for release.

And then he gave it to her. Gave it to them both. It burst over them like the avalanche, and this time she did not try to fight the swirling, tossing sensation, but tumbled willingly with it, with him. Her climax closed off every semblance of thought.

What must have been aeons later, Lenore became aware of Jon leaning over her, tracing that long curl of her hair over her breasts again, teasing her with it. She opened her eyes slowly, met his smiling gaze and said, "What did you do to me?"

"I loved you, Lenore."

Made love, he meant. She knew that. But even knowing it, her heart leapt with joy at the thought of his loving her, despite the impossibility of it.

"And I will love you again," he said, just before a whistling sound drew his attention and he smiled as he turned them both. "But now, would you like to meet some friends of mine?"

Lenore would not.

She was stark naked in a strange place, had just shared unbelivable sex with an alien, and now he wanted to introduce her to friends? She bit her lip, totally unwilling to share him—to share this place—with anyone else. Though she heard another whistle, she saw no one anywhere along the shore, or in any kind of boat in the water.

"What friends?"

"The *mazayin.*" Jon stood and pulled her up by the hand.

"*Mazayin?*" She repeated the word as he had said it, with the accent on the center syllable. She felt she was becoming much more adept at using the odd bits of his language, though she despaired of ever achieving the musical quality of his tongue.

He swung a gesture at the sea before them. Now, in addition to the birds that danced on its waves, she saw the dark fins of some kind of swimming creature just cutting the surface of the water, approaching at great speed. Still holding her hand, Jon walked from the resilient ground cover over the hot, shifting sand and stood at the creaming edge of the surf.

The animals cavorted near the surf-line. Larger than dolphins, smaller than orcas, the deep blue shade of their sides lightened to silver as they rolled, revealing inky-black double fins on their backs.

"The *mazayin* enjoy company. Come and meet them. We will swim with them." He smiled into her eyes. "For a time," he added, and her insides quivered at the promise she heard in his voice. Half of her was intrigued by the thought of swimming with the animals he called *mazayin,* but the other half wanted only to lie with him again in that soft vegetation, to be alone, to once more realize the totality of satisfaction she had found in physical union with Jon.

Still, Lenore let him lead her farther into the water. Together, they waded waist-deep. The sea, or lake, or whatever it was, wrapped around her body, warm, silken, and as sweet-smelling as the air, but with different overtones—vanilla, cinnamon, and a hint of lemon. It was totally unlike any water she had ever experienced. Even its texture seemed special, softer somehow, more limpid. A *mazayin* glided close by stroking her thigh, and, startled, she crowded nearer Jon, but the creature was no threat. It smiled at her and . . .

It sang!

Its song was not one with any words she could understand, but she was aware of the rhythm, the rhyme of its music. Something compelled her to reach out and touch it. Its hide was soft, like the finest kid gloves she had ever owned. She stroked it and then, to her amazement, it dove and came up under her, lifting her fully from the water. She clutched the fin before her, felt the one behind her flatten and curve to support the small of her back. The beast submerged until she was breast-deep and then, suddenly, she, still astride its back, was flying across the surface of the water. Jon astride another *mazayin* was right beside her, leaping from wave-top to wave-top.

She was one with it, their minds, their bodies, their emotions linked and harmonized. She sang its song, danced its dance, knew its joy and took a deep breath without knowing why she must, and held it. Down, down, down they dove through crystalline depths where fantastic creatures swam among long, waving fronds of rainbow-tinted luxuriance.

A galaxy of stars burst before her, around her, within her, as the *mazayin* exhaled a vast bubble of air for her to breathe, and then they continued on, each turn of the creature's body opening new vistas to her. Light reflected in diffused patterns as she looked up at the silvery surface, refracted as she looked down, and out, and inward, absorbing a kind of beauty she had never seen before.

Suddenly, they went sweeping upward again, leaping free, back into the sparkling air. As she drew in another breath, she realized she had never once felt stifled, not for an instant feared for her life. With the *mazayin*, she had explored a world even more alien than the Maxfield Parrish vista in Jon's *Kahniya*.

Again! she begged, and once more she and her mount with Jon and his flew across the surface of the sea. At times she was immersed up to her neck. Other times, she saw water droplets glistening as they poured down her legs and off her toes, splashing to the surface many feet below as her *mazayin* leapt free of the sea.

She felt no fear, only an incomparable sense of freedom, of oneness with the *mazayin*—and with Jon, as if the unity of the beasts opened a link between the two of them, psyche to psyche, soul to soul. She glanced over at Jon and saw her own delight mirrored in his face.

Her hair whipped back. Spray flew. She laughed from unadulterated joy. Birds called and a great chorus of *mazayin* song filled not only the air, but her heart. She threw back her head and sang their wordless song from the sheer delight of being alive.

At her silent pleading, they once again descended beneath the surface, circling a reef of coral with colors so intense she held her breath, though the *mazayin* had just given her another bubble to breathe from. Never had she felt such a staggering sense of familiarity, almost of homecoming. This was her place, one she knew she would want to return to again and again, no matter what it took. And she knew, too, that she would want to return with Jon, that without him, the magic would not exist.

Even if he could not love her as she wanted to be loved, could not be her lifelong mate, she would stay with him for the duration of his time on Earth. And if he left her with a child, she would love it, cherish it, learn with it, and someday, tell it the truth of how it had come to be.

On a tiny islet, hardly more than a shallow part of the sea, the *mazayin* left them for a time, going off to feed on the sea growth far, far below. Their song faded to a faint, lilting murmur.

With their feet buried in soft sand, the sweet-scented water supporting them, Jon lifted Lenore until her legs were around his waist. She made no protest, only looked into his eyes as he gazed into hers. Bending his head, he kissed her breasts, her neck, her stomach. He laid her out in the water so she floated before him, linked only by her legs around him, and traced hot patterns over her skin with damp fingers. He dipped them inside her, bringing her close to the verge of ecstasy, then grasped her thighs and pulled her to him, entering her with exquisite slowness that left her writhing and gasping, straining to get closer.

He tugged her legs farther apart, opening her wider as he gave her everything she wanted. When he was finally deep within her, he stayed very still, holding their slick bodies together, letting only the slow, undulating motion of the waves move them against one another. It was a peerless consummation, him so large, yet so still within her, filling her completely, only the gentle movement of the waves as they rocked and floated her creating an extraordinary sensation. When her climax began in small, quivering flashes of heat that built and swelled and finally overcame her in a rush, he joined her in the release, letting her body float free again but for that scalding point of union, throwing back his head and shouting his relief to the sky above.

"Jon . . ." She could scarcely stand, but he supported her, leading her to an even shallower spot where soft, slick seaweed cushioned them as they sat, letting the ripples wash over them as aftershocks did the same.

"I have never . . ." she said, leaning her head on his shoulder.

"Never what?" His murmur was close to her ear. His hair dripped onto her cheek. She licked away the drops, loving the taste of the water, the taste of him.

"Never known anything like that."

"Nor have I."

She lifted her gaze and looked at him, shaking her

head. "You must have. I suspect you Aazoni are much more . . . accomplished in such matters."

He stroked her hair back from her face, and she felt the streams of water from it trickling down her back. "I have some . . . controls," he admitted. "But somehow, with you, I seemed not to be able to maintain them for long."

"Which is probably a good thing. My heart might have stopped dead if you'd controlled yourself, controlled our joining, denied us both release any longer."

He laughed softly as he cupped her face between his two hands. "No it wouldn't have, my *letise.* I would never let that happen."

The *mazayin* returned then, and Lenore wondered whether Jon had called them or whether they had just known their presence would no longer be an intrusion on the privacy of the people who'd had other games in mind.

How long they swam and played, dived and leapt with the *mazayin* the second time, Lenore never knew. Time had crystallized for her, but the psychic animals knew when hunger pangs began to gnaw at her, for they turned and sped back toward the island, which was nothing more than a distant blur on the horizon. Long after the *mazayin* had left her and Jon back in the shallows she endured a fierce longing to return to that sandbar, far out of sight of land, where there had been only her and Jon and the water that surrounded them.

As Jon showed her what fruit to collect from three different shrubs and with a *florentia* shell dug nuts from beneath a *belgrina* tree, the warm winds dried their skin and hair.

Looking into the shell, she saw the shimmering mixtures of shades Jon had claimed he found in her hair. As the light winds tossed her tresses, blowing them across her eyes, for just a moment she thought she saw what he could see. For just a moment, she felt beautiful.

She touched her skin, finding it as silken and smooth as the water had been. She felt as if she had been treated to the most luxuriant spa ever created. Inside and out. Simply looking at Jon was enough to make her shudder with want again, desire such as she'd only dreamed of—but not until he had entered her dreams. She pushed that thought away. What he had done, what she had done, the bond they had formed, both physical and emotional, seemed far more real than anything even in the dreams.

With broad, reddish leaves from the *belgrina* tree as impromptu bowls filled with a variety of fruits, they reclined in the mossy growth and fed each other with the sweet, succulent food.

It satisfied both thirst and hunger, but somehow honed a different hunger in Lenore. And, she knew without being told, in Jon, too. She leaned over and kissed his warm shoulder, feeling him quiver beneath her touch. She ran a hand up his bicep, lifted the other and cupped his face, marveling again at his lack of beard, and turned him toward her.

"I want you to kiss me," she said.

"I want to do much more than kiss you," he replied, but continued to hold back.

"Then do whatever you want," she invited him.

He did whatever he wanted, and miraculously, it was what she wanted, too.

"Now is it my turn again?" she asked.

He laughed at her eagerness. "Soon it will be, but first, we will rest." He laid his hand on her forehead, stroked gently from temple to temple, and when she awakened, they were back in the bedroom in her Port Orchard apartment.

She touched Jon's face, slid her hands into his hair, so thick and soft to the touch it was like exploring the pelt of an exotic animal. She wove her fingers through it, reveling in its texture.

"Where did you take me?" she asked. "Was it real or a dream?"

"It was real while we were there. My *Kahniya* helped me to recreate it for us."

"But where was it?"

"A place neither of us have ever been before," he said.

"How did your *Kahniya* know to take you there if you had never been there before?"

His smile, so tender as to make her chest ache, the caress of his fingers on her cheek, suggested that however improbable it seemed, his feelings went as deep as her own. "That's not what I meant, *letise*. The physical place is one I have visited many times. It is an island in the Sea of Lancore on Aazonia. But where you and I went . . . that was unique. To both of us." He rolled to one side and drew her with him, her head on his shoulder. He brushed her hair from her face.

"Did we . . . uh, did we do what I thought we did, or was that an illusion you created?"

His smile curved his beautiful lips. "*Letise*, we did everything you remember. The only illusion was the physical surroundings."

"The *mazayin* . . . ?"

"Yes, they were an illusion. I have swum with them many times. That, I shared with you." He paused long enough to kiss her again, long enough to make her

197

quiver with need. "But not as we shared our bodies with each other. That was very real."

"I'm glad," she said. "Because it's a kind of sharing I have never known before."

"Nor I. Even without *baloka,* you and I together reached heights I had only thought I might be capable of." He shivered, and she reached down to pull a light cover over them. "To go so far without *baloka* is not something I ever expected."

"Baloka?"

"The kind of sharing true lovers experience when joined physically, emotionally and mentally. It is what bond-mated pairs strive for and, often after much time, achieve. Some are more fortunate and find *baloka* from the beginning of their mating and know without waiting for it to develop, that they are to be bond-mates."

She bit her lip. "Have you ever been . . . bond-mated?"

"No. Nor have I known *baloka.*" He became very serious, his eyes deepening to a shade verging on teal. "With you, *letise,* I would find it. This, I know."

"Jon . . . we are . . . you and I are not—cannot be—mated. Not in any meaningful way." She drew a line from his broad brow down over the ridge of his nose, pausing at his lips until he parted them and took her finger inside. Slowly, she pulled it free. "You'll leave when your Octad is complete and you've found your sister. I know this. You know it. We have no future."

He closed his eyes for a moment. "I know that," he whispered. "Do you think I want to leave you now that I have found you?"

"I don't know."

Capturing her in his arms, he rolled her over top of him. "I will not want to leave you. I will never want to leave you. If the only way for you to know that, to understand it fully, is for you to come into my mind, then do it, *letise.* Let me give you all that I can."

"Then it wasn't the red sea bird that said those words to me. It was you. Why would I hear it, but not sense your request?"

"You would," he said, "if you would come into my mind. It's open to you, *letise.* You need only enter."

She drew in a tremulous breath. "I . . . don't know how."

His fingers encircled her wrists as he rolled her back over until he was on top of her. Drawing her hands up, he placed them on his temples. His hair tumbled over her fingers and wrists. "Close your eyes," he said. "And feel. See. Know. *Everything."*

Chapter Thirteen

Lenore allowed him to give part of his mind into her keeping. She felt herself becoming ... different ... changing, becoming ... him, while never for one moment losing her own sense of self. She felt, as a woman, his kisses, the hard thrust of his tongue, but also felt the softness a man feels when his lips take a woman's, the gentler, more tentative response of her tongue to his invasion. She felt the pulsating heat of her own need, and savored his delight when his fingers again found a welcome in the slickness of that desire, desire for him, need that matched what he felt.

Through him, she felt the tightness, the hot, smooth wetness of her as she enclosed him. Bright blues and pale lavenders, and greens of a hundred shades, along with reds and pinks and golds swirled in an incredible blend as she felt what he felt, her muscles contracting around him, holding him when he pulled back, releasing him with reluctance, then welcoming him back when he plunged into her. Orchestrations of music pulsed and sobbed, whispered in barely audible notes like a softly played panpipe, rose as sweet and pure as early-morning birdsong then ascended in crashing crescendos, each achieving greater and greater might than those preceding it.

Then, she knew the time was near for him, possibly even nearer than it was for her. With one last, lingering stroke of his fingers, he slid them out of her, glided their moistness—her moistness—over her most needful part, held them there, scarcely moving them as he bracketed that center. She experienced his pleasure in feeling her tension build as her body quivered while the tip of his penis hovered at her entrance. She knew his intense desire to see into her mind and felt, as he felt, the agony of having to deny himself the fullness of the *baloka* he was certain he would discover with her.

And then he entered her, feeling hard and large and rigid, with heat she knew for the first time in her life as a man could know it, building at the base of his spine, heat he struggled to control while she moved erratically beneath him, around him. She knew it was she who tossed and bucked, trying to find a rhythm her frenzied body could not create without guidance, and knew it was his hands that clamped on to her hips, holding her still. She perceived his appreciation of the silk of her own inner thighs as he shifted his grip toward her knees, penetrating deeply. She knew when he sensed he was not making the exact physical connection she required, and knew the moment he knew that they must turn, roll together, letting her find the best position for her deepest satisfaction.

His rapture in their union felt as if it were happening

within her as the pool of heat that generated in the small of his back, expanded, gathered force, threatened to burst free while he strived to control it. She knew the effort with which he contained that force, reveled in his strength and determination. She sensed the depth of the emotional connection he wanted to share with her, recognized his need to complete it and almost . . . almost allowed him into her deepest places, but then her own physical response took over.

Her heart raced as she shared his exultation in the ever-increasing spasms of her muscles as they clenched around him, released to allow him to pull back, gripped him again before he could retreat too far. She reveled in the uncontrollable surges of almost-pain as they drove their bodies together again and again, the rhythm steady now, growing more and more rapid as they climbed together up a slope toward a golden promise of reward. Her body stiffened and held him in its grip. Her head tilted back until her throat was so taut only a high, thin cry of release could force its way out. As her limbs shuddered into limp repose, her heart still raced, her lungs still strained, she felt the hard dam of his hold break. She knew the joyful, triumphant moment when his release came, and experienced with him the hot, blessed liberation of all he had held back. The hot tide of it flowed from him and into her and then there was nothing but an incomparable inner peace . . . and her own mind to celebrate it.

A long time later, she looked up at him.

"I didn't know it could be like that . . . for a man. So . . . intense."

"It may not feel like that to every man," he said. "Nor may it feel like that to me every time. If we were in true sharing, it would be different, I'm sure."

"You mean, if I had let you into my mind."

"Yes."

"I almost did."

"I know. You do not yet have enough confidence in me to give so much of yourself."

Suddenly, a wave of ineffable sadness washed over her, and she knew it emanated from him, knew he had made no attempt to disguise it from her. "That lack of confidence hurts you," she said, her throat tight with the desire to cry. Was it her desire, or his?

"It does not so much hurt me as it saddens me. On your behalf. There is a wonderful world of knowledge awaiting you, if only you had the confidence to tap into it. If you could but know the truth of what you want, you could have it."

"You mean I could have a baby if I wanted it enough." She wondered, with an excitement that verged almost on awe if her union with Jon could possibly have resulted in pregnancy. What would his child—his child and hers—be like? If only it were as physically beautiful, perfect, as he. . . .

He broke into her whirling thoughts. "More than that, Lenore. Much, much more than your desire for a child."

"Then . . . what?"

"I cannot tell you. You must learn it for yourself."

She gazed into his eyes for a long moment, trying to read his thoughts. She even went so far as to thread her fingers into his hair and cup his head in her hands, hoping for entry, but his smile told her it wasn't going to happen. He had shared with her once. He would do it no more until—unless—she shared with him.

She wanted, again, to weep for the loss of whatever might have been had she the courage to accept the full sharing he wanted with her. Instead, she drew his face to hers and shared a deep kiss with him.

Making love, even without the mental union he had offered her before, was stupendous. But she knew, when it was done, it could have been a much more intense experience. If only . . .

But no. She was not ready for that. She would never survive if she opened her mind to his.

She shivered as she remembered the very intensity of entering his consciousness. She let the power of their earlier coupling wash over her, knowing all too soon he would be gone; all too soon she would be left with only the memories of their joining to comfort her.

"Though I know I must, I do not want to leave the place of wonder we have created in this room," he said. "I want it to be part of me, as you will be, always." He held out his hand and bade her to watch. She blinked as a small pool of light began to grow in the hollow of his palm, pulsating, gleaming, shimmering. The light it cast reflected in his eyes, turning them as soft and luminescent as would candlelight.

Moments later, with infinite care, he lifted the bead between finger and thumb and laid it gently against the other beads of his *Kahniya*. "My first *Aleea* of you," he said. "It is one I will treasure above all."

Lenore choked on a tightness in her throat and attempted to speak. She could find no words with which to explain—even to herself—what he meant to her. Instead, she leaned over and kissed him. When he would have deepened the kiss, taken her on another journey to fabulous realms, she pulled away.

"Jon . . . stop now. We have work to do."

He blinked, as if drawing himself back from an edge. "We do?"

"Yes. Remember? We're supposed to be searching for your Octad."

"Yes. Yes, of course." Though his tone was brisk, she knew somehow his reluctance to leave her bed was as deep-seated as her own. But she must remember, whatever happened, that Jon did not belong to Earth, nor to her, that his time here had a purpose and a duration she could not influence.

"We will access your holographic projections of what is happening in this world?"

"We'll do that, sure, but there are other ways, too," she said. "The holo doesn't report everything. I can track 'anomalies' on the web." She reached for her robe, but before she could touch it, it whipped away from her and disappeared. Once more, she felt long hair caressing the bare skin of her shoulder blades. She leaned her head back, shook it, and enjoyed the sensation.

"How long were we on your island?" she asked.

"Not nearly long enough." He filtered his fingers through her hair and let it fall forward over her breasts. "Please, leave it thus, Lenore. You like it. And so do I. And do not clothe yourself. We are private here, are we not?"

"Until I start having to go to direct contact with others through my compad. Unless I leave the video feed off. Though if I do that, I may not get the truth we are seeking. Plenty of people refuse to talk unless they are face to face." She grimaced. "I'm one of them."

"When that time comes," he said, "I will create the illusion of clothing for both of us."

Lenore laughed. She liked the idea of being clothed in illusory garments. "Will I see yours?" she asked. "Will you see mine?"

He smiled in understanding. "Not unless you and I choose it that way."

Daringly, she said, "I choose that we not see each other clothed."

It would be kinky maybe, but certainly titillating, to know that she and Jon were bare naked while giving others the appearance of being clad. And she wouldn't have to give up the pleasure of looking at him. She could only hope she'd be able to resist the temptation of touching him every second of the day.

The expression in his eyes told her he had no intention of making it easy for her. With a jolt of desire, she accepted that she did not want "easy" from him.

"There!" Jon's hand shot out to stay Lenore's lest she move on from the site she had accessed in her swift browsing. They had been at it for most the night. They'd checked everything from strange appearances and disappearances, from items inexplicably missing from securely locked premises, to police reports of public nudity in places it was not allowed. Lenore had even searched the word "vagrancy," but found so many reports it would have taken months to sift through them.

But now, for the first time, Jon seemed galvanized by something. "The magician. Let's study him."

"Jon, it's just a small country fair. He's probably not very good or he'd be a star, not entertaining gullible audiences from surrounding farms."

He peered closely at the man on the stage. He wore a long black cape, a wide-brimmed hat, and as they watched, he released a tiger from the cage before him, paraded it in front of the crowd that sat below a make-shift stage on the grassy slope of what appeared to be a natural amphitheater. Then, with a flick of his hand, the tiger was replaced by a small, yapping white and black dog that danced and bounced and turned somersaults. The magician held out a ring from which flames suddenly sprouted, and lowered it toward the little dog, who leapt through it, landing safely on the other side.

All right, so maybe he was better than Lenore had anticipated, but still . . . there had to be more likely candidates than this!

The magician whirled in a circle, his cloak spreading out, the flaming ring creating a faint mask of smoke around his head, and when he lowered the ring once more, it was not the dog, but the tiger that jumped through it and back into its cage. The man gestured, drawing his rapt audience's attention to a point in midair two meters before the stage. There, the little dog lay curled on a pink satin cushion, apparently floating in space, a matching pink ribbon in the fur between its perky ears.

A hand gesture brought the dog and its cushion back to center-stage and with another flick of his cape the man made the dog disappear. It was replaced by a slender woman dressed in a blue gown brushing her long hair with a silver-backed brush that gleamed and glittered as if some invisible stage lighting were capturing diamond facets and casting the light in sparkling rainbows over the backdrop of deciduous trees.

The little dog was in the tiger's cage, standing quietly on the back of the big beast. Another gesture and the man stood alone on the stage while the audience cheered, whistled, and applauded. He swept off his broad-brimmed hat, bowed deeply, tossed the hat to the front row of spectators, then stood erect as they began to drop in coins and bills.

"Zareth!" Jon said in triumph.

"You're sure? You recognize him? His face?" The man in the holo image lacked the bronze skin Jon had. He also lacked Jon's stature and presence.

"No . . . no, he'll keep his real identity disguised, just in case, but I know it must be him. Where is he?" he demanded of Lenore.

She swiftly ascertained the location of the performance. "A place called Jonestown in Tennessee," she told him.

"Show me."

She brought up a map, pinpointing the place. "Dress," Jon ordered. His urgency flung her into action, and she raced to her room, dragged on a jumpsuit, and shuffled her bare feet into shoes. When she returned to the living room, Jon was watching a replay of Zareth's performance. He was still naked. He glanced at her. "I need clothing, too. Can you get it for me?"

She stared. "Can't you just create the illusion of it?"

He shook his head. "For some time after we translate I will not have the strength left to create that illusion. It will drain me too deeply to make the translation. Zareth is scheduled to give another performance in one hour, but still, we must hurry."

The hat, now overflowing with donations, had been passed back to Zareth, who whirled his hand over it and created a small cyclone of cash that spun high, then slid neatly into a capacious pocket of his cloak. With his hat back on his head, he somehow made the lights go out and faded into the darkness at the rear of the stage.

"Wow! He's something!" Lenore said, but Jon was no longer paying any attention to the holo. He was busy studying the topography of the location she had found for him on the map. Somewhere in the area of Tennessee with low ranges of hills, much agricultural land, forests and pastures, it appeared serene and beautiful and quite sparsely populated in that zone.

"We must hurry," he reminded her, and she dashed out.

It took her very little time to purchase what she thought he'd need, and even less time to return. He dressed as she quivered with fear of what was to come. When he finished changing, he took and held them tightly.

"Will it hurt?" she asked.

"No. But you may feel . . . inchoate for a moment as we complete the translation. I will be with you." He placed his left hand and her right on his *Kahniya.* "You will be in no danger."

Oddly, she believed him. There was a moment of darkness, a brief sensation that there was no up, no down, no weight, no true sense of direction. Lenore fought nausea, choked it down, and realized that her feet were once more on solid ground and she could see the moon sailing overhead.

They were in the amphitheater where Zareth had given his performance. Only—it was empty. Nothing remained, not even a hint of litter to show that a crowd had gathered there to watch a magician work, not even a stage, though the grass still held the impression of where it had stood.

"Gone!" Jon whispered, and Lenore sensed his frustration.

"I guess it wasn't a live broadcast," she said. "What we need to do now is find someone who can tell us when your friend was here. Over there"—she pointed—"there are lights. Someone we can ask."

"Yes," he said, sliding an arm around her. "Work with me now, Lenore. Fix on the lights. We will go there."

She ducked out from under his sheltering arm. "You work with me now, Jon. Those lights are less than a hundred meters away. I can see people moving on the street. Why take the risk of materializing in front of some curious bystander? Let's just walk into town as if we've been out for a stroll."

He looked almost scandalized by the notion, then grinned. "I bow to your superior knowledge of the way to do things on Earth." Taking her hand, he began walking with long, even strides she found difficult to match.

In a busy café where a crowd of young people occupied one end, filling and spilling out of several different booths, and older, quieter people sat at tables near the front, Lenore and Jon took seats at a bar. "We have to order something," she said, sotto voce. "What would you like?"

"I do not know. Coffee?"

"Coffee it is. And apple pie, I think. With ice cream. Translating makes me hungry."

His intimate smile told her translating—or something—made him hungry, too, though perhaps not for pie. When the server rolled over to halt before them, Lenore passed her wrist over its scanner and ordered. The cost would automatically be debited from her credit account.

While they waited, Jon murmured, "How do we learn when Zareth was here?"

"If it was Zareth," she reminded him.

"I am sure it was. No one else is that expert."

"I've seen some pretty good magicians in my time," she retorted as the server placed two large cups of coffee before them. "Only it's sleight of hand, Jon, not real magic."

The server slid two plates of pie, still issuing steam

around the cold scoops of melting ice cream, across the counter.

Jon cut off a forkful and held it out toward her, his face patient. Suddenly, she realized what he was waiting for. She grinned and gently pushed his fork back toward him. "Not here, pal. In public we each feed ourselves." Picking up her fork, she cut through the melting ice cream and hot pie and placed a bite in her mouth, reveling in the contrasts of texture, temperature, and flavor. "Mmmm . . ."

Jon did the same, and repeated her "mmm . . ." He did the same with his next bite. And the next. She strangled a laugh.

"It's not necessary to say that each time."

"Oh. I thought that was the way to express appreciation—to share our pleasure in public. It is a pleasant sound, that 'mmm' you make. It vibrates right here." He tapped his chest.

"Drink your coffee, Jon." She nearly choked on hers.

When she had finished her pie—and he his, with no further sound effects—Lenore spun on her stool and faced the three people at the nearest table. "Hello," she said, taking her compad from a pocket and laying it in plain sight on her knee. She introduced herself and Jon, giving him the first last name that came to her mind—Francis, which was Caroline's. "My assistant and I are in search of talent for a show we're putting together for HoloNatUnited. We saw the holo of the magician who entertained at your latest county fair. Can you tell us where to find him?" She scanned the café as if hoping to find a black-cloaked man in the shadows.

One woman spoke with a shrug. "The county fair? That was more than a week ago. You must have been watching old material. Anyway, he's not local. He's also long gone. And he was a cash-taker."

She added that last with a strong dose of suspicion. Cash-takers and -users were growing fewer and fewer as the years passed, and were little trusted, even in outlying agricultural preserves. Most people preferred the safety of chip transactions, which offered a foolproof means of tracking sales and ensuring the honesty of vendors. Though many kept some solid credits around for just such oddballs as itinerant entertainers. "He just came," the woman said, "and then he left. No one arranged for his appearance. It wasn't advertised. Don't even know what brought him here. Except maybe hunger for an audience."

A man at her table laughed. "Which he got after that little demo he put on right out there in the main square. And his show was good. You have to admit that. The guy had a great act."

Several nods and murmurs of agreement sent a ripple through the crowd. Even the noisy youths in the back had fallen silent as they listened to the conversation. Probably more than half of them could see themselves being recruited for a part in the new show if the magician couldn't be found.

The server rolled over and refilled the three cups of the table's occupants, then tilted its urn over the cup Lenore held out. A glance at Jon showed her his coffee was hardly touched, and he had on his vacant look. She wondered whose brain he was poking into. As long as it wasn't hers . . .

"Did the magician say where he was going next?"

"No. Simply took our coin and was gone. And he'd promised us another performance the next day. We sent out notices over the net to every town in a five-hundred-klick radius, with vids of his performance. Must have been one of those you happened on. Had a pretty big crowd show up, too, and then he didn't come through after the two acts he put on for us that first evening. Don't even think he intended to. He didn't so much as spend the night in our hostel so far's I know."

The indignant spokeswoman turned to a man at another table. "Did he, Roth?"

Roth shook his head. "Didn't so much as poke his head in the door. 'Course, I wouldn't have let him in without a reading of his chip, and I'd be surprised if he even had one. Prob'ly from one of the rebel tribes. Most of those wanderers are. They go out and get coin to buy goods on the black market."

Lenore nodded. Rebel tribes existed, she knew. They lived deep in some of the forest and mountain preserves, self-sufficient survivalists who refused to use embedded chips or allow their children to be so equipped. There were some things they couldn't provide for themselves, though, so they resorted to an ancient Gypsy means of obtaining them—stealing. When they were caught, they were chipped, of course, and trained in a lucrative profession. Most soon learned it was an easier way of life than the hand-to-mouth existence they had known before.

"Any other communities close by that plan spring celebrations or have had them in the past weeks?" she asked. "He might be making the rounds."

Several people named a few other towns, and Lenore nodded, then tapped her compad to stop its recording. After thanking the townsfolk and fending off pleas for auditions from a few, she and Jon left the small café.

Back in the empty amphitheater, Jon's eyes took on the blank look that told her he was searching, seeking,

213

probing. It seemed to go on for a long time while they stood in the sultry night, under a sky where a few stars shone. Was one of them in his place and time, she wondered, gazing upward at the twinkling lights. And if so, which one?

Finally, he blinked and looked down at her, his face unreadable now the moon had gone behind the trees.

"I cannot reach him. Either he is very successfully screened, or he has gone from anywhere near this location."

"So, now what?"

He took her hands again, putting one of them just beside his *Kahniya*. "Now, we return to your house and eventually to our search. But first, you will need sleep. Translating is draining, even for me. For you, I know it was much more than that."

"No it wasn't. I didn't do anything. I was simply . . . along for the ride."

He touched her face with his fingertips, and she heard the smile in his voice. "That is not true, Lenore. Your mind melded with mine to make the jump through time and space."

She stepped back out of his reach. "How could it? I don't have the right kind of mind for that."

"Ah, but you do. Remember, I said at the beginning you were very receptive to the Aazoni mind? That tendency helped you to link with my *Kahniya* when there was need. It will be easier this time. It will grow easier for you each time, if you will but let my *Kahniya* guide you. It would be easier still if you allowed me to help you create one of your own."

She shook her head. "I'll pass."

"As you wish," he said, but she heard the regret in his tone. Then there was that moment of disorientation again, the sensation of nausea, and she was suddenly standing weak-kneed in her own living room.

She sighed as Jon drew her close, holding her, supporting her, easing her transition back to reality in the confines of her home.

Reality . . . deep sadness flooded her. They knew now with some certainty that several of the Octad lived. Minton, Zareth, Jon . . . if they could locate Zenna, they were halfway there. And if some had survived that risky translation, surely others had, too. Lenore felt guilty for wishing that Jon would never complete an Octad. She released a tremulous sigh.

"You need to sleep now," he said, his lips against her temple.

"I need you to hold me."

"Are you saying you want me to sleep with you?"

She looked up at him. "Yes, that's what I'm saying." She smiled. "And if you think I'm using the euphemism you learned not too long ago, you'd be right. I want to sleep with you. But I also want to have sex with you."

His smile was tender, so tender she thought for a heart-stopping moment, he was going to correct her and use the other term he had learned: make love. He did not. "You are very tired, *letise.*"

"We'll see. I know only that tonight, I need you with me. Close."

"Yes," he said. "I, too, need that. It is an unfamilar emotion to me, but still very real." As his gaze lingered on her face, and his hands tangled in her hair, she sensed his despair and that his need to be held close was at least equal to her own.

Together, they walked to her bedroom. This time, their clothing did not disappear as if by magic. Jon slowly slid his hands up under her tunic, cupping her breasts, toying with her hardening nipples until she gasped and swayed. She reached out and unfastened the zip in the front of his jumpsuit, peeled it back and explored his chest.

"I am not as tired as you seemed to think I would be," Lenore said.

"So I see," he said. Slowly, with exquisite tenderness, he made love with her. When it was over, she could only gaze at him, trying to catch her breath.

"I wish I could bottle those feelings," she said at length. "I wish I never had to let them go." *I wish I never had to let you go.*

"You can keep them," he said. "If you let me build you a *Kahniya* you can have an *Aleea*, and in it we will place that memory. We can create many *Aleeas* for you, and you will have them forever. And anything else you might want to recover and keep."

She gazed into his eyes, reading the promise in his words, taking strength from the calm in his face, his tone, his smile. And if it was all she would ultimately have . . .

"I think I would like that," she said.

"I would have to enter your mind."

"Would you do it as skillfully, as beautifully, as wonderfully as you have entered my body?"

"My *letise,* I would project to your mind with the same care as I have tended to your body." He traced the shape of her left eyebrow. "I would cherish it as well. If you feel any discomfort, any fear, I will know and retreat at once. This, I pledge to you."

For a long moment, Lenore hesitated, then whispered, "All right. You may come into my mind and create a *Kahniya* for me, so I will never, ever lose you."

Chapter Fourteen

Gently, then, so softly she was scarcely aware of it, she heard him—no, sensed him—in her mind. He gave her pictures that were familiar to her, scenes she thought she had forgotten. Views of her childhood. She remembered the son of a housekeeper, felt again a four-year-old's elation at winning a footrace against him though he was six months older. She experienced the joy of learning how to swim, the satisfaction of operating a car for the first time, the pleasure of watching a drawing emerge from the end of her pencil, paintings take shape from the strokes of her brushes and colors on canvas. . . . She had all but forgotten her girlhood creativity. Recapturing the wonder of it was like a miracle.

With Jon's guidance, she wove in and out of her own memories, going deeper and deeper, further and further back until she knew herself as an infant, nestled close to warmth, sustenance flowing into her as she suckled, absorbing a total, unconditional love such as she had never since known. Her tiny fist clenched a single bead of light and—

"No!"

Her voice tore from her in a harsh scream as she fought against a memory too fraught with terror to be sustained. Jon guided her back to more tranquil times, holding her there while her tremors eased and then ceased.

Later, she slept.

When she awoke, she remembered all of it, even the fear, the shock of having that monumental love ripped from her. Where had it gone? The thought occurred and almost on top of it, the answer: *It has not gone. You hold it in your hand.*

Feeling a warmth in the palm of her hand, she opened her fist, lifted her head, and stared down at the small bead of light lying there. She reached out to touch it with a forefinger, then jerked back, her motion sending it rolling from her hand to almost lose itself in the folds of the sheet.

Carefully, Jon retrieved it between finger and thumb and set it into the small hollow at the base of her throat. It remained there, feeling as if it were part of her. Though she sat up, it did not roll out. Eyes wide, she stared at her image in the mirror over the dresser and watched in awe as two glistening tendrils began to grow from the bead, one on either side, to encircle her neck, imparting a deeply warming comfort. It flooded her from the inside, made her feel strong, whole for the first time in her life. Again, she experienced immense love that knew no beginning, no ending, that simply . . . was.

She stared at Jon, who gazed calmly back at her. "Yes," he said. "It is your first *Aleea*. It is the one your mother gave you. It was always there. I merely helped you recover it."

"My . . . mother?"

"Your Aazoni mother."

Lenore squinched her eyes tight as a shudder of horror rattled her body, but Jon's strong arms held her close, his gentle persuasion touched her mind with comforting care, calming her fears. Or, almost. Some were too deep-seated, too strongly ingrained.

"Did you know?" she asked. "I mean, before you came into my mind just now?"

"No, but I suspected. From the beginning, I've known your talents were superior to those of most non-Aazoni. As they grew, though, each time we translated together, I began to wonder. And now I know." He smiled and touched her face tenderly. "Now we both know."

She, for one, did not want to know! It was too much!

"Does my father know I am . . . am not—" She bit her lip, unable to go on, and around her neck the warmth of the *Kahniya* somehow soothed her. "Not human?" Was that the reason for his lifetime of coldness toward her?

"You are human, Lenore. As human as you are Aazoni. It is the human side of you that has such deep fear of your father."

"What?" She stared at him, shivered again, not wanting to open that door. "He is an emotionally repressed man. I am not fond of him. But I'm not afraid of him, for heaven's sake." Sudden anger welled up in her, overflowed. She jerked free of Jon, scrambled halfway across the room.

"He wasn't the one who abandoned a helpless infant. That was my mother. My *Aazoni* mother, as you would have me believe. At least he stuck around to see to it I

219

was raised with some semblance of stability."

"In boarding schools you hated." Jon's statement was an indictment of her father, one she felt obliged to defend.

"I needed to be properly educated so I could take my place in this world as a self-sufficient adult, which is all he ever expected of me. He wasn't in a position to provide a home for me, but he did the next best thing."

"So, you're telling me you care for your father. That you believe he did right by you?"

She tilted her chin up and flicked her hair back. The way he'd phrased the question told her not to bother trying to lie. "Do I care for him? No, I do not. No, I don't think he did 'right' by me—except by his own lights. I realize many other men in the same position would have responded differently. But fear him?"

She snorted disparagingly. "Not likely! A self-sufficient adult has no reason to fear her only parent. He may not have been loving, but he never, ever hurt me."

Except she failed to add, by his very coldness. That had never ceased to hurt, especially when compared to the warm memories Caroline had shared of her family life with her parents. True, Caroline had attended the same school as Lenore, but as a day student. At night, she went home to love and caring and nurturing. . . .

"You do feel fear of him, *letise*." Jon's unequivocal statement broke into her thoughts. "Whether it's justified or not, you feel the same kind of fear as your mother experienced when he learned what she was— and what you are."

"What?" Lenore leaped up, strode across the room, and back again before whirling to demand, "Are you telling me she married him, had a child with him, and didn't even bother to tell him the truth about herself until . . . afterward?"

She planted her hands on her hips, facing him, fury driving her, sustaining her. Fury, not unmixed with fear of the unknown, or maybe fear of the known she did not want to acknowledge. "Didn't you tell me Aazonis valued truth above all, that without it, there is no honor? Where was her so-called Aazoni 'honor' when she did that?"

"She told him, Lenore. Your memories of your early time contain the words they spoke when he finally did come to believe what he had previously preferred to ignore. When he no longer had any choice but to see the truth of what she said, he was very afraid and very angry. He said many things in your hearing. He tore you from her breast. Literally and physically. You remember that. You recall the fear: his, hers, and yours. When he cast her out and refused to allow her to take you, you shared her pain."

She covered her ears with her hands as if that could block out what she preferred not to know. "I have no such memories!"

Jon merely looked at her for a long moment. "You do, *letise.*" Then, "May I show you?"

Sudden, tense dread infiltrated her every cell, and she backed away until she was tight against a wall. There was nowhere else to go, but still she refused. "No!"

The quavering tone appalled her. Where was her personal dignity? What had happened to her hard-earned self-control? She drew in several tremulous breaths, still facing Jon with outward defiance she had to struggle to maintain. She did not want to believe him. But how could she not? That small bead of light was there. She felt its warmth, longed to touch it, to reenter the world it encompassed, but dared not because along with that deep sense of connection to something wonderful had been the horror of having it stripped away.

When she thought she could trust her voice, she asked, "Why would my mother have left me?"

"She had no choice."

Lenore wasn't buying that for one minute. "Garbage! There's always a choice. If she was Aazoni, with all the attendant powers you Aazoni seem to enjoy, how could she be said to have had no choice? Surely she had greater mental capacities than my father. Couldn't she have simply dematerialized both of us?"

"No, she could not. She could not risk your safety, so she had to leave you with your father."

"How can you possibly know that?"

"I looked at the memory she left in your *Aleea.* I could do nothing but, if I were to reclaim it for you."

Lenore tried to steady her mouth, which was inclined to tremble. "Thanks for nothing."

Jon arose from the bed and came to her, wrapping her securely in his arms, holding her tightly against his strength. She realized how much she needed the comfort and resented the need. After a moment, she pulled free. He, who could have forced her to stay simply by utilizing his size and physical power, let her go.

She stared at him for a long moment, arrested by internal conflict, trying to make sense of everything she felt.

His revelations were too much. They posed too many questions. She needed time to digest this new information. She wanted to be alone, wanted to let the sensations, the memories, if that's what they were, come at her in tiny increments, short, unthreatening scenes she could adapt to one by one. The phrase, "tore you from her breast," was far too melodramatic to believe.

Except . . . when she had been there, when Jon had taken her deep into the pit of her own memories and she'd emerged from them with a scream of terror, clutching a single bead of light . . . what she had fled could easily have been described as exactly that. The emptiness, the unresolved grief she had always felt, made more sense when seen in the context of having been taken from her mother.

But no. Her father prided himself on being truthful, as much as any Aazoni supposedly did. He, like she, admired the consistency of numbers, the right-or-wrong of them, the truth in the answers they could give. Had he actually taught her that, or was her craving for their integrity something she had inherited from him?

But . . . had she also inherited her long-neglected artistic bent from her mother? Were those buried memories the reason she had been able to accept—far too easily, she now knew—Jon as who and what he was?

But why would her father have lied? Because he thought she wouldn't believe him? That made a lot of sense. If he had told her as a child, she'd have considered it a fairy tale. If he'd told her when she was an adult, she'd have thought he'd gone nuts. Nevertheless, she couldn't accept that he had known this about her and failed to find some way to tell her.

"I think what happened," she told Jon, "is she never did tell him what she was."

He stood there, impassive, but slowly shaking his head, as if waiting for her to finish drawing her own conclusions before he snatched more of her foundations out from under her.

"I think she got tired of slumming on poor, primitive Earth and returned to Aazonia. That would certainly account for my father's belief that she joined a commune and they all committed suicide. Translating away from here could certainly be misconstrued as 'reaching a different plane of existence.'" A vast wash of sorrow threatened to engulf her. She steeled herself against it, thrust it away by sheer force of will.

"You think, then, that your mother may be alive—on the home-world?"

Lenore didn't know what she thought. "Can you . . . Can any Aazoni come and go? Do they ever? I mean, other than criminals and law-enforcement officers. Is Earth a . . . an Aazoni tourist destination?"

"I know that over the centuries since we first began to visit Earth, some Aazoni who have come, perhaps as part of a study-group, have been trapped on Earth if a member of their Octad met with accidental death. Some, while awaiting rescue, made lives for themselves. Your mother might have been among them, *letise.*"

He reached out and stroked her hair back. For an instant, she let herself lean into his cupped palm, then jerked away from him.

"When your father sent her away, she might well have found enough other Aazoni to form an Octad and go home again. Yet, however much she would have wanted to take you with her, no infant can tolerate the rigors of translation."

He pressed a finger against her bead, sending a trickle of energy deep into Lenore's soul.

"She told you she intended to return when she was able."

"Did she say return from where?"

"Not that I can detect. But if she did go back to the home-world, something must have prevented her coming back for you. I read her intention to do so clearly in here, Lenore. I wish . . . I wish you would see for yourself."

She shook her head and pushed his hand away from her *Aleea.*

He continued. "As I have mentioned, safe windows for translation are infrequent. When this one closes, there won't be another for ten years. Often they are as much as fifteen, even twenty years apart. True, our time is measured differently, but your mother, if she lives now, would know you to be an adult on Earth and perhaps thinks you'd not be amenable to meeting with her."

Lenore wanted very much to resist, to deny, the possibility she might have a living mother on some distant planet—or in some "space and time, not here, not now." Though the thought was too overwhelming, she had no option but to let the conviction that Jon was right grow in her heart.

"Would she have been allowed to come back—simply because she wanted to? Or would she have needed a better reason than merely having left behind a half-breed child?"

"No Aazonia laws would have stood in the way of her returning" he said. "All citizens may do what they choose, live where they wish, so long as they cause no harm to others. Some who have first come as students of your cultures, have returned to Aazonia with such fond memories of Earth they elect to make this their home. They opt for the simpler lifestyle Earth offers, the more . . . fundamental one. A place like Earth or other worlds where mindlink is uncommon, is more comfortable to some Aazoni."

"More *comfortable* for *them?*" Lenore dragged on her robe, wrapping it tightly around her as she paced across the room and stood with her back to the window. "I don't give a damn about their comfort! I feel . . . violated, Jon. On behalf of all humanity. To know that there are aliens—have long been aliens among us and we didn't know it—to learn suddenly that there are people who pass as human yet can get into our minds without our knowledge, horrifies me. And to know I was born to one of them horrifies me even more."

"Aazoni do not take from unwilling minds," he said. "Nor do they give to unwilling minds. But they have contributed much to humanity over the centuries, donated willingly and generously of their knowledge, shared and contributed . . . many things."

"Oh yeah? Like what?"

"Are you," he asked silkily, "familiar with the name Leonardo DaVinci?"

"DaVinci?"

"And many others—Marconi, Houdini, Watt, and Lister?"

Slowly, she she lay back down on the bed, an arm over her eyes. "I suppose," she said, "it was the Aazoni who built the Pyramids, who cut those long, straight lines in the jungles of South and Central America? Who carved designs visible only from space?"

"Why, no, as a matter of fact," he said, lying beside her, but not touching her. She felt his side of the bed depress and steadied herself so she wouldn't roll against him. "The Pyramids were built by a much older race than the Aazoni, and the ruins known now as Incan, were left by explorers from a culture that arose in a different sector. A large party of them was lost and hoped to lead rescuers to their location with those designs and lines they created."

She let her arm slide off her eyes, looking at him with

ungovernable curiosity. "And were they rescued?"

"Eventually." He drew one fingertip along the sensitive skin of her lower lip. She had to rub away the sensation with the edges of her teeth. "It was the Aazoni who found them—long before my time, of course, and returned them to their own space and time. They were grateful."

She laughed, then choked on the laughter. "Jon ... it's the strangest thing, but I actually believe you. I mean, about DaVinci and the others. Everyone said he was before his time—a visionary. He drew working models of helicopters, for heaven's sake, before there was even fixed-wing flight."

Then, rolling up on one elbow, she looked down at him. "Why would an Aazoni know about flight in aircraft when you can just translate yourselves from point A to point B? What would be the reason for that? And why would he try to tell humans about it long before their technology was ready to build what he drew?"

"Aazoni do not require flight," he said, "but many other peoples do. Perhaps he learned from one of those races. As to why he might have attempted to educate humans regarding this, I cannot say. Truly, he should not have. Perhaps he never meant his drawings to be seen by other eyes."

"Well, they sure as hell were, and they puzzled a lot of people for a lot of years."

Lenore dropped back down onto her pillow, staring at the ceiling, silent, thoughtful, wondering.

Jon rolled toward her and lifted his upper body against the headboard, reclining on three pillows that had not been there before. "*Letise*, tell me what else it is you want to know. I sense a great question burdening you."

227

"How can the union of an Aazoni and a human create a baby? We aren't the same race." She firmed her chin when it threatened to wobble and met his steady gaze. "I don't even know what you really look like. I mean, is this—the way you are now—nothing more than a form you adopt when you're on Earth? Are you really green, with scales and a long tail?"

He laughed. "*Letise,* this is my real form. The only one I have. Human and Aazoni are cousins, descending from a common ancestor. We did evolve in a slightly different manner, and on different worlds, but there are few physical differences in our bodies. "Except," he added, flicking undone the firm knot she had tied in her bathrobe sash, opening the front and touching her breasts, her belly, her thighs with a broad, firm palm, "the very important ones between male and female."

She shivered at his touch and in defiance of her own needs, tugged her robe closed again, knotting it even more tightly.

"And did the union of my mother and my father produce what we would call a mule? A sterile being—me—without the capacity to have children?"

"No," he assured her. "You are fully functional in every way."

She pulled in a long breath and let it out slowly, feeling as if a large weight had been lifted from her chest. "Good."

"You are finding it easier to believe me."

She nodded. "Strange as it may seem, but yes, I am. I'd be a fool to keep denying things, wouldn't I, with all the weird and wonderful evidence you've placed before me."

"But you will believe me more and will know more about what's possible from a union between a human and an Aazoni, if you allow us the full bonding found only in *baloka.* Now I know your true heritage, I understand what my *Kahniya* has been telling me."

"What has it been telling you?"

He was silent for a time, perhaps even morose. Then, so softly she could scarcely hear, he said, "That you could be my true bond-mate."

"I cannot be that to you any more than you can to me," she said. "Your time here is too short, Jon. If we share this . . . this *baloka,* how will I survive when you leave?"

"How will I?" he countered. "I only know I must leave. I have a duty, *letise,* one I cannot ignore. But I— we both—you and I, have a right, a need to know each other as deeply as we can. To store that knowledge in *Aleeas* for our *Kahniyas* to keep. Will you share that with me, Lenore?"

She wanted to! Oh, lord but how she wanted to. As frightening as it might be, to say no was beyond her. She met his gaze.

Yes, she told him without speaking and saw joy leap into his eyes. It quivered through her, too, knowing she had reached out mentally to him and he had heard/ sensed her response.

She looked down at the robe she wore and wished it away. It stayed exactly where it was, sash tied as tightly as she had pulled it just moments before.

Her gaze flew to Jon's amused one. "It won't go away."

"You must crawl before you can walk, *letise,* and walk before you can fly. Allow me?"

She could only nod helplessly. She would allow this man, this alien, anything, she thought.

His mind opened to hers, as hers opened to his,

united, blended, even as their bodies and spirits joined. Lenore gasped, half-frightened by the intensity of what she felt, but unable to deny her own need to go forth whatever the outcome. She wanted to experience true *baloka* with Jon regardless of the consequences.

Jon's mind was as beautiful inside as his body was on the outside, and his touch within hers as gentle as his hands on her flesh, yet as commanding. Carefully, as if she were a child just learning to take her first steps, he guided her along paths of melding so deep, so soul-fulfilling she knew her life had only ever been lived on the very surface. Whatever happened from this point onward, having discovered her true depths, she would never be satisfied with what had been before.

What they created together was a blend of harmonic music that pulsed and sobbed and reached crescendos before fading out to nothing more than a whisper. Then as their minds and bodies played against each other, those whispers gave way to new notes, deep bass tones, and high, laughing tremolos of pure joy. Each new note, each tonal change created a coalescing of color and light, along with nerve-tingling physical sensations that reached deep into her psyche, bonding irrevocably the essence that was Lenore with the essence that was Jon, until one was the other and the two were one.

When slowly, slowly, Lenore come back to her own individuality, it was to know that she had grown within beyond any manner she could truly comprehend. She was no longer Lenore Henning—or not the Lenore Henning she had been before—but someone much greater, larger, wiser, and more complete.

Feeling a touch on her face, she opened her eyes and saw Jon smiling into hers. She tried to speak, but found she had lost her voice somewhere in that incredible union. It mattered little. To her amazement, she no longer required it.

Are we . . . are we . . . The thought she tried to form remained incomplete. She had not yet achieved the full power of Aazoni nuances and was afraid she might have misinterpreted the significance of their joining.

Almost, letise. The thought drifted across her consciousness. *Only the formalities remain*. She felt the question arise in her and sensed Jon's silent reassurance. He rose to his knees on the bed, drew her up into the same position, facing him. Both sat back on their heels. He let his hands fall to his thighs as he searched her face, searched her inner self. Then, slowly, he lifted his left hand and touched her lips with with his fingertips, each finer in turn, then repeated the gesture with his right.

My pledge to your soul. The words sang into her mind.

He dropped his hands. Following his lead, Lenore mirrored his actions, touching his lips with her fingers, one by one, slowly, and with the same sense of reverence and ceremony she had felt in his touch. *My pledge to your soul*.

He laid his left hand over her heart. She laid hers over his. She knew the rest of the vows, as surely as she knew of his love. His mind and hers repeated together, *My promise to your life*. They leaned together as one, pressing closed lips to closed lips. *I offer my covenant to your body*.

Without her volition, her hands rose to his shoulders as their lips parted. His fingers wrapped over her shoulders. Their minds whispered as one, *I accept your pledge. I welcome your promise. I embrace the cove-*

nant we have given to each other, for now and forevermore.

Lenore continued to gaze into the depths of Jon's glowing eyes, sensing the fullness of his love for her and hers for him. "We are bond-mated." She didn't pose it as a question. She spoke the words in triumph, in gratitude, and in awe.

"We are bond-mated," Jon assured her. "For now and forevermore."

What it meant for their future—their impossible future, Lenore didn't know, and Jon didn't say, but sometimes as the days passed, she found him gazing at her with deep longing and sadness in his eyes. At those times, he shielded his mind from her completely.

Over the next few weeks, they translated and searched all the towns where fairs had been held, or were being held, but never with any sign of Zareth or others of Jon's Octad.

As the clock of the open window between Earth and Aazonia ticked down, Lenore forced herself to control her growing hope that the Octad would never be reassembled. To take her own happiness at the expense of others' would be too wrong. Once, when she let the yearning surface and beam forth, she knew she had projected it for Jon to see. He held her and told her without words that he shared her longing for them to remain together, that he, too, felt guilt for that secret wish.

Still, they searched.

When they weren't physically searching, they spent time net-surfing, seeking out other possible leads. Though they followed up, often by waiting until night and translating to the different locations, each proved either to be easily explained in Earthly terms, or simply false, another tabloid exaggeration.

Jon was right. Each translation became easier for her, though after three in one day, she was weak, scarcely able to stand.

She was never too weak to make love.

Jon awoke from a deep slumber and lay watching Lenore sleep. Her face was, for once, serene, and he was glad for that. He had given her peace, if only for a time. And she . . . she had given him a great deal more than peace. While she had accepted her Aazoni half over the past weeks, had accepted the powers it gave her, she was still reluctant to let him help her delve deeper. Her early memories of her mother and their parting still terrified her. Not once had she accessed her birth-*Aleea,* to revisit the unconditional love he knew she would find within it.

He knew that even their *baloka* could be richer if she would but let it, allow him into her mind all the way. But, he decided, sadness permeating the thought, it was likely better for her if she did not.

What they had together could not last. His obligations would take him from her, and in the ten years before he could return, he wondered whether she would choose to bury the memories of their bonding. If he were to return during the next available window between their worlds and find her mated with someone else, he was unsure what it would do to him.

He'd known of no other bond-mate union that had been broken but by death.

Now, knowing he had permission, he gently stroked over her mind, through it, seeking memories she would cherish, to build her another *Aleea.* She had only three *Aleea*s so far, the one from her mother, the one he had given her of their time with the *mazayin*, and a duplicate of the one he carried of their bond-mating enhanced by *baloka*. Unlike most Aazoni she did not have an *Aleea* from each parent because her human father was unable to make one for her. There were many memories for her to recover, so he filtered gently, seeking out the better ones—but then he hit a snag.

Something captured him, held him helpless as he experienced the teasing giggles of a small child, one who danced just out of sight, keeping to the shadows, tempting Lenore—or her mind—to follow. Lenore tossed restlessly in the bed at his side. Her mouth moved as if she were pleading or protesting.

Jon tried to contact the mind of the child, certain now it had to be Zenna hiding in her memories. That clear, infectious giggle was hauntingly familiar to him, but with the conduit of Lenore's mind the only way to connect, he could go no further than Lenore was able to take him.

Would it be far enough? The other presence seemed so close, almost tangible. Hope sprang high in him, and a desperate need.

Come out, he ordered the child as would a kindly parent. *Show yourself!* And for a split second, much too short a time for him to grasp and hold, he saw the bounce of tawny hair on narrow shoulders, glimpsed a bright blue garment reflected in the bright blue of Zenna's eyes, but then it was gone, flooded out by a much more powerful presence, filled with evil, with anger, with death.

Rankin!

His sensing the other man snatched him away from the gentle child-mind. With rapier focus he homed in on Rankin, battling for supremacy and was fought back by an indescribable blast from which, for a terrible moment, he had no defense. It left him open, vulnerable, in that first second, and worse, it did the same to Lenore.

Instantly, as she cried out, her body twisting into a convulsion, Jon wrenched free of Rankin, clamping down hard on his mind, blocking access to the criminal he should have been following. But not while Lenore was in danger!

The seizure continued to turn her rigid, vibrating her limbs against the mattress however carefully he tried to enter soothing thoughts, giving assurances of safety. Did Rankin still have hold of her mind? He could not tell. She had erected a block so powerful he couldn't penetrate it. Or had Rankin erected it to keep him out? What was the other man doing to her mind? Was he stripping it of all knowledge, using it as a means to reconnect with Jon?

Though her mouth opened in a silent scream of terror, he dared not interfere with whatever defense mechanisms she might be creating for herself. Her brown eyes remained wide but sightless, and he sent out a blow, smashing it indiscriminately toward where Rankin's had originated.

He felt resistence, pushed harder, felt Rankin give and then cave in.

He glanced again at Lenore, still twisted, her body locked into contortions.

Her heart stopped. He started it again.

He inadvertently let his alarm for her safety beam out in an uncontrolled burst, a plea for help, for Wend, who could heal.

In that instant, another presence overwhelmed him totally.

It overwhelmed him with gladness, with relief, with the sense of connection that had been missing since his Octad had broken and Fricka—*Fricka!*—tumbled naked to the floor beside Lenore's bed. And then . . . Fricka's signature wavered, collapsed, though her body, scratched, bleeding, badly damaged, remained.

A gurgling groan jerked his attention back to Lenore as she continued to convulse in dreadful spasms. He saw as much as he felt her consciousness leave her body, and cried out, grasping her shoulders, shaking her, as the rictus eased, leaving her limp and flopping like something dead. He sensed no patterns from her brain as again, her heart froze, unable to continue beating.

Wend! His mind bellowed again a wild and terrible projection made without care for who else might hear, who else might zero in on his desperate cry.

Wend! Come to me! Help us! Now!

Jon's instinctive call for the Octad's medic had an effect, but not the one he had wanted. A scream of outright rage at his presence flooded Jon's mind. Rankin again! And stronger, much stronger, as if he were nearer. He was coming after them!

Swiftly, Jon acted, flinging the rage back tenfold, blasting it through the atmosphere with killing intensity. Even as he did so, he reached out with his mind and gathered in Fricka, reached out with his arm and cradled Lenore, then translated away. Out. He knew not where, he cared not where. He knew only that they must be gone from the spot where he had so carelessly let down his defenses, blasted forth that cry for help and let Rankin in.

His powers nearly depleted, he felt himself thud to a hard surface. Under his head and right shoulder, something cushioned him as his own body cushioned Lenore's. He glanced blearily around, but it was dim and his *Kahniya* had not enough strength to illuminate it properly. The place felt and smelled vaguely familiar to his all but scattered mind. He tried to focus on something recognizable but found nothing.

The substance under his head and shoulder was loosely woven brown, cream, and orange threads, much like the mantles worn by the Grales. That told him nothing. He knew he couldn't have translated to their time and place, despite the enormous jolt of fear he had experienced at the thought of losing Lenore. Not without an Octad.

Of Fricka, there was no physical sign, but he knew she was there—or what remained of her was there. Her essence ran weakly through his mind, struggling to remain connected with him.

He automatically ticked off the seconds since Lenore's life-signs had faded to nothing. How long did he have? He could start her heart again, her breathing, but it was her mind that most concerned him. He knew he could not bring her back unaided. He needed two intellects. He really needed Wend, their medic, but she was not with him. All he had was Fricka.

He must cure her so she could help him recover Lenore. Deftly, having done this many times before with others, he melded his mind to the fragments of Fricka's, building, knitting, patching, feeding warmth and strength and positive thoughts into her. Until, at last, she flickered, almost formed, on the floor at his side, and then was there, growing ever more solid.

As her corporeal self took shape, she gazed at him, still stunned, but he couldn't give her time to fully recover. With his fingers playing her *Kahniya* in a clumsy and only partly effective imitation of Wend's expertise, he imparted to Fricka the urgency of his need to help Lenore. He formed a physical bridge between the two women, gave Fricka threads to hold, tenuous ones, but vital, while he reached in and carefully, skillfully braided in the most tattered ones within Lenore. It took great effort on both their parts, but when she began again to breathe, when her heart took up a slow but steady beat, her mind to function as it should, he knew they had won.

The knowledge gave him added strength, strength he shared with Fricka, with Lenore, further depleting his own until, at last, Lenore merely slept, her mind whole, her body restored to what it should be, operating correctly in every sense. Rolling apart from her, he covered her with the Grale-like fabric to keep her warm, knowing her newborn *Kahniya* would not be equal to the task.

He aimed a swift thought at Fricka, instructing her to remain cloaked, to maintain a surround, not to project so much as a glimmer of their presence beyond these walls . . . wherever these walls might be.

The power of Jon's psychic surges as he battled against Rankin swept over Zenna, sending her reeling and smashing into an open storage compartment, bringing a cascade of filled drug vials tumbling around her. They broke, smashed, spilled their deadly liquid across the floor, and she clasped her daughter, holding her close to keep her from harm.

She felt herself falling, falling, falling, swinging and twirling as if she were a leaf caught in a cataract as the two men fought. Jon, with his bare mind, Rankin with the aid of the amplifier, fortunately close to depletion from a recent translation. But slowly, with great concentration and determination, she steadied her descent, struggled against almost irresistible forces that wanted to drag her out of it and into the battle on Rankin's side at his demand.

She knew B'tar had been put down in the first instant of Jon's response to Rankin's probe. He was of no account, but she refused to let herself be used against her brother, no matter what.

She somehow regained her center, calling on her *Kahniya* to support her, to strengthen her, help her torn senses to reconverge within herself, to collect the spirit of her daughter and protect it with her own powers.

That first incredible force of Jon's energy might not have been aimed at her, but the effect was the same as if it had. All that had saved her from destruction was the fact that he was her birth-mate, and hence she was insulated by her intimate knowledge of him. In it, she felt his fear, his anguish, as well as his fury as he refocused his power and squashed Rankin like the insect he was.

She picked herself up from the floor, wiped her hand across her top lip, saw it streaked with red; her nose streamed blood. She tasted it in her mouth. Her tongue was lacerated from where she had bitten it. Her eyes felt as if they had been half sucked from her head, or pushed, perhaps, by the pain that still screamed there.

Still holding Glesta close, both mentally and physically, she grabbed a cloth from a nearby rack and held one end to her daughter's face, pinching the bridge of her small nose to staunch the bleeding. Applying the other end of the fabric to her own nose, she cast her gaze swiftly around the room, seeking Rankin and B'tar.

She found the former crushed into a corner as if by

the force of a heavy, physical blow. He had dropped the amplifier, rendering him much more exposed to the power of Jon's undiluted second surge. Not only his nose spurted blood, but his ears showed trickles of it, too, and he was deeply unconscious, his mouth lolling open, also bleeding where he had sunk his teeth into his tongue.

B'tar showed little signs of life, yet Zenna knew he lived.

Between the two men, under a table near Rankin's bunk, lay the amplifier. Zenna lunged toward it, but pulled back swiftly as she saw it was coated with the viscous fluid rendered from the salal leaves. To so much as touch it with unprotected hands, to breathe the fumes of that drug could be deadly.

Carrying her limp daughter, she translated herself and Glesta to a camp far out in the Arizona desert, one they had not visited for some time.

She and Glesta rematerialized in cold, star-filled darkness, with blowing sand filtering around them. Slowly, aching in every joint and muscle, she made her way into one of the adobe huts where there was shelter from the wind. There, still dizzy, she lurched to a bunk with Glesta, her precious child, who lay curled in a fetal position, alive, but just barely.

Cradling the small form, she rocked her, humming a soft, familiar tune, one that comforted her as well. With infinite patience, she peeled back the protective layers Glesta had instinctively created to secure herself. Presently, she sensed a tiny glimmer that was the essence of her daughter's consciousness. She fed light into it, and warmth and strength. With one hand pressed to the beads of her *Kahniya,* the other against those of

Glesta's, she gave the child back her knowledge of herself, knowledge of Zenna, of Minton.

The sun had risen on the desert before Glesta returned to herself.

Her eyes flickered open. She smiled. "Mama."

Tears of gratitude stung Zenna's eyes. "Yes, my love, my *letise*. Mama is here. You are safe. We are safe."

For the moment, she did not add.

Chapter Fifteen

Lenore woke to find herself lying, inexplicably, on the living room floor in the log house in the mountains, with a half-completed afghan, the crochet hook still attached, covering her. She blinked her eyes and focused on the shape of another person who sat propped nearby, her back against the front of the shabby old sofa. Though it was nearing twilight, she could see the woman was naked. Lenore shook her head. Was she having another weird dream? Somehow, she sensed this wasn't the woman from her earlier dreams.

She fought loose of the covering she wore and struggled up as far as her hands and knees, then dropped back down again into a crouch as she spotted yet another person in the room.

This man wore a powder-blue ski suit of shiny, form-fitting material. The sleeves, revealing strong forearms covered with glistening hairs, were much too short.

With it, he wore no hat, no gloves, but, as unlikely as it seemed, he did have on a pair of red ski boots—still attached to the skis—Skis, in the cabin! She shook her head, but the vision remained.

Long orange socks protruded from the tops of the boots and had been drawn halfway up his lower legs. He propped himself on his poles, looking as confounded as she felt, and stared at her.

At once, she realized her nudity and grabbed the afghan again, pulling the loose ends of it up in front of her while scrambling backward in an attempt to free the rest of it pinned beneath her knees. She was so damn weak! Her head spun dizzily in response to her hurried actions, and she stayed very still for several minutes, waiting for the room to stop tilting. Slowly, she rocked back onto her heels as she somehow sensed the skier meant her no harm. At least, he appeared to be immobilized, making no move toward her or the other woman.

Reassured that the man posed little threat, Lenore turned her attention back to the woman who remained slumped in front of the couch, her eyes closed. There were signs of injury on her skin, but even as Lenore watched they began to heal.

Around the woman's neck was a circlet of light. . . .

In a flash, it all came back. "Jon!" she wailed in dismay, looking frantically for him.

At Lenore's sudden cry the woman's long lashes whipped up to reveal silvery eyes glowing intensely under a wide forehead. Dark, shiny hair lay in deep waves that touched finely arched eyebrows. She was impossibly beautiful, with high cheekbones, a small, pointed chin, and almond-shaped eyes. Whoever she might be, like Jon, she had to be a perfect specimen of whatever she was. Another Aazoni? A member of the Octad?

She glanced at the man who still stood, as motionless as an ice sculpture, his face appearing frozen in disbelief. He, too, was larger than life, incredibly well put together, with broad shoulders, narrow hips, and long legs. His hair was black, thick and curly like the woman's. It was longer than Jon's, and his dazed eyes were so dark a brown they, too, could have been black. He also wore a necklace of light, a few beads visible where the neck opening of his ski jacket had failed to close tightly.

Lenore clenched her teeth to keep them from chattering, and wrapped herself more closely in the afghan. The crochet hook fell to the floor, rolling away. She watched as it disappeared under the cold pot-bellied stove.

"Where is Jon?" she demanded.

The woman didn't speak, but Lenore knew, without understanding how she knew, that Jon was all right. He was simply . . . recovering.

"Regaining his corporeal state?"

The answer, *yes*, occurred in her mind and Lenore accepted the mental communication. She no longer had the desire or the strength to fight against the telepathy.

I am Fricka. Over there stands Minton. I sensed him during our translation and managed to create a surround strong enough to include him. You are Lenore. Jon was very angry that I killed you. It was not my intention to do so. I apologize.

"Killed me?" Lenore rose unsteadily to her feet, pulling herself up with the aid of an upholstered chair. She tripped on the blanket she wore, stumbled, and flopped down on the seat of the chair.

"How did you kill me?" Oh, yes, she'd definitely gone

down the rabbit hole—or maybe just around the bend. The last thing she remembered, she and Jon had been in Port Orchard. And now she was back in the cabin with a strange man in not only a ski suit, but boots and skis as well, and an even stranger, naked woman who claimed to have "killed" her? That part was madness, of course. Because she felt alive. Or at least half-way alive.

But hungry. And thirsty. And weak.

In my eagerness to reconnect with Jon and the rest of our Octad—her gesture included the skier—*I failed to control my* willayin. *I heard Jon after all this time of silence and simply leaped that way, leading with my* willayin, *without thinking of possible consequences. That was very wrong of me, and Jon has a right to his anger.*

"Your what? *Willayin?*" It occurred to Lenore that it was becoming easier to wrap her tongue around Aazoni words, even to add the drawn-out, almost hummed, consonant at the end, as Fricka had.

My ability to seek and find the others of my Octad. With it, I create a surround that is supposed to bind us together. During our translation to Earth, I failed. Shame clouded the thought. *It is my specialty, the reason I belong to an Octad.*

"Oh. Like Zareth's ability to delude through illusion, your special talent is *willayin.*" Certainly. Of course. It all made sense now.

Zareth? You know where he is? This time it was the thoughts of the skier, Lenore knew. She glanced at him. His face was animated. He stared at her, his eyes alive with eagerness. *Jon has found him?*

"No, we . . . saw him. On a holo. But we could not reach him before he disappeared again."

Judy Gill

That is all my fault! A thread of lament ran though the other woman's projected thought. *Had I not been injured when the solar storm tore apart the Octad, I would have found Jon much sooner. It is my task to gather everyone if we become separated, just as Wend is there in case we are injured. She is our healer. When my arrival killed you, Jon called out for Wend. His power was such that he gave away our position, alerting the criminal we seek, so Jon had to translate us to this location. I think. I do not know how we would have come here otherwise. But since neither Jon nor I had the strength to meld and carry yet a third, we all arrived naked. May I, too, have a covering? It is cold here, and my Kahniya is not yet recovered fully enough to keep me warm.*

"You," Lenore accused, "are talking inside my head."

Why, yes. Since you are receptive, I choose not to waste strength I need for my recovery in vocalizing. This disturbs you?

Lenore laughed as she rose and got a bright green and white serape from Caroline's last trip to Mexico and tossed it to Fricka, who wrapped it around herself. "Not half as much as it disturbed me in the beginning to think Jon could dip into my mind whenever he wanted to."

But he has promised not to go further than you are willing to permit, Fricka assured her. *No Aazoni who has given such a promise will ever break it. When we were rebuilding you after your death, I was the one who had to hold the threads that are your . . . your deepest substance. Jon would not. He could do only the mending. I could know much more of you than he does had I let myself accept the knowledge—remember it. I did not, of course. Like Jon, I am aware only of what you freely offer.*

I accessed none of what is in there—she gestured at Lenore's *Kahniya*—*because that is intensely private. Some of your memories and knowledge, Jon accessed before you decreed he could not. It gives him great pleasure to accept the contact you do permit him, but he wants more. It grieves him not to have it.*

Lenore huffed out a large puff of breath. "Well, it grieves me to think of anyone digging around too deep in there." *Even myself,* she did not say aloud, though suddenly she wanted to touch her *Kahniya,* to let herself fall into the safe and lovely memories the beads contained—at least those two that included Jon.

But now was not the time.

She gave Fricka a hard look. "Are you two snooping, or merely talking to me?" she demanded, including Minton in her sweeping glare.

Fricka's silvery eyes widened with hurt. *We would not snoop! We would take only what is needed to make sure we are fully answering your questions. To snoop is not*—

"Is not the Aazoni way," Lenore finished aloud as the other woman's thought filtered through her mind.

"Ah . . . you know that," Fricka spoke aloud this time, displaying a delicately melodious voice. "Jon has taught you some of our ways."

"As many as she would let me," Jon said, and Lenore gasped as he regained his corporeal state at her feet, as magnificently naked as the first time she'd seen him. He sat up while Lenore tried to decide where to look. It was one thing for the two of them to be naked together when they were alone, but to have him thus with another naked woman in the room plus a fully clad man embarrassed the hell out of her.

"What is this place we have come to?" he asked, ris-

247

ing lithely to his feet as if he had never had to deplete himself to "mend" her.

Tugging her afghan closer around her, Lenore stood, too. "This is the cabin," she said. "Don't you remember it?" She gestured to the door on the left. "Through there is the room where you slept." She waved a hand toward the archway. "The kitchen where we ate."

Jon smiled. "Ah, yes. Of course I remember now. My mind is not all . . . collected."

"After such a swift mending of one unconscious woman and one dead woman, followed by an unplanned translation like that, and scooping me up on the way by," Minton said, making Jon swing around to face him, "it's no wonder you were depleted."

"I did not guide that translation," Jon said as he wrapped an arm around Lenore's shoulder. "Lenore grows more powerful each day." He smiled into her eyes. "You knew we needed safety, *letise,* and you brought us here."

She stared at him. "I did no such thing! According to Fricka, I was dead. She had killed me. She thinks you are angry."

"Fricka did not kill you!" he said, his demeanor expressing shock at the notion. "It was Rankin who did that. But," he added, "it appears even Rankin's malice was not as strong as I'd thought. Enough of your spirit remained intact to bring you to your place of safety."

He turned to the other woman. "Fricka, I was angry, it is true, but not with you. If your unexpected arrival had done damage to Lenore, I would have been furious with you. But it did not."

"Nevertheless, I should have approached with more caution and less enthusiasm. I am Aazoni, not a child or a foolish *patán,*" Fricka said.

A *patán,* Lenore remembered from one of her excursions with Jon, was a long-haired, red-brown creature similar to a tailless monkey. They were cute to look at and mildly telepathic, but made poor companions as they were completely untrainable. *Patán* could be used as a mild reproof for an impish child—or as a deadly insult to an enemy.

"Will you forgive me for that error?" Fricka continued, folding her long, slender hands in a prayerlike gesture under her chin.

Jon bowed. "Fricka, I forgive you."

Fricka stood and let her serape drop to the floor. She bowed deeply. "Jonallo, I thank you for your forgiveness."

Despite the Aazoni formality and ritual, Lenore's prosaic, human stomach growled loudly. "I think we should all have something to eat." *Not to mention getting dressed!*

Jon, she knew, was always as hungry as she was following translation—and not just for food. Unfortunately, with two other people in the cabin, she knew that there was only one appetite of his—and of hers— she would feel at ease in satisfying.

Jon turned and gazed again directly into her eyes.

"Sharing?" he asked, then laughed softly as Lenore felt heat rise in her face. Their sharing of food always led them directly into a far more intimate kind of sharing. *Baloka* . . . The word seemed to hover, unspoken, almost unthought between them, but the emotions, even unexpressed, were as intense as ever, the yearning as great.

When we are more than two, we still share, though the sharing is . . . different. The words, Jon's words, occurred in her mind, privately, she hoped. She also hoped she wasn't unconsciously projecting for the other two to see exactly what she was feeling, thinking, wanting.

You are not, he assured her. *I have given us a cloak of privacy.*

More relaxed, knowing that, she returned his smile, wondering if he could keep all their communications private from others if he so desired.

Of course. And that is something I will teach you to do also, he told her, then spoiled her state of composure by adding, *Tonight. When we are alone.*

"Jon . . ." A note of warning. She would not spend a night in bed with him while others were in the house. Especially not telepathic others!

He laughed softly. *Fear not,* letise. *The others wouldn't want to be privy to our personal discussions or activities. It is not the Aazoni way.*

For which she would be eternally grateful!

But . . . "It is not the American way to exclude others in the room from a discussion," she said aloud. "That would be as rude as whispering behind someone's back. Fricka, Minton, are you hungry? May I offer you something to eat?"

"I am very hungry," Minton said, "since I have not eaten in four days and have been traveling hard in search of either Zenna or Jon. After Rankin found me during my last translation, I prefered to remain on foot, with my mind shielded. But I have not yet mastered the art of making these . . . skis?" he looked at Lenore as if she had the answer—"move gracefully except on snow, and they are very difficult to walk in. I found them especially so in the forests I traversed as I tried to follow the land in the direction my *Kahniya* told me I would find Jon. Can you assist me, Lenore? I'm certain you can explain these conveyances to me. I will need to make them fly again if I am to move around with any speed on Earth, or even inside this dwelling. Speed does not appear to be one of the talents that traveled with me."

Lenore tried not to laugh. "You can't 'fly' with them indoors! You'd break your neck! In fact, you're not supposed to use them except on snow. Take them off, for goodness sake, then you'll be able to walk." The notion of him traipsing unknown distances of forest preserve with skis on his feet—and no snow under them—was stunning. "And you'll be more comfortable if you shuck the boots, too."

Minton sighed and looked disconcerted. "I cannot remove them. I have been trying to do so since I left the snow-covered ground. These extremely hard shoes seem to be permanently fastened to my feet, as well as to the skis, which do not move well without snow."

Lenore had to laugh. "I just told you, they aren't supposed to."

So, maybe these Aazoni supermen weren't as invincible as she'd thought. Marching over to him, still clutching her afghan to her breasts, she pressed the concealed button to release the electromagnet that held the boots to his feet and the lower one that kept the boots in their bindings.

Gratefully, he slid his feet out of them, wiggling his toes inside the socks that went halfway up his lower legs. He tugged them off, and she realized then that the ski pants' legs, like the sleeves of the jacket, were much too short for him. In fact, the entire outfit was too tight, which explained why he hadn't zipped it fully, thereby leaving his *Kahniya* exposed, something Jon had made sure neither he nor she did in their various translations.

For heaven's sake! If the guy was going to create the

illusion of clothing, why didn't he do it with garments that fit?

Lenore shook her head. "Why didn't you simply make them disappear?" she asked.

Minton blinked at her as if she were speaking a foreign language, which, she supposed, she was.

"I cannot make things disappear," he said, and unzipped the jacket, tugging it off. She saw he wore no kind of undergarment beneath it. "That is Zareth's task."

"I see." She tried not to see that he was also unzipping the high-waisted pants of the ski suit. "And what is yours?"

Mercifully still wearing the pants, though they gaped open as far as his navel, their shoulder straps dangling down toward his knees, he slumped to the chair where she had been sitting. "I have none," he said and buried his face in his hands. "I am here only to recover my bond-mate, my Zenna. I am poorly equipped, mostly untrained in the ways of an Octad. This was my first off-world translation."

He looked up, his face tortured. "It was not you, Fricka, who broke the translation. It was I. I sensed Zenna's presence and lost my concentration." Standing, he stood before Fricka and bowed. "Fricka, I beg your forgiveness."

He turned and did the same to Jon. "Jonallo, I beg your forgiveness."

Jon and Fricka both bowed in return, and oddly enough, it didn't seem so terribly strange to Lenore that two naked people and a barefoot man in the bottom half of a too-small ski suit were completing such a formal ritual in the living room of her and Caroline's mountain retreat. "You are forgiven," Jon and Fricka said in unison.

Then Jon added, "Though forgiveness is unnecessary, as is shame, among any of us. It was the storm that interfered with our translation, not the failure of any one person."

Minton looked hopeful. "But now that we are three the task of locating the others will become that much easier." It was almost posed as a question—a plea for reassurance.

Jon treated it so. "It will, my brother. Though we must take great care, as Rankin is aware of my presence."

Minton shuddered as he projected a brief image of the ugly, angry entity that had plunged him deep into the snow, creating an avalanche. "And of mine."

"I do not think he has yet sensed me," Fricka said. "So if you two search from within my surround, once my *willayin* is stronger, we have a greater chance of being undetected. Now we are three, we will surely succeed in collecting the others."

"One moment," Jon said. He dropped his arm from Lenore's shoulder, stepped in front of her and bowed formally. "Lenore, will you join us in our search?"

Lenore suppressed the impulse to bow in return, and an even stronger impulse to giggle like an idiot. A *patán?*

"I thought I already had."

Jon smiled slowly. "Why yes. That is correct."

He turned to Fricka and Minton. Minton stood again and completely stripped out of the pants. Lenore held her breath and fixed her gaze on Jon's familiar face.

"Lenore and I have been searching together for several days now," he continued, as if it were completely normal for another man to strip naked in front of her—which she supposed to him it was. "We have followed many different leads, but to no avail. However, now with the two of you combined with the two of us, we have become a powerful four, and our task will be less onerous."

"Wrong," Lenore said, this time unable to hold back a splutter of laughter that had its roots deep in hysteria, "this time, for the first time ever, I have to believe that two plus two makes only three and a half. I . . . I can't wait to tell my f-father." Her splutter became a gale, which ended in an uncontrollable series of choking sobs.

Jon cradled her close. "Toor-a-loor-a-loor-a . . ."

"Wait a minute!" she blurted, recovering swiftly and swiping the backs of her hands over her eyes. She glared at Jon accusingly as if it were all his fault.

"Can you explain exactly why my supposedly Aazoni mother would have known an Earthly lullaby?"

Her question was met with such a barrage of surprised mentation, questions bombarding Jon from both Minton and Fricka. She cringed under it until she felt, with gratitude, Jon provide a shield to protect her. Their surprise, their . . . joy in this knowledge still came through to her, but with less daunting intensity. It was not that they were intruding, merely that they were curious. It reminded her, oddly, of the way the child's mind had felt when it accessed hers.

Clutching her hands together, holding the afghan close to her suddenly chill-prickled skin, she realized the child was probably real—and very likely Aazoni. Also, probably, as Jon had originally thought, it was his sister, peeking cautiously out from a childhood safe-place.

Before she could question him about this, he spoke aloud.

"Lenore had—maybe still has—an Aazoni mother. That much we know," he said, gently touching the central bead on her *Kahniya*. She felt a tingling in her chest. It seemed to be reaching tendrils right into her heart. She recoiled from the sensation, pulling back from Jon.

He dropped his hand away and the tingling, along with some apprehension she didn't recognize until it was gone, faded. She was not ready to further explore her relationship with her mother—or that of her parents from her mother's point of view. She doubted she ever would be.

"More," Jon added, stroking her arm soothingly, "we do not know. Lenore and her mother were separated when she was only a few weeks past birth. Though her father is fully human, Lenore is a singleton, hence she has stronger powers than she would have had as half a birthmate duo—even with only one Aazoni parent. Still, these powers are very new to her, very strange, and must be treated with delicacy, as if she were a fragile newborn."

Lenore closed her eyes as she rejected that, too. Suddenly, she didn't know what she wanted—to be treated as a human with extraordinary powers, or as an Aazoni, willing to take her place, to whatever extent she could, among these strange new cousins of hers. But whatever she ultimately decided, she would not turn her back on these people who needed her help. If she had a greater potential than she had ever anticipated, she would reach out and try to achieve it.

No. I am not fragile. I am not newly born. And I want to learn.

Yet even as she deliberately, fiercely projected the thought, unsure whether she was doing it correctly, if it was reaching the others, she felt a quiver of trepidation pass through her at her personal defiance of accepted Earthly wisdom. Only Jon's steadying presence gave her the courage to continue to reach out, to hold open a portion of herself to the other three Aazoni.

Chapter Sixteen

Why, Zenna berated herself, had she not taken the time to glove her hand, to mask her face and snatch up the amplifier when she had the chance? Sick with the knowledge that in her impulsive flight, with her panic-driven lack of forethought, she had missed a chance, she briefly considered leaving Glesta and returning to the Pacific Coast camp. Maybe the two men would still be incapacitated by the blow from Jon's mind.

But no. It would be too late. A whole night had passed. They could be awakening even now, searching for her. She kept a tight cloak around herself and her child.

"The Other . . ." Glesta frowned as if trying to remember something. "Someone . . . something hurt her. Maybe Rankin."

"You reached her?" Zenna asked, trying not to allow

Glesta to sense the urgency of her need to know. "Did you talk to her?"

"I found her again, Mama. I guess she wasn't lost," Glesta said, her small face reflecting both glee and confusion. "I told her I had missed her. I asked her where she had gone. I said I wanted her to play. She was laughing, Mama. She was happy to be with me, too, and kept trying to find me. Then a different Other One came."

She frowned. "When he came, I couldn't hear our Other anymore. I could only hear him." She looked puzzled. "Mama, his name is Jonallo. He thought your name at me. He told me to show myself."

Zenna went cold as her suspicions were confirmed. "And did you?"

"No, Mama. I hid, not to tease like I do with The Other, but because he made me . . ." Her nose wrinkled.

"He made you what, *letise?* Afraid?"

"No-o." Glesta sounded very unsure. "Not afraid. It was like I knew him, but he didn't know me. He was looking for you. And then Rankin was there all angry and wild and scary, trying to kill The Other and Jonallo, and Jonallo pushed very, very hard, pushed me right out. Then came the big hurt, and I went to where you told me was safe. I stayed there until you came to get me. Did Jonallo want to hurt me? Jonallo is in here"— she touched her *Kahniya*—"but he is never like that, Mama. Why was he angry with me?"

"He was not angry with you, my love."

How could she explain to her daughter who had been raised on stories of Jonallo, her mother's wonderful birth-mate, that he had just tried to wipe them all out, Glesta, Zenna, Rankin, and B'tar? And why?

If Jon had followed Glesta's mind back to Rankin's camp, he must know who was there. He had not tempered his power, not aimed it in a fine but lethal manner at the true enemy, but had used it indiscriminately in a broad sweep against all in Rankin's vicinity. Now all doubts were gone: Jon was not here on a rescue mission. He had come to kill.

And he had brought Minton! Of that, she was certain. It had not been coincidence that she had sensed her bond-mate's signature. But why was he on Earth with Jon? Because Minton had finally overcome the difficulties he had detected with the amplifier she had devised? Did he have the other prototype operational? Had that enabled him and Jon to travel without an Octad? Or, did Jon have an Octad, one into which he had blended Minton?

That made no sense. Minton, like she, was a scientist. He did not concentrate his talents on translating through time and space and between worlds. She wasn't even certain he was capable of traveling with an Octad to another planet. Nor was she, which was why she had set out to build the amplifier in the first place.

Did Jon hope her love for Minton, Minton's for her, might force her to give away her position? Had he told Minton the truth behind his coming to find her?

No. Surely not. Yet, she was forced to fight down uncertainty and despair about her own bond-mate's motives in joining Jon's Octad. If in fact he had; perhaps just Jon had amplified.

"I do not know why Jonallo hurt you, Glesta, but I'm certain it was not his intention," she said presently, once her flying thoughts had calmed to a degree where she was capable of speech. "Besides telling you to show yourself, what did he say?"

"I can't remember. It was all so . . . big, what happened. I was very frightened. He is not a gentle mind, Mama."

But he was, he always was with me, Zenna wanted to protest. Only with criminals was he harsh. Except . . . now he saw her as a criminal, so his time of being gentle with her was done.

Zenna wanted to weep with despair.

Instead, she soothed her daughter. "Now, you must let me in to where I can see what you saw, feel what you felt. I believe because you were open to her, since you sensed The Other before you sensed Jonallo, the two might be together. I must know where they are." So she could translate herself and Glesta, as soon as they were both strong enough, far, far from this desert camp.

She must also wipe all knowledge of Jon and Minton from Glesta's mind and *Kahniya* lest the child need to hide again, and did so in a memory her mother had given her that contained either of them. Jon and Minton had now become the enemy just as much as Rankin and B'tar. Remaining cloaked from them until she could somehow, she did not know how, find a way to get Glesta to The Other, was mandatory—unless Jon was in control of The Other. If that were the case, all hope of ever finding a home for her daughter was gone. Unless she could create a safe place for the two of them somewhere here on Earth.

Hiding Glesta from her brother and her mate was the only way to keep her daughter secure.

But, though she tried, Glesta's understanding of the events just past was too fractured and immature to be of use. All Zenna could evoke was a faint echo of that massive surge of power that had sent her flying, that had nearly killed them all.

Sudden panic struck. Even if Jon could not find her, he could find Rankin again. Rankin, who would surely be searching each of their camps in swift succession, looking for her and Glesta. She must leave here at once! She must translate, blind, to a place she had never been, to which Rankin had never been.

Gathering herself, holding Glesta, she drew a deep breath and—was knocked flat on her back as Rankin materialized, landing right beside her, naked. His nose, ears, and mouth were still showing traces of dried blood, the amplifier in his hand and fury blazing in his eyes.

She flung her daughter's mind into a safe place and shielded herself as best she could from the mental pummeling Rankin began to deliver.

With three other minds entwined with hers, the newcomers questioning her, learning about what she was doing, Lenore created a meal with meat, vegetables, fruit, noodles, rice, and sauces, wanting a wide variety of choices, hoping to appeal to all tastes.

While she did so, Minton, who seemed to be the most adept with that particular talent, sent each dish as it was prepared, drifting out of the kitchen. She watched from the corner of her eye as they sailed serenely though the air and turned the corner of the hallway, disappearing from view. Where, she wondered, were they going?

To a place of comfort. Jon answered her unspoken question while he made coffee, giving Minton and Fricka a sense of what it tasted like, the way it affected the cerebral cortex. Both stood near the machine, drawing in the aroma, Fricka eagerly, Minton less so. Feeling self-conscious, Lenore offered Minton a selection of herbal teas merely by allowing him access to the way they tasted to her. He chose a peppermint–rose-hip blend, and she made it for him.

As the food and drinks became ready, all went waltzing away through the air. Following them, leading her guests, Lenore found dinner arranged neatly on the roughly circular maple burl coffee table in the living room, around which was strewn a veritible rainbow of stacked, large silk-covered cushions with long, dangling tassels.

The three Aazoni joined hands, Jon and Fricka reaching out to link Lenore into the ring. Gracefully, after encircling the table three times, they sank to the pillows, reclining. After one stiff moment, Lenore leaned back, too. Jon plumped a pillow behind her back, making her even more comfortable.

He reached for a dish of hot beef and noodles, fed her a forkful, then handed her the bowl. Without being told, as though it were a ritual she had performed before, Lenore understood what was expected of her. She turned and fed Minton, who in turn fed Fricka. When Jon had his mouth full, Fricka took up a dish of steamed vegetables and offered Lenore a bite. And so it went, the sharing of the meal, back and forth, around and around. Lenore lolled there, wrapped in a sense of security such as she'd never experienced, a sense of belonging, of community, where all were equally accepted by the others.

It was only later she realized that while a lively conversation had accompanied the meal, not a single word had been spoken aloud.

Presently, Jon stood, drawing Lenore up with him. "I

am ready for sleep. Lenore, where do you wish Minton and Fricka to be?"

Aazonia would have been her first choice, but beyond that, Lenore didn't care. She knew only that she was not about to relinquish Jon before she had to. She showed Fricka the room Jon had occupied on his first night in the cabin, and Minton one of the others upstairs. She would have made up the beds, but Jon indicated it was not necessary. She watched in awe as Minton took care of the task, sending sheets, blankets, pillows, whatever was needed, from the linen closet to the room. She had no doubt at all that the linens would land exactly in the right order, in the right positions, fully tucked with hospital corners.

Minton just seemed like that kind of person.

In her room, Jon parted her lips with a deep kiss that he held for an inestimable time before lifting himself away from her. "Today has been a difficult one for you. And for me. I will not permit my impatience to endanger you or our cause. Tomorrow, we must continue our search. Tonight we both must rest."

She smiled as she slid her arms around his neck. "But before we rest . . . How impenetrable is that shield of privacy you have created for us?"

He laughed. "As strong as we need it to be. Come to me, Lenore. Come . . ."

"Can Fricka keep us in a surround if we return to Port Orchard?" Lenore asked the next morning when they had all collected in the kitchen, drawn by the aroma of the fresh coffee she had brewed. Breakfast was nearly ready.

Jon nodded. "Not yet. But in a few days. Why?"

Lenore began to place prepared food, plates, and cut-

lery on a tray, only to have them float from her grasp
and wend their way into the living room. Obediently,
carrying her own mug of coffee, she followed them,
sinking to the silken cushions that had appeared there
the night before.

"Since it was from there that you sent out your call
for the others of your Octad, if they heard, won't they
go there?"

"I think not," he said. "They sensed me, of that there
can be no question." He looked rueful. "No living Aazoni on Earth—or maybe even nearby worlds—could
have missed my mental bellowing. Those not of my Octad or family might not have recognized it as having
come from me, specifically, but they would have known
someone was here and experiencing great anger and
distress. But now the Octad members also know Rankin
was not far from there. I think they will avoid that
place."

"So how will we connect up with them? And how,"
Lenore asked, as the thought occurred, much later than
it should have, "did Rankin know you were there?"

"I followed you into your dream," he explained.

"I don't remember having a dream that night." Night
before last. Had it really been so recently she had been
'killed' by the force of Rankin's malevolence, had met
Fricka and Minton, had ended up back here. "Did I
dream of the child or the woman?"

"You dreamt of the child Zenna once was," Jon explained. "She was inside your mind, *letise.* She had
been searching for you and could not find you until you
were back in the place where she first contacted you. I
suspect she—and undoubtedly Rankin—are not physically distant from Sector Seattle. She was happy to find
you again. Her delight, and yours, were unmistakable."

His eyes closed for a moment. "As was mine, to find her. I bade her show herself, and she did. I saw her, merely a glimpse, just enough for me to recognize her, but in doing so, I exposed myself and you to Rankin."

His voice cracked. "That precipitated his attack, which forced me to beat him back, to thrust him away from us. In doing so, I may have caused irreparable harm to anyone in his vicinity. His power was much stronger than I had anticipated."

"That is possibly an effect of the amplifier, if he was connected to it when you sensed the child in Lenore's mind and in following the signature, allowed him to glimpse you," Minton explained, his face drawn and pale as if he had not rested well. "We will need to take great care that he doesn't find us again."

"Then how will we find him?" Lenore asked. "And Zenna?"

Jon and Minton exchanged a glance. Minton squeezed his eyes shut for a moment. Lenore sensed his great agony. "I think," he said, "we will not find Zenna again."

Lenore stared at him as he opened his dark, suffering eyes. "Hold on! Are you saying you think Zenna could be dead?" she asked, astounded. "What possible reason do you have for that belief?"

It was Jon who answered, Minton seeming incapable of speech, even thought, so deep was his gloom. "Since no Aazoni could have missed that projection of mine, Zenna, in whatever place or time she was, would have heard it. Even from a safe-place in childhood, she would have come to me—if she were able. That she did not, has not . . ." He didn't finish, didn't have to.

Fricka, however, did. "It is unlikely, Lenore, that a child, even a child in safe-hiding, could have survived the conflict Jon and Rankin projected. If she did, if she resumed her adult state, Rankin, knowing Jon is here, has probably killed her by now so Jon couldn't find him through her again."

"What would have driven her into hiding in childhood? Could it have been our arrival? Is she afraid of us?" Minton asked, clearly aghast. "Is it possible that, if her essence still lives on that level, she's afraid to come out?"

Jon reached a hand to his birth-mate's husband, gripping the other man's shoulder. "I do not know." He swallowed visibly and added softly, "But I do not think it's possible her essence lives . . . anywhere. As Fricka said, no unprotected child-mind would be capable of enduring what Rankin and I sent forth. Our *Kahniyas* will keep seeking hers, of course. We will, at least, have that of her." His voice broke.

"That is all we can do," Minton agreed.

Lenore placed a hand on Jon's chest, feeling the steady beat of his heart, much slower than her own, feeling, too, the despair emitted by the others.

"Lighten up, people." She couldn't believe their negativity, their loss of hope. "My supposed child-mind survived the onslaught," she reminded them. "I can't believe you would have come so far and suffered so much only to fail. I don't like your defeatist attitude, talking about your *Kahniyas* finding hers and recovering it. It's almost as if you want to fail!"

"We do not want to fail," Minton said. "But if all we can recover of Zenna is her *Kahniya* we will have to be content with that. With it, she will never truly die for us, and it becomes clearer and clearer that when Rankin knew we were both here to rescue her, he killed her."

"That would have been when the avalanche happened?"

Minton nodded.

"But it was *after* that I had the dream of the child, the one Jon followed me into, the one that alerted Rankin to our whereabouts in Port Orchard. If indeed it was the child Zenna was who has been reaching out to me, she was alive following the avalanche."

Jon looked sorrowful. "We know that, *letise*. We know she still lived then, Lenore, at the time of the avalanche because Minton sensed her adult presence in the moment of his connection with Rankin. But now . . ." He shook his head sadly.

"But now . . . *what?*" Lenore demanded. "Why are you so sure she has to be dead now?"

"Because there is no sense of her—for me or for Minton, the two closest to her. Her *Kahniya* and mine are intertwined. I cannot find her hidden in any of her memories. Not so much as a hint. There are very few, if any, that the two of us do not share."

"And my *Kahniya* knows hers intimately, too," Minton said. "We have *baloka*. After that initial contact, our *Kahniyas* should have kept us within reach of each other if not actually in touch."

He fingered his, as if searching. "But they did not," he said, dropping his hand from its play over his beads. "There is a huge void where Zenna should be. What Jon saw, in your dream, was likely nothing more that an echo from her *Kahniya*. It will live on for some time unless Rankin destroys it."

"He will not," Jon decreed heavily. "He will use it to draw us in."

"Dammit, I still think she's alive. I . . . sense it somehow," Lenore insisted.

"If she lived, why would she cloak herself from me, her bond-mate?"

"Or from me, her birth-mate?"

"I can't answer that for either of you. All I can say is I feel, somewhere deep inside me, that she is alive. Alive and waiting for you to help her. Maybe she's stuck somewhere in that childhood where she went to hide and needs one or both of you to pull her out of it. It is almost as if I can . . . see the three of you, reunited."

She sighed and smiled weakly. "My father would say it is just wishful thinking." But . . . deep down, she knew that since her deepest wish was for Jon to somehow be able to stay with her forever, his finding Zenna and the rest of his Octad would make that impossible. So . . . how could it be wishful thinking?

Jon stroked her brow with his fingertips. "I wish I had the means to see in there without frightening or hurting you. If you have the gift of prescience, you may be right. But as Minton says, why would she hide from us?"

Lenore couldn't answer that. Nor, it seemed, could anyone else.

She drew a deep, steadying breath and held Jon's free hand tightly. What if she did she have a special gift that was only now unfolding, like a butterfly from its chrysalis? She had never noticed herself having hints or felt omens of things to come. But did she, on some level that was only now beginning to blossom, have the ability to sense the future?

It became important to know. It became more important to know than to continue hiding herself from herself.

"I think I would be less afraid now, Jon. Try. Please try. I will do my best to let you search as deeply as you must."

"Later, *letise*. Now, we will prepare plans for locating our Octad members without alerting Rankin. Fricka must regain much strength, and all of us more geographical knowledge before we can leave here again."

"How will you approach Rankin?"

"With great care and great stealth," Jon replied. "Fricka's surround will give us much-needed protection. As we collect the others, their individual talents, added to those we already have, will offer us more defenses. And, of course, the more of us who are united, the stronger we will be."

"If we can find them," Lenore said, squashing her guilty hope that they never find the others. That Jon be trapped on Earth with her forever. To prove to Jon, Minton, Fricka—and to herself—that she would continue to assist with the search, regardless of the fact that the outcome threatened her happiness with Jon, she said, "Where do we start?"

"We go back to where Zareth was," Jon said. "Even cloaked, as he must be, he surely felt my command. He, as are the others, as Minton did when he learned the perils of translation within the field of Rankin's enhanced range, will be making their way overland in search of me. He will not have traveled far."

Zenna awoke to another desert dawn with a glowing golden sky streaking high above sharp, black mountain peaks, visible through the narrow window across the single room. Glesta, still sleeping, lay curled beside her, tight fists nestled under her chin. She soothed the sleeping child's troubled mind, casting strong reassurance over her, promises she didn't know whether she would be able to fulfill. But she must try!

Rankin, as exhausted as any of them by the travails

of the previous day, still slept, the amplifier cradled as close to him as Glesta was to her. Could she get it?

Stealthily, leaving Glesta on the bed, she slid off the mattress and crept toward Rankin, careful not to stumble on the hard-packed earthen floor littered with detritus blown in on the desert wind. And just as careful to keep from crossing the narrow band of sunlight beginning to peek through the window in the adobe wall. She wanted to cast no shadow, to cause no change in the level of dimness. Three steps away . . . two . . . one. A swift lunge, and she would have the amplifier. Another, to grab her child, and she and Glesta would be gone.

Patán! She berated herself silently. Why had she not carried Glesta with her? Did she risk waking her now and having her make the leap to her side? Glesta had some levitational abilities—more than Zenna herself—but were they developed enough yet? In secret, she had been working with her daughter to help her enhance the talent. But could she expand the privacy bubble wide enough to reach out now to Glesta, or would her probe escape, alerting the sleeping men?

She hesitated, deciding, one foot poised to place itself in position for the final stride that would put the amplifier within her reach.

The time was now! She made that last long stride, grasped the amplifier and as she did so, heard Glesta cry out. She whirled.

B'tar held the child, one arm around her middle, clutching her struggling body to his, oblivious of her heels drumming against his thighs, her torso twisting as she flailed her arms in a futile attempt to claw at his eyes.

"Mama! Make him put me down!"

269

"You heard her," Rankin said, and she tore her gaze from the sight of her captured child. To see him still lying in exactly the same position, but now with his eyes open, a baneful smile on his face. "B'tar will let her go—when you return the amplifier to me."

Still, Zenna hesitated. She held it. She controlled it. Could she, somehow, use it to translate the four of them back to Aazonia, this minute? She fed her mind into it, linked with its intuitive fibers and felt it waver. She backed out of it swiftly. No! It lacked the stability to translate four minds.

Translating only two with it was perilous enough. She could not, would not, risk her daughter's life this way. Slowly, defeated, she held out the amplifier to Rankin.

He smiled again, sitting up, then standing. He shook his head, refusing to accept it. "You wanted it," he said. "So you keep it." He crossed the room and lifted the still struggling child from B'tar's rough hold. "I," he added, "will keep this. Fair trade?"

"No!" Zenna shrieked, flinging herself bodily at him.

He sidestepped her, allowing B'tar time to block her physically. "Oh, I think you'll agree. I think you will have to. The device grows more unstable with each inter-world translation, does it not? Even I can sense that. It requires tuning, Zenna. Tuning only you can perform, since it is keyed primarily to your mind."

"I can tune it no further," she said. "It is going to die, and those connected to it, also. If not in the next translation, then in the one after that."

"You will have to tune it differently, then. Already, it has the power to amplify my thoughts, to cast my net wider. Now I want more from it."

"It has no more to give!"

Rankin tossed a terrified Glesta toward the overhead beams, and caught her as she came down, holding her upside down by one foot, swinging her from side to side like a pendulum, eying the thick adobe wall as if measuring the arc of travel her head would have to make in order to miss—or hit it.

Zenna sent quieting thoughts to her daughter, whose struggles ceased as she slid into a safe place. Zenna sent her even deeper, into a place Glesta had never been before, into one of her own hide-outs, one where she had even, on occasion, hidden from her brother, just to tease. There, she knew, not even Jonallo could find the child.

Despair flooded her. The amplifier could be fine-tuned no more. She had done as much as she could to it. It was due to fail. It would fail. And if Rankin continued to insist she repair it so they could make one more trip, she also knew she—and he—could die. She flicked an exploratory thread into the cesspit that was his mind and knew, knew he expected only one more translation out of the amplifier.

His escape trip.

That he would readily sacrifice B'tar, she had long known. He had no scruples. B'tar, who considered himself Rankin's partner, was nothing but a tool, however weak, to use. Rankin would abandon him in a flash, if that best served his own purposes.

The only way Rankin could get back to Aazoni and his amassed wealth was with the amplifier. And to use the amplifier in this way he needed Zenna, even—maybe especially—if it killed her in the process. The one holding the device, the one whose mind was linked most intimately with it during translation was the one most at risk. The passenger—Rankin in this case—would likely survive.

Unless—The thought horrified her. Unless he tried to

link himself to it and took Glesta as the supporting mind.

So. It was to be now. Or was it? That fine connection she had maintained, however horrible it was, with his mind, told her he had a germ of a plan. She couldn't begin to read what it was, but sensed his glee, his growing belief that there was another way.

What other way, she could not ascertain. Nor could she trust Rankin's machinations. . . .

Deep within the cocoon of safety where she had sent Glesta, she fed the knowledge that her own time was nearly over. When it was, when her maternal signature was no longer a part of Glesta, then the child was to slip out of that safe place and find The Other. That Jon might be in contact with the potential foster mother was a chance she had to take.

Surely, he would be compassionate with an innocent child, even if he was sure her mother had betrayed every code of honor. And Minton . . . he would want their daughter. Even if, without the amplifier, it would be impossible for him to take Glesta home, he would want her safe and loved until she was old enough, strong enough, to make the translation as part of an Octad. Minton, or Jon, or both, would return for Glesta in time.

Her preparations, her decision, had taken only a split second, and now she looked again at Rankin, still swinging the apparently lifeless child in ever widening arcs. Her tawny hair whipped against the pale wall. With the next swing, her skull would connect.

"All right!" She leaped to catch Glesta in midarc. "What do you want me to do?"

Moments later, as Rankin finished explaining, Zenna gasped. "I cannot do that!"

"You will," Rankin informed her, holding Glesta's limp form, upright now, but with one hand at the back of her fragile neck, the other cupped around her chin. "And you will do it now." He nodded at the amplifier. "Tune it as I have ordered."

"If I do, then you will never get home."

His smile sent a shudder through her. "When I have your brother, your bond-mate, and whoever else they may have brought—or the other amplifier, if that is how they traveled, then I shall have no difficulty returning to Aazonia."

Still, she dared to defy him. "Where you will be captured and put to death if you refuse repatterning."

"Repatterned, I would have no knowledge of the life I now enjoy. Repatterned, I would be unable to make use of my wealth." He tightened his hands perceptibly around Glesta's neck. "I will not be captured, Zenna. You will see to that."

He flung a vicious mental stab at her, which, aided by the amplifier, sent her reeling out through the partially opened door, to land with her back against a tall saguaro. Its spines dug into her viciously, but their pain was nothing compared to the pain of watching Rankin stride through the door with her helpless child still dangling from between his hands. "Quit arguing and get to work." He looked down at Glesta's limp body. "Unless you have decided to risk your daughter's life."

Scrambling to her feet Zenna left her *Kahniya* to take care of her physical wounds, and without acknowledging her captor ducked past him to return to the hut. There, she wove her mind into the intricacies of the amplifier, creating from it an entirely different device.

Rankin knew when she had succeeded. There was no way she could prevent that. As the amplifier caught Jon's essence, it transmitted that to Rankin, who laughed in soft triumph as she stepped outside into the bright sunlight bearing his new weapon. He tossed the child like a rag doll to B'tar, who nearly missed.

Put her inside the other hut, Rankin ordered. *Keep her out of my sight. And away from her mother*. He snatched the amplifier from Zenna's hand and let his mind bite into it, mentally projecting all it permitted him to see—simply to torment her.

Helplessly, Zenna tried to block out what Rankin blared forth, but was unable. She yearned to hide far inside herself, to join Glesta in oblivion, but could not.

"Jonallo," Rankin gloated. "Ah, and as I thought, your beloved bond-mate. Does it not feel strange to you, after all these years, to read his signature so loudly, so clearly? To see him standing as he does, looking so close, yet knowing he remains oblivious to your presence, Zenna?"

She refused to answer, and he grabbed a fistful of her hair, yanking it viciously. "Speak to me, woman!"

She spat on his feet.

He flung her away, leaving her lying in the baking sun. "Ah!" he said. "But they disappear, their signatures blocked. A surround, do you suppose? Now who would Jonallo have chosen for that task? Who has the most powerful *willayin?*"

Though she strived to retreat, to keep him at bay, the new and different focus of the amplifier made that impossible. "Fricka. Fricka of Nokori," he said, picking the information right out of her mind. "An old childhood playmate of yours and Jonallo's, am I right?"

She did not deign to answer, but both of them knew he did not require her to. He knew without her confirmation.

Moments passed while he let the amplifier's strength

pick out another, and another of Jonallo's Octad from their different points on Earth.

"Zareth," he said, "and Ree. Soon, Jonallo will find them. Oh, the pickings will be good."

In three long paces, Rankin stood over her, bombarding her with the knowledge that he had most of Jon's Octad pinpointed, that he could pick them off whenever he chose. Grabbing her hair again, he yanked her to her feet. "The moment they are together, you will speak to them," he said. "You will call them to you with the amplified voice of this device. They are five. We are three. Together we complete an Octad."

She defied him. "I will not."

"Then your child dies."

"If she dies, you have no further hold over me, do you?"

That, finally, gave him pause. He backed away from her, keeping out of her reach, both physically and mentally.

But Zenna knew he was not done.

There were others of the Octad still out there. Who would they be? And where? With the amplifier, it was only a matter of time until Rankin discovered their hiding places. She closed her eyes.

In having retuned it to his specifications, she had sentenced the others to death.

Chapter Seventeen

The next three days passed swiftly in the mountain cabin.

Jon's team used the time to heal and rest. An air of anticipation hung over the group, as if they prepared for an upcoming battle. Lenore knew they were readying themselves to recover the remaining members of the Octad and complete their mission.

She longed to ease their suffering, to help Jon find his sister. She seemed unable to conquer her mind, though. Jon tried repeatedly to penetrate the powerful barriers Lenore could not break down within herself, barriers that, once breached, would permit him access to her deepest places—and information as to Zenna's last sure location.

Each attempt left her exhausted and frustrated, because she knew there must be information inside her mind that would help Jon find the place where Zenna had been—the place where Rankin would still surely be. However, a part of her resisted so strongly Jon feared he would harm her unless she, herself, could break through the blocks she erected each time, and offer him a safe way in.

"It will come, *letise*," he assured her after each session. "We approach closer with each attempt. You were so swift to protect yourself from Rankin's rough probe, you instinctively blocked—and without restraint. What we must do now is dissolve your protective defenses, little by little, but this is new to you, and while you say you are not an infant, in many ways, you are the same as an Aazoni newborn. To force your development too quickly could destroy you."

Lenore could only believe him, trust him to know things she could not possibly know. But still, each time she fingered her *Aleeas*, returning to the places she and Jon had visited together, she was more and more tempted to enter into the one her mother had given her.

In there, would she find the means to allow Jon full melding? If she let him touch it, let him examine those memories minutely, let him borrow from the knowledge her mother had left in her, couldn't he protect her from whatever it was she feared so deeply? Many times, while they lay close and warm in the glow of *baloka*, she wanted to suggest it, but that deep sense of privacy, her human need not to have her mind invaded, held strong, making her shudder. Instead, she enhanced her new powers by focusing on *Aleeas* where she knew she could be safe and happy.

"Jon," Fricka said the morning of the third day. "My *willayin* is strong again. I am ready to move us in whatever search pattern you wish."

He considered for a moment, then shook his head.

277

"I think we must separate to cover more area in less time. Minton, you will seek Wend, of course. As birthmates, your minds will link more easily than any others." As he spoke, Lenore caught the sense of despair he projected, because of his belief in his own birthmate's death.

She is alive! Lenore insisted. *Jon, I know this.*

But . . . did she? Or was it simply that she longed to give him peace in whatever way she could? Never before had the mental comfort and emotional ease of another been so important to her. She yearned with a terrible intensity to give him relief from his internal pain, to succor his heart. Was that a function of love, of . . . *baloka?* She reached out soothing thought-fingers to him, felt his gratitude, but knew she was accomplishing little. How could she? She was not a healer. She was not even a full Aazoni.

She, being half of Earth, was of small use to him. She could not even become a member the Octad, should they discover one of the others to be permanently missing. Nor could she travel to Aazonia with Jon when he left. It was not possible for her, with her limited powers. Perhaps, in time, much time, if she developed, it would be possible. But not soon. Not soon enough.

Grief closed off her throat, grief she kept locked within herself, lest it escape and he sense it. She refused to add to his already heavy burden.

"First, though," he said, "We must risk the return to Lenore's other home now that we are in better condition. Fricka, will you create a surround in which we can move undetected?"

Lenore felt less disoriented on their arrival back in Port Orchard. Was that due to the security of translating within the surround Fricka's *willayin* had created, or was it simply that she was growing more skillful herself? Stronger, more accustomed to this strange manner of transportation?

"We will require clothing in order to move around inconspicuously here on Earth," Jon said the moment they rematerialized, all naked, from the cabin. "Lenore, can you provide it for the others, as you did for me? It will need to be durable, as we have no way of knowing what situations we might encounter with each new translation."

As before, it took her little time to meet his request. When all were clothed—he and Minton in identical, dark blue one-piece garments with plenty of room for their shoulders, and enough length for arms and legs, and Fricka clad similarly to Lenore in a paler-colored version of the suits the men wore—Jon declared them ready. But for sustenance. "We must eat and drink before we leave and check Lenore's machines for news of mysterious happenings."

While Jon and Lenore prepared food, and Fricka made the coffee she had come to enjoy greatly, Minton stood leaning against the table. He lifted first one foot then the other, twisting his ankle from side to side, admiring the soft but strong ankle-length boots he wore now. "These," he said with a grateful smile aimed at Lenore, "are far superior to the ones I found in that dwelling under the tumbling snow."

She had to grin at him over her shoulder as she tossed salad in a large bowl. "I'm sure they are. At least you can walk in them."

"I expect to be doing little of that," he said and sent the finished salad into the living room where their dining cushions already lay heaped on the floor. "Within a surround, I will translate wherever our investigations tell me there is something to be investigated."

"We will translate only under cover of dark," Jon decreed once they were reclined and sharing food. The holo tuned to a tab viewer at one end of the living room was reporting news of oddities from all over the world. "And once in a location, we will walk or travel in other Earthly manners so as not to attract attention. In addition, we will meet back here each day to report in person."

When they were finished eating, and Minton had sent the clutter away, Lenore waved on a different holo newsie where she thought they might find more information.

"Stay tuned," the image of the announcer said, tossing her improbably purple hair back from her face, "Next up, we have live footage of a naked woman who is, even as we report it, causing a near riot in Berlin."

Then, for five frustrating minutes, she showed commercials for everything from better nutrient pastes with "more flavor, more vitamins and minerals, and fewer carcinogens" to reduced prices on jumps to Moonbase, and a wide variety of other thirty-second dribbles of "important" information.

Then, finally, the holo showed a long shot of a woman running along what appeared to Lenore to be an invisible tightrope over a canyon between two enormously tall buildings. She gained the sanctuary of a rooftop while thousands gawked from the street below or hung from windows to stare aloft.

As a police helicopter landed near her, she sprinted across the rooftop and stepped out into what could only be thin air. Continuing her dash, she crossed high above another street. As drivers tried to avoid surging crowds or gaped upward at the spectacle, vehicles smashed together, ending in untidy heaps, cluttering the streets for blocks. Three more police helicopters and several news choppers circled a distance from the woman, each hovering over a building, as if waiting to see which one she would next approach.

A close-up revealed no wire under the sure and steady strides of the tall, naked woman with flaming red hair.

The voice-over intoned, "In some undetermined manner, this woman you see here, live, in the privacy and safety of your own home, has crossed from one side of the city to the other, evidently walking on air. Is this some kind of magic? Is it illusion? Is it—"

"It's Ree!" three voices called out in unison as one of the newsie cams managed to capture her full face.

Jon leaped to his feet, dragging Lenore with him. "Berlin. Where is this Berlin?"

All Lenore knew was that the unfamiliar city still used streets, not glideways within the downtown. She keyed her compad to search. "There are three. One in the European Union, two others in the North American. Of those, one is in the Great Lakes Corridor, the other the Atlantic Seaboard Corridor."

She popped a few more keys and established contact with the newsies in each of those three, did a quick search for the words "Berlin," "woman," and "naked."

"Bingo!"

"That signifies success?" Fricka asked, crowding in to peer over Lenore's shoulder at the image on the screen.

"Yes. Your friend is in the Great Lakes Corridor, Sector Madison, and"—she did a rapid rewind of the holo—"unless I miss my guess, she's trying to escape from someone. The cops, I'd say."

Another police chopper landed on a roof in the

woman's path. Ree made an immediate ninety-degree turn in midair and aimed her fleeing feet at another building, this one lower.

"Can she really run in the air like that?" Lenore marveled at the unlikely sight. "Why doesn't she just fly? Or disappear?"

"She is not running on the air. She is a caster."

"A caster?"

"She is able to cast. Just now, she's casting a filament upon which to place her feet. Disappearing at will is not something she can do. She will dematerialize if she is ill or injured and her *Kahniya* is unable to hold her corporal state, but for Ree, fleeing is the best option just now. She must be too depleted to translate alone. We have to get to her." Jon spoke rapidly.

"Fricka, a surround, now. For the three of us."

"Not so fast," Lenore jumped in, clinging tenaciously to Jon's arm so as not to be left behind. "I'm part of this team, and if Ree is in trouble, escaping from someone, you're going to need a person on hand who's better equipped than any of you to deal with Earthly authorities. What if they catch up to her before you reach her? If you go, I go."

"She is right, Jon," Minton said. "I had great difficulty with the Earthly beings I was forced to deal with. Several times I had to translate out of tight situations. Each time, I grew weaker. As it appears Ree is now, too weak to translate."

Jon took no time to decide. "A surround. For Lenore and for me, then." When Fricka would have protested, he raised a controlling hand. "Your *willayin* is not yet strong enough for a long translation with all of us contained. Take yourself and Minton to where Lenore and I saw Zareth. Leave signature trails for him. If he lives, he is cloaked. He might be seeking. Leave him small surrounds, with directions to get here."

He stepped apart from the other two, still with Lenore clutching his arm. "Now," he said, and there was that moment of disorientation, then Lenore was high on a rooftop, with the buzz of helicopters filling her ears. Jon was at her side and the red-headed woman raced toward them, her eyes wide and wild, her face filled with terror. Lenore felt Jon reach out to her mentally, felt him capture the panicked mind, and then they were three within their surround, and the helicopter buzz was gone. She was back in her own living room, half-collapsed against a chair.

She blinked rapidly at the newsie as the purple-haired woman said excitedly, "You saw it with your own eyes! Two other people appeared from nowhere on the rooftop with the fleeing woman, and the three of them disappeared! This is not a trick, folks! This is not our cameras fooling you! What you saw was real. And unbelievable. And you saw it here, live, on JRLO in Berlin, Sector Madison!"

The shot showed that pandemonium continued on the streets and in the air. The confused choppers still hovered over the buildings, fighting for room in the confined air space. The scene appeared exactly as it had only seconds before . . . except now, there was no naked woman running from rooftop to rooftop.

Lenore stared at Jon. Had they even left? The naked woman who lay in a heap on the carpet, quivering slightly like a dog asleep and dreaming answered her question.

Help me. Jon's plea filled her mind, blocking the hysterical voice of the announcer who danced from one foot to the other in the corner of the room as she gave a recap commentary along with an instant replay of the action.

Lenore knelt. *How?*

Give strength. Show peace. Project safety. Enter Ree's mind with me.

It was easier than she had thought it would be, and took less time.

Ree awoke, gazed at Jon, and tears filled her eyes. *Jonallo . . . I have been so alone.*

No longer alone, Ree. No longer apart. You are safe. Safe with me, safe with Lenore, my bond-mate.

Ree looked at Lenore through tangled wet lashes and dashed the tears from her eyes. They were a lovely shade, as clear a turquoise and as limpid as the Sea of Lancor.

Bond-mate? You had no bond-mate. Bewilderment seeped from her. *Jon, how long have I been lost? Are we too late? Have we missed the end of the window? Where is Restal?*

Jon smiled and propped cushions around and under the woman, making her comfortable as Lenore covered her with a blanket. Her *Kahniya* winked and twinkled, flickering with the purple light reflecting off the holo announcer's startling hair. Lenore waved the holo out of existence the better to concentrate on the conversation between Jon and Ree.

It was not so much a conversation as an outpouring of information that Ree absorbed as quickly as it was delivered. When Jon was finished, she smiled, reaching out a hand to touch Lenore.

Welcome, cousin.

"It is she who must welcome you," Jon said aloud. "For this is her home, on her home-world."

"I do welcome you," Lenore said.

"And I?" spoke another voice. Lenore whirled. Minton and Fricka stood supporting a man a few inches shorter than Jon. He looked nothing like the magician she'd seen as a holo-image, yet somehow, she recognized him.

She felt momentarily light-headed. "Yes, Zareth. I welcome you, too."

She tried to smile and make it genuine as she counted the Aazoni. Where there had been only three, now stood five.

Three more to go, and the Octad would be complete.

Letise, letise, *we will find the strength somehow to do what we must . . .*

Lenore looked at Jon, read the sorrow in his eyes and whispered aloud, "I know, my love. I know."

But she did not know where she would find such strength.

The next to be found was Vanter, a man much older than the others, and according to Jon, one of the most experienced trackers alive. If anyone could find traces of the others, he would. Vanter had picked up one of the faint trails Jon had left, and over the past several weeks, had stealthily followed it, taking great care always not to alert Rankin.

Now, the old man sat in quiet solitude, almost a trance, Lenore thought, for many hours each day. Periodically, he would join them to eat and drink, but always he returned to his. . . . ruminations? She assumed he was using his great skill to search for the others. As the days passed, she wondered, how exactly he traced them.

The others seemed to accept his long silences, to trust that he would succeed. Jon, she knew, was becoming increasingly aware of the passage of time. All too soon, their one, narrow window would close. If they didn't find the missing members . . .

Lenore longed for more time. More time for them to find the remaining members of the Octad, more time for her to spend with Jon. But she realized the futility of her wishes. The most she could hope for was that her new friends would make it home safely. She tried to convince herself that it was the best thing for Jon. He needed to return to his own planet, his own time and space. He was hers for those last few days, and somehow, she would have to make that suffice.

At odd intervals, the others disappeared singly or in pairs leaving Lenore to tend to Vanter's needs.

Then, one day just as everyone else had assembled for a meal after their various treks, Vanter opened his eyes and looked fully alert for the first time since Lenore had known him.

We must go to a desert, he decreed, facing Lenore, directing his thoughts at her. *There, we will find Rankin.*

"Rankin? What of the others?"

The others will come. Vanter had never used audible speech in Lenore's hearing. She didn't even know if he could. *But in the desert, Rankin awaits.*

"What desert?" she asked.

Vanter gazed at her for a long time. *A desert with hot days, cold nights. There are few trees but many cactuses. Steep mountain peaks rise from the bare earth. I see it. I sense from you that the aroma from the trees is that of pine. The cactuses are of several varieties, the names of most unknown to you. There is one that grows tall. It rises straight from the ground as a fat cylinder, with upraised arms for branches. One is broken. You have seen it. You know it.*

Into her mind he planted a vivid picture. "Saguaro?" Lenore said. It was the only cactus she knew by name, and the one he showed her did have a broken limb. And it also, oddly enough, looked familiar to her, though she was certain she had never seen it before.

That is your name for it, yes. You must show me where it is.

"That particular cactus?" She gaped at him. "But . . . that's not possible. There are millions of them. There are many desert areas where they grow," she protested, looking to Jon for help. A frown of concentration creased his brows as if he were searching either her mind or Vanter's. The latter, she hoped. It was enough knowing Vanter had been digging through her thoughts all these days, without her even suspecting it.

You know where it is, the old man insisted. *You have followed Zenna's* Kahniya *to that place.*

"How could I have?" Lenore knew she had not. "The only time I sensed Zenna was in my dreams, and she wasn't in any desert, but here, somewhere in or near the Cascadia Corridor, in a forest clearing with the ocean visible through the trees. And not a cactus in sight!"

Nevertheless, her essence speaks in your mind of desert terrain and of that particular plant with one broken limb.

Hope surged like a palpable tide through the room. Jon spoke almost inaudibly. "Zenna? Are you saying she's alive?"

I cannot know that. I sense only her Kahniya's *signature through your bond-mate's mind.* His dark gray gaze, penetrating and clear, connected with Lenore's. *May I look again, deeper?*

After a moment, she gave him silent, if reluctant consent. As Vanter's gentle probes fluttered through her mind, they seemed less intrusive than she had feared. How long he searched her, she could not tell, but when he released her, she was weak with exhaustion.

She knows. The knowledge is in there, but she blocks me. She gives me nothing I can follow.

"She gives as much as she can," Jon defended her.

But she has more. To find, to track, to be sure, I must be allowed to seek deeper within her, to break the blocks she has erected.

Jon's arms tightened around Lenore. "No."

Then we will not succeed. Vanter's thought carried the heavy weight of despair as Jon carried Lenore to her bed.

But . . . Zenna's essence. Is it of her, or only of her Kahniya? Lenore, despite being on the verge of sleep, recognized how deeply Minton longed to know if there was a chance Zenna lived and how it grieved Vanter not to be able to tell him.

I believe it is of her living self. I will continue my sweeps. . . . The old man's thought followed Lenore into sleep.

The next day, with Fricka's *willayin* firmly in place, creating a tight surround for all of them, the party of searchers moved out, translating to every desert the maps told them were within reach of a strong *Kahniya* such as Zenna's. The areas were vast and empty. Even Vanter had to admit that.

Wherever Rankin is, he is so well hidden I cannot track him. Jon, I must send out a stronger probe. I must break through the carapace of his shield. Meld with me. All meld with me, join me in my tracking. Help me!

Jon shook his head. He was still the Octad leader. "No. We will find Wend and Restal first. Then, with a full complement, we will track Rankin and defeat him. If he is so heavily shielded, he cannot sense us unless we are right on top of him. As long as Fricka can maintain our surround, and Zareth our invisibility, we could be in his lap and he would not know it. Keep trying, Vanter. He's out there—" Jon waved a hand at the desert where they all stood. "I know that. If not this desert, then another. The next one, maybe. I trust your instincts, Vanter. And we will locate him. He doesn't know we are here. And when we find him, Ree and Restal will cast hoods over both him and B'tar. They will not escape."

"Your birth-mate's hunting party grows," Rankin said in satisfaction, sneering at Zenna, "This is a far superior tool you have devised for me. With it, I can choose which of them will live, and which will die. You have done well, Zenna. I may, after all, let your child live. Would you trade her life for that of your birth-mate, or your bond-mate?"

He paused, apparently in thought, though he kept the power of the newly tuned amplifier shielded fully from her except when he projected what he wanted her to know.

"Your bond-mate, I think," he decided for her, as if she had ever really been offered a choice. "I will need Jonallo for the translation to the home-world. At least, for the initial stages of it."

His smile was pure evil. "I'm certain you left enough of the translation functions intact to get yourself home . . . in the faint hope that you would somehow regain possession of the amplifier."

His being right did not endear her to him, but she resolutely kept her cloak firm, not letting him past a certain point. He had no idea how much she could hide from him, and for that she thanked the genetics that had bequeathed her much greater personal strength than he could ever hope to attain.

While maintaining a tight mental lock on the part of her psyche he could reach, he still managed to feed a large portion of his mental capacities into the amplifier, and laid the visions out for her like holo images, wavering in the desert heat. "There, you see. Your birthmate is reestablishing his Octad. I believe I will let him continue."

Through her unwilling connection with Rankin, Zenna saw through the loose surround with which Jon kept his group guarded, unaware of how much stronger it would need to be to hide their presence from Rankin. She longed to warn them, but could not.

She saw Jon, Minton, Ree, Vanter, Zareth and Fricka— and another. She clamped down tightly on that, not to let Rankin glimpse the stray, startling information that leaped into her mind. The woman was . . . The Other! She felt ill. The Other, there, physically beside Jon and Minton, and by the look of the surrounding terrain, not far from this location.

"He did not translate to this space and time with only seven," Rankin mused, "and one of those a weakling."

Zenna was glad that while he recognized The Other had deficiencies, he did not realize that she was an addition to the original Octad.

"One is yet missing."

Which one? B'tar's terrified thought filtered in.

How would I know which one? Rankin was scathing. *I have no way of knowing who else he has brought on this little venture of his. Now, leave. Tend to the child. Keep trying to reach her essence wherever her mother has buried it.*

"Who will it be?" he went on, speaking aloud again as he faced Zenna. Half his capacity was tied up in the amplifier. "Shall we see, Zenna? Shall we, ourselves, collect the last member of Jonallo's Octad and use him for our own purposes?"

Again, she remained silent, neither helping nor hindering, simply . . . biding her time, watchful, waiting, hoping, however slim that hope might be, that he would lower his guard for a moment. And that before he did, he would not find the one small gap she had left in the amplifier's shield on the chance she could infiltrate.

"There!" he said, from within his link with the amplifier. "Restal."

That wiped the smile off his face. She felt his sudden apprehension, exulted in it. He, like she, had knowedge of Restal and his powers as a hood-caster. If Restal could get near enough, if he could pinpoint Rankin's location, he could cast a hood that would contain Rankin's mind, rendering it incapable of projection.

She gasped in pain as Rankin's amplified mental capacities linked abruptly with Restal's. It was as if a huge, unrelenting hand gripped the hood-caster's heart. It squeezed, holding it, stopping it, squeezed once more for good measure, and Restal dropped. A moan escaped Zenna's throat, hidden under the raucous sound of Rankin's triumphant laughter.

She snatched at his moment of elation, seizing the opportunity to pounce, but he was too quick for her. With one blow, he flattened her to the ground. Reaching into a pouch at his side, he withdrew a hypospray and pressed it to her neck.

She felt nothing, heard only a faint "psst!"

291

As the drug infiltrated her system, leaving her helpless, only half aware, she heard him laugh. "Now, they are only seven. They cannot leave Earth without me." And Zenna knew she would never see her family or her home-world again.

Restal's glad cry of recognition and connection gave way to a gurgling, strangled one of shock and agony, swiftly followed by his death-tone. Lenore reeled under the impact of its projection. Vanter's form flickered and wavered, so hard did Restal's demise hit him. Fricka steadied the surround as Jon caught the old man, balanced him, held him together, while Minton and Zareth supported Lenore. Ree collapsed to the hard ground, unconscious, overwhelmed by the loss of her mentor.

Vanter's anger flooded from him. Its power helped Lenore recover as it swept through the group. *Rankin!* The old man spat the word into the minds of the others. *He killed Restal. Just like that. He stopped his heart. But how? How can he have such power?*

"The amplifier?" Minton asked. "Could it be used in that way? As a tool of death, not just a means of translation?" He seemed to be talking to himself, thinking aloud. "How? What would have to be done to it to create such a device?"

Zenna . . . Vanter's certainty was clear. *Her living essence is in it. She caused it to behave in that way.*

Both Jon and Minton rounded on him. *Zenna?* Their mutual joy in his certitude that she lived did not prevent their instant denial of Vanter's statement. "She would not create a tool that would give another the power of death over others. She would die first, herself."

But she lives, Vanter insisted. *I felt her. She is with*

Rankin. A part of him, an integral part of it. A part of his . . . power."

"She might be *in* his power," Minton snapped. "She is not, I assure you, part of it."

Vanter sighed and nodded. *Perhaps it is as you say. But it makes no difference. With her power and his linked through the amplifier, Rankin has more than all of us put together. Especially now we are missing two.*

"The Octad is missing but one," said a husky feminine voice Lenore had never heard before, and she watched a slender woman, shorter than herself, fly into Minton's arms, where she nestled like a fledgling returning to its nest.

Wend! The thought came from nowhere and everywhere, carried on a wave of pure gladness.

Fricka, strengthen the surround, Wend said from within her birth-mate's embrace. *Much evil is afoot. I sneaked in under cover of Restal's translation. I felt Rankin reach out, felt him still Restal's heart in a way I did not know was possible.* Her voice broke. *I tried to restart it, but could do nothing. All we have of him is this.* She stepped back from Minton, showing them Restal's *Kahniya* draped over her hand. She bent to the slowly recovering Ree, laying Restal's *Kahniya* on the other woman's chest. *You will take it to his family, Ree. As his student, it is your duty.*

Ree only stared, and Lenore sensed she was still deep in shock. The hood-caster closed her eyes again, but her face seemed less strained. Was Wend healing her even as she turned back to Jon?

"How can she take it home to Restal's family?" Fricka asked, slumping against the trunk of a tree in the copse where they stood, trying to take advantage of its sparse

293

shade. "Restal is gone. We will never get home without the full Octad."

Jon and Lenore shared a swift glance and a momentary sensation of sweeping, guilty exultation before Wend spoke sharply as if to drag Fricka from the despair she was quickly sinking into. "We will rescue Zenna as we came to do. With her, we will be eight."

"You confirm Vanter's belief?" Minton's hope grew stronger. "Zenna lives?"

"Zenna lives." Wend's tone left no doubt.

"But where?" Jon asked. "Did you sense where she is? Where Rankin is? Exactly, I mean. Can you lead us to their location?"

"No. He has something that makes him entirely more powerful than any one Aazoni should be. That is why we must remain within the tightest of surrounds and well-cloaked. Vanter must do the tracking, with Zareth to hide him from view."

"Yes." Lenore felt Jon's distress lessening, felt his strength returning. Was this the effect of the healer?

He stood straighter, his face hardened, his lips tightened, his chin squared with resolve. He was, without doubt, once more in full command of his team.

"Fricka, can you maintain a total surround with our help?"

"I can." Fricka's voice quavered. She steadied it as she rose. "I will."

"And Ree . . ." Jon crouched beside her, touching her brow with his fingertips. "Will you manage to hood two captives unaided?"

Ree nodded slowly. Her eyes, as green as Jon's, stared round and hurt from a face still white in contrast to the blaze of her hair. "I can . . . try. Restal would expect it of me."

Jon raised her from the ground with one hand as he stood.

"*I* expect it of you."

She nodded, looking healthier, more sure of herself by the minute.

"Zareth . . . you are ready to do your part?"

Zareth looked suddenly like a Marine snapping to attention before his commanding officer. "I am. I will create a diversion the minute we have a lock on Rankin. He will not know whether he sees illusion or reality."

"Vanter?"

Ready. I will track Rankin. I will find him for you. He cast a narrow glance at Lenore. *With luck.*

"Not with luck. With your own skill." Jon's tone was hard, uncompromising. He held Vanter's gaze for a long moment until the old man nodded, tacitly agreeing not to molest Lenore's mind for needed information.

"Minton?"

"I will do what is required of me to rescue my bond-mate."

"Then we will return to Lenore's home to refresh ourselves with food, drink, and rest."

The seven Aazoni—and Lenore—joined hands and translated from the edge of the Mojave.

It was not until they had all eaten and she lay beside a sleeping Jon that Lenore let herself think of how he had polled each of his teammates as to readiness for the task at hand—and had asked nothing of her.

It was, she knew, because he felt she had nothing of value to contribute.

Slowly, carefully, she reached out a shaky, inexperienced probe to Vanter, inviting him in. . . .

*   *   *

He was gentle to start with, his touch so soft she scarcely knew he was there . . . until he met resistance. Then, as if he were a crowbar and her mental barricades no stronger than rusted gates, he forced them open. With a scream of pain mingled with terror, Lenore struggled to escape, blaring forth a spray of torment, a wordless plea for Jon, for his protection, for succor. She felt his presence, felt Vanter struggling with him for precedence, and then . . . they were both gone.

Lenore whirled through a dark abyss shot through with ugly streaks of red like blood, of deep purple like bruises, of green like putrescence. Her body slammed hard against something as another mind raked through hers, raping, tearing, snatching out pieces here, chunks there, casting them carelessly aside even as she attempted to repair the breaches in her barriers.

It was no good. She couldn't keep him out. It wasn't Vanter. This much she knew. The signature was the one of total evil she had sensed once before, the one that had inadvertently killed her. It would kill her now. It could, but it didn't. It simply . . . took from her.

She sensed the man's malevolence, knew his mastery over her was complete, felt him using her terror to batter at Jon, to demand his presence if Jon wanted surcease for her. With each clawing probe into her mind, she knew she was crying out to him, though she tried not to. She had to hide. She needed to protect not only herself, but Jon. She must not let Rankin use her this way! Something told her that. *Someone?* Yes. But who? It was a person she should know. Vaguely, she recognized she had felt that person's fear at other times, fear for the life of . . . a child? The fear was the same now, but it was *her* life in jeopardy, not that of a child, unless she was the child?

Was the person who wanted to protect her a mother? *Her mother?*

In her traumatized condition, she could not find answers to her questions, could only go where she knew it was safe. Following a persistent, annoying nonvoice, an order she only felt but understood she must obey—or die, she raised her hand. Slowly, it moved, heavy, heavier than the world, but she forced it to raise from the hard-packed dirt where she now lay, moved her fingers, digging them into her own skin to help them creep from her side, up over her chest, until her finger touched, for just the necessary instant, that single bead that would take her home.

Deeper, deeper, she slid into that home, a home she'd forgotten existed, a home open only to the unborn. She crawled inside, curled there, warm in the enveloping fluid, floating, at peace, leaving the Rankin-taloned attack far behind. On one level, she remained aware of his rage, his fevered attempts to drag her from her haven, but she refused to leave because there was safety.

My child ... my beloved. The voice filled her soul. She sensed somehow a presence, not so much a memory as a knowing. For a time she floated, gathering stamina, then she was out of the fluid world, cradled close, nestled to warmth, sustenance filling her body and mind.

She heard all the words her mother had ever spoken to her, accepted the knowledge of who she was, what she was, why she was. She recognized the love Careel had felt for Winston Henning, man of Earth, the love he had felt for her, and for their daughter. She grew to know intimately Careel's sadness at Winston's refusal to accept her for what she was. She was there during the discussions between the two, not part of them, but aware. She suffered with Careel, suffered with Winston who thought his beloved's mind was unsound.

And then, she experienced his disbelief, swiftly followed by terror, then anger, the day he came in and found his infant daughter hovering near the ceiling above her crib. Levitating!

She cringed, as did Careel, at his scream of anguish when he finally accepted that his wife was sane—sane but not of Earth, that his child, the child of his heart, could never be wholly his, that she had talents that would take her from him. His horror burned deep within Lenore, his revulsion at what he had helped to create.

A monster. A hybrid. An unearthly mutant. His mind, set to deal with facts and figures, could not handle such an aberration.

Careel fought him, fought his prejudices, worked to appease him, but to no avail. She clutched her child in her arms, pressed her hungry mouth to a breast to still her terrified cries. And then . . . and then *she* screamed as the baby was dragged from her grasp, forcibly taken from her. Mother/child combined could not overcome the determination of a demented man, not without doing him irreparable harm.

Careel, loving them both, could only leave, giving her child the most precious gift she could, her one *Aleea*, planted deep in her mind for later retrieval, and a solemn oath she would return.

And then, for Lenore, the memories stopped. Of Careel, there was no more, only an echo of the strong, unending love of a mother for her child.

Mama, mama, mama . . . The words were hers . . . and yet not hers.

The child! The child of her dreams. Enough self-awareness returned for her to recognize that child, to know that they were both in great danger, to know that somehow, before Rankin, with his horrendous capacity to do harm, could claw his way to where they were, she must act.

Gathering herself, she sent out a thought to the child and the essence that was . . . *Glesta* . . . flooded her mind, mingled with the child that had been Lenore. The sum of the two, combined were greater than the parts.

Glesta, whimpering, crawled in to the safe cradle of Lenore's mind as they fed each other strength. It took time, time to build rapport, time to create trust, time to reassure the child that was Glesta, time to rebuild the child that had been Lenore, to reclaim the woman Lenore had become. But when it happened, when the mending was done, the melding complete, there came a surge of pure energy. It carried unexpected vitality, held spare power. Power Lenore knew was hers to employ. She rejoiced in it, in her new-found certainty that she could win. She could, if nothing else, save this child. In doing so, she would save what was left of Careel.

You must go, she told the child, recognizing the truth even before the thought formed. *Glesta, I must send you from here.*

My mama. . . .

Your mama sent me to save you. She wants me to take care of you for her. I am The Other, Lenore.

My mama, my mama, my mama. . . .

And mine, Lenore said, mingling the *Aleea* of Careel with those already in Glesta's mind. Then, with a dint of effort she could only hope would be adequate, she gathered herself, narrowed her focus, locked it on what she knew of Jon and . . . thrust the child from her.

Judy Gill

Her last conscious thought was knowledge that Glesta was gone . . . gone to a better kind of safety, with Jon.

Jon staggered under the impact of a small but solid body smashing into his chest. Instinctively, his arms came up to hold it, and he looked down into a face that was Zenna's—and not Zenna's. *Who?* he demanded. *What?* But the child could not reply. He could make no sense of her. In her mind was only terrified gibberish, incomprehensible babbling, and the repeated word: *mama, mama, mama. . . .*

Jon sensed the shocked confusion of the others within Fricka's surround, felt them crowding physically closer, mentally probing, trying to get a handle on this newcomer. Wend stepped in, brushing their minds and bodies aside, pulling a cloak over herself and the child, blocking out even Jon.

He let her take the little girl, watched the concentration on her face as she used her superior healing powers as a calming influence, sifting through the confusion to sort knowledge the child carried. Finally, Wend broke into a broad smile.

Stepping forward, she handed the small, unconscious body to Minton. "Minton, this is your daughter, Glesta."

The instant babble nearly overwhelmed Jon, but again Wend's calming authority, her rapid but succinct explanations settled the group.

Minton, tears streaming down his face, stared at the child whose existence Jon knew he had never once suspected. He stroked her hair back, tenderly administered to her mind. Jon followed Minton into the mind of his birth-mate's child, approved as the other man fed her bits of himself, bits of his memories, sifted through hers for all her mother had told her.

His gaze swung to Jon's, stunned, and for a moment, the two continued to stare at each other. "She had no knowledge of either of us," Jon said to the others, who had politely kept themselves apart from this family union. "None at all."

"But of Zenna, yes?"

"Yes, Wend. Much of Zenna. And of Lenore. We have Rankin pinned. Through Glesta, Lenore has sent us his exact location."

But, he couldn't help wondering, was it already too late for his sister . . . and for his love?

In stealth, shielded by the protection of Fricka's *willayin,* the cover of Zareth's illusion, and the power of their combined minds, five Aazoni slipped across the desert. They left Wend behind, still working on the unconscious child, carefully, skillfully peeling back the layers of her protection, freeing her from the protective chrysalis her mother had created for her, and in which she had safely remained when Lenore had flung her.

In the crystalline desert air, the encampment appeared closer than it was. Making their way toward it on foot was slow, tedious for those accustomed to instant movement from one spot to another. But, now they knew of Rankin's enhanced abilities, his power to kill with a mere thought; they could not risk him detecting their approach. To translate would surely alert him that the group he "sensed" as still being huddled under the trees was nothing more than one of Zareth's illusions.

Still within the surround, they safely reached the first of the adobe huts. All was quiet. Jon slipped apart from the others, a shadow masked by the other shadows Zareth created, and peeked inside the building.

B'tar! He lay in a heap on the floor, as if he had been

301

flung by a powerful force against a wall, only to slide down and stay put. Jon spared him only a glance. He was of no account and clearly out of commission, but there, on a bunk at the side of the room, deep in real shadows, he saw Lenore.

Deeply unconscious, she lay as in death. Only the faint rise and fall of her chest told him she still lived. He dared not reach out to her physically, lest her unconscious mind respond to that touch and signal Rankin of a change in her neural patterns. He dared not reach out to her mentally either. To do so, he would have to break out of Fricka's surround.

There was no physical sign of Rankin in that hut, nor in the next. Jon was forced to clamp down on Minton's inadvertent howl as he spotted Zenna lying in the dusty soil, bruises covering her face and body, blood running from wounds, a limpness about her that spoke of more than mere unconsciousness.

Carefully, Minton lifted her, cradled her close, rocking her to and fro, telling her that Glesta was safe, healthy, healing, that they were together, they were going to go home. Jon felt her fogged brain begin to respond and bade Ree to cast a hood over her and Minton, to contain their uncontrollable gladness.

Yes, they were together. Yes, they were going to go home. He closed his eyes, visualizing Lenore lying alone and unconscious in that hovel not ten meters away. How could he leave her like that? How could he leave her at all?

But he must. Time was running out. The window was about to close, and he had yet to find Rankin and dispatch him. It was his duty to his people that he fulfill the task for which he had come. Rankin had to be stopped.

But . . . in stopping him, Jon would be forced to leave his bond-mate to die.

Grief overwhelmed him, spilled forth, and in that moment, Rankin pounced from out of the sky.

The criminal's amplified mind struck out at Jon, flinging him across the open space between the two adobe shacks. Rankin materialized in the middle of Fricka's surround, sweeping it aside as if it were of no more substance than a *welligan*'s nest.

Jon recovered quickly. *To me!* his mind roared. *With me! Together!*

Zareth sent a bellowing herd of *grumpion* stampeding down on Rankin, who dodged instinctively, leaving an opening for Jon, with Ree's help, to send him rocking back onto his haunches. Before he could recover, Fricka had him wrapped in a surround. He fought, pummeling her, trying to keep his mind attuned to the amplifier.

Zareth created a clap-banger right over Rankin's head. He dropped the amplifier, cupping his hands over his bleeding ears. Jon, this time joined by Minton, smote him again, forcing his mind into instant retreat.

The battle raged on as Rankin recovered the amplifier, melded with it, aimed its might at the opposing forces. But they were too many, coming at him from such different angles. He couldn't hold his focus long enough to vanquish any one of them. One moment he thought he had Jon, but realized he held only the illusion of his primary enemy's mind. The next, he felt Vanter slip from his grasp, only to blindside him with a painful mental jab.

Then it would be Ree's turn or Minton, or Jon again, or any of the five in concert. As the *grumpion* herd bore down on him again, he struggled to hold his position, to convince himself they were not real. But somehow they were, and they were upon him, their sharp hooves trampling the ground all around him, kicking up choking dust, obscuring his physical vision. The thunder of their passage, the stench of their bodies, the heat of their breath all over took him.

He curled into a ball to protect himself, and unexpectedly, B'tar seized the moment—and the amplifier— by dashing into the herd only Rankin could see and feel and smell.

With it in his hand, he forced his inadequate mind into its inner workings, trying to meld with it as he had learned from watching Zenna and Rankin. But he was inept.

Rankin knew at once what his partner was trying to do.

With a shriek, he dove for the other man, his hand connecting with B'tar's ankle just as the other man managed to operate the device, setting it into translation mode. It stuttered, hesitated, and Rankin forced B'tar's mind out of the way, struggling with him for control, but it was not B'tar whom he had to fight.

Zenna, coming out of her drug-induced stupor, linked with Minton, linked with the amplifier. The two of them, knowing the device so well, misaligned it completely, destroying it. And with it, both B'tar and Rankin.

Their singed, corporeal forms dropped at Zenna's feet.

Carelessly, she stepped over them, still clinging to Minton's arm. "Brother," she said to Jon, bowing low before him. "I thank you for coming to my rescue."

Jon embraced his birth-mate, holding her close, lending her some of his poor, remaining strength. They both did better when Wend and Glesta, the latter now fully restored, materialized beside them. Zenna scooped up her daughter, pressing her tightly to her breast.

With one hand on Minton's *Kahniya* and the other on Glesta's, she gave her child back the memories of her father, the memories she had hidden for so long to protect Glesta and herself. She repeated the same with Jon's *Kahniya*, and then her own. She trembled violently with exhaustion, but was clearly determined to join her loved ones before she succumbed to her body's needs.

Cradling her between them, Jon and Minton eased her to the ground, where they sat holding her as she held the child, a family once more, bonding. The others of the Octad, while remaining within reach should their strength be required, took their minds out of the link, offering the privacy none of the three reunited family members had thought to build.

"My sister," Jon said, finding it hard to use his voice when he wanted only to reconnect mentally, deeply, fully. But the child needed to hear this, to be assured of her welcome, as well as her mother's, and he was as yet unsure of her capacity for full understanding. "My sister, you have suffered much. I will regret until the end of my life being unable to come to your aid sooner."

"It was likely worse for you than for me," Zenna said, also using audible speech. "The times that Rankin forced me to translate to the home-world were the hardest because I knew you were there." Her gaze swept from Jon to Minton. "And I could not, dared not, reach out to you. Either of you." Black pain clouded their small gathering for a moment before Zenna controlled it, but Jon felt Minton's response to that pain and saw the physical evidence of it, read the remorse emanating from him.

The tears in Minton's eyes spilled over. "You feared me."

Zenna spoke gently, without censure. "I feared for our daughter. I refused to take any chances with her safety. She was all I had of you. I wasn't sure you still loved me after all our arguments over the amplifier. But even more important, I could not forget all the hurt that surrounded our union when we thought we could not have children."

Minton moved apart from their close grouping, sitting several feet away, his hands dangling loosely between his drawn-up knees. His deep regret lay around him like an almost visible cloak of misery. Jon wanted to reach out to him, but knew that this was the time for his birthmate and her bond-mate to come to terms with their differences.

He began to slip apart from them, but Zenna's thought tendrils captured him, demanding that he stay to bear witness.

"I should have known you would never have left voluntarily without telling me first. I trusted you would never use the amplifier for illegal purposes." Minton said. "But I thought maybe you had left because you no longer wanted to spend any time in my company. Perhaps you had sold the amplifier to support yourself. I never should have doubted you. We are bond-mated."

Zenna smiled. "Our bond-mating was beginning to waver and lose strength. I know that, Minton. I knew it then." She drew a deep breath. "The fault was mine. I know that now, have known it since the very day I was taken from Aazonia. Our bond-mating had been damaged by my anger with you for declaring our device unreliable, for your walking away from our research, branding it as dangerous."

"I feared for your safety if you persisted."

"I thought you were giving up on me because I couldn't get pregnant. When the healers assured us we were both physically capable, and that it might be a psychological problem, I blamed myself."

Minton's eyes showed shock. "*I* never blamed you for that. I hold myself responsible for so much, Zenna, for abandoning you in the lab, for not detecting Rankin's evil. How could I not have sensed his dishonesty, his blatant disregard for right and wrong? The low value he placed on the lives of others."

She reached a hand toward him, but he made no move to take it. It was as if he didn't see it, wouldn't see it. Jon sensed her mental reaching, and sensed, too, the barrier Minton erected against it.

Despite that barrier, Jon knew of Minton's inner strife, watched and even felt the physical difficulty with which the other man finally turned his head and gazed long at Zenna as if trying to read the truth in her mind. When she opened it fully to him, Jon did slip free of the tenuous bonds with which she held on to him, leaving her alone with her mate. He reached out and took Glesta so that Zenna was free to move to stand before Minton.

"Minton, it was my own preoccupation with the lack in our personal lives that left me careless, open, and vulnerable," she said, reaching to where he sat, folding her fingers through his and urging him to his feet. "That distraction allowed Rankin to capture me. I was searching deep within myself, trying to discover what of my nature was preventing my conceiving our children, and not paying attention to the fact that he was managing to cloak himself from me. Rankin had been watching me, waiting, since you denounced the amplifier and absented yourself and your expertise from the project. As

307

did all of our other lab assistants, he knew the Committee for Scientific Advancement would soon stop the research. As a man with his nefarious sideline, he also knew he must act quickly if he were to succeed in capturing the device for his own use. He administered a drug that incapacitated me, then used my unconscious mind to make that first translation with the amplifier.

"It was during that trip to Earth that Rankin detected my pregnancy. With the help of the amplifier and my unconscious state, he was able to sense things about my body of which I was not even aware. From that day forward he threatened to hurt Glesta, first as an unborn baby and then as a young child, if I did not help him.

"The fault," she concluded, touching his face with her fingertips, "was not yours, my mate. Never yours. And my joy upon learning of Glesta's coming was something I ached to share with you because I knew it was the one gift I could give you that would mean the most. But because of our child, I dared not make any attempt to seek help when I was on the home-world. Rankin held Glesta hostage to ensure my good behavior. I beg you to believe me, beg your forgiveness, beg for your love again."

"That, you never lost," Minton said. "And it is I who must beg forgiveness for ever doubting your love for me."

The two embraced for a long, silent, and Jon hoped, healing moment, then separated, connected only by linked hands as they took the few paces necessary to reach his side.

"Glesta," Minton said formally, bowing to the child Jon held. "You are my daughter. I waited long for you. I was not able to give you the benefit of my memories as is your birthright. I wish to do so now." His hands twitched as he struggled not to reach for his first-born. Jon felt the strength of the restraint with which the other man held himself back lest he frighten the child with the force and intensity of his longing to know her, to have her know him.

Minton touched his *Kahniya,* stroking his fingertips over it, and proffered one glowing bead of light. It winked on the palm of his hand. Glesta did not reach for it. She merely looked at it, and then at Minton. Finally, as if satisfied by something even Jon was not privy to, she smiled and finally spoke, a trifle impatiently. "Papa, you may touch me."

With a groan, Minton took her from her uncle, stroked her hair as his gaze roamed over her face. He was open for all to see, his emotions shining forth with the golden energy of love as he bonded with his child. Carefully, he curled his palm and fingers, creating a miniature trough. As his fingertips touched the mother-bead of Glesta's *Kahniya,* the father-bead rolled down the shallow slope and nestled close to the first one.

Glesta's eyes squeezed tightly shut for a moment; then she popped them open, along with her mouth. "Oh!" she said. "Oh, Mama! There is so much more. Help me." Smiling, Zenna slipped into the other side of Minton's embrace, wrapping one arm around him and the other around her daughter.

"It will come, *letise,*" she said. "Soon, it will all make sense."

"It all makes sense now," Glesta informed her as she gazed at her father. "It is just more than I ever knew there was in this world."

"That, my dearest child," Minton told her, "is because there is so much more than just this world on which you were born. There is another world I want very much to show you."

He looked at Jon. "With your uncle's permission."

Glesta met her uncle's gaze with a wide blue-eyed blaze of complete trust.

"You are my mother's birth-mate. We had to hide from you so Rankin could not find you and kill you." She beamed. "But you are strong. Very strong. And you were angry. You roared louder than an entire herd of *grumpion.* You made Rankin go away, and now Mama and I can go home with you and my papa."

Jon looked from the child to his birth-mate, sorrow eating into him, sorrow he felt Zenna trying to alleviate. But even her closeness could not eradicate it.

All these years apart. He stole them from us. He stole the moment of your child's birth from me, from our parents, stole the knowledge of her growing mind. You suffered, my sister. You were alone when most you needed my support, the support of your bond-mate, the strength of family unity.

"I am not alone now," she said aloud, but under that, he sensed that she knew the depth of loneliness he felt. *I grieve that you are, Jonallo. Had you not been forced to search for me, you would not be in this torment now.*

Had I not come to search for you, I would not have found my bond-mate, he told her. *Whatever the outcome, for that reason alone, I can have no regrets.*

"Jonallo," Glesta said, oblivious to the communication between her mother and uncle, "can we go home now?"

"We can go home," he said, though his heart was breaking. "And we will. But first, I need your help." He looked around his Octad. "Everyone's help. Lenore lies in there, near death. I cannot leave Earth until she is whole again. She has gone into hiding. It may take all of us to find her and bring her back."

"I know where she is, Jonallo," Glesta said, sliding down from her father's arms. She led the way into the adobe hut where Lenore lay with Wend in close attendance. The healer's hand spread over Lenore's brow, as if she hoped her presence would prevent Lenore's essence from slipping completely beyond reach.

Standing close beside her, Glesta touched the central bead on Lenore's *Kahniya*. "Come," she said, reaching to take her uncle's hand. "Follow me, Jonallo. I will lead the way to where your bond-mate waits."

Lenore stood facing the eight adults and one child, formed in a semicircle before her. All were naked, as was she. This time, it didn't bother her. Why worry about her body being exposed to them, when her mind was even more so? Oddly, that didn't bother her, either.

Zenna was the first to bow deeply, formally. "Lenore of Earth and Aazonia, I thank you for the care you gave my child." She stood erect and pressed an *Aleea* to Lenore's *Kahniya*. "To remember us by."

Lenore returned the bow, then briefly stroked the new light bead, feeling the tingle of it extend into her heart. "I will never forget."

One by one, the others thanked her, gave her a memory of themselves, beads she could dip into whenever she chose, to know them better, to visit their pasts— since she could never visit them in the present, nor in the future. Even within an Octad as powerful as Jon's, Lenore could not translate that far through time and space. This, they all knew, was a final goodbye.

Then, Jon was before her. He did not bow. He did not thank her. He merely put his hands on her shoulders and held her as he gazed into her eyes, into her mind, one last time.

I would like to go first, she told him. *I cannot bear to stay and watch you leave.*

And do you think I can bear to leave you? he asked. She shook her head, but both knew he had no choice. *I will return. In ten of your years, I will come to you.*

Lenore nodded. *I will wait.*

Ten years might seem like a lifetime, but it was not. A lifetime without Jon would be an unendurable eternity. Ten years she could manage because she must.

She smiled at Jon, then at the others. "I'm not very good at this yet. I hope you'll offer me a boost."

In the next instant, she found herself, not at home in her Port Orchard apartment as she had expected, but in the mountain cabin.

The smile, she noticed as she caught a glimpse of herself in the mirror, was still on her face. Had they sent her here, or had they merely given her, as she'd asked, a boost to get her started? Had she, of her own volition, come here to her safe-place? She liked to think she had.

Carefully, though her *Kahniya* was getting more proficient at seeing to her needs for warmth, safety, and direction, she laid a fire on the grate in the pot-bellied stove. As she crouched to light it, she saw her crochet hook just under the front of it. After retrieving it, she sparked the striker, igniting the kindling, and watched the happy flames dance upward, filling the cavern of the stove with a golden glow.

It reminded her so strongly of another cavern, filled with firelight and a golden glow that she sank back onto the floor, lost in memories that had no need of *Aleeas* to bring them forth.

Still, she touched the one given her by her mother,

no longer afraid of what it contained, and let herself slip into its comfort for a few precious moments, gathering strength from the affirmation of self she found there.

She visisted the *mazayin,* laughed and sang with them and with Jon. She nibbled at the sweet fruits that grew on the tips of the branches in the fern forest. She smelled nut bread baking in an oven and sipped the sweet waters of the Sea of Lancor.

No, she would not be lonely. She had all those memories, but she also had a life of her own, a life she would fill with things that would please her.

She picked up her unfinished afghan, set the hook into the yarn, wrapped the first loops around it and pulled them through. As she continued, she watched the pattern emerge, bright, straight edges, zig-zagging from one color to another. There was satisfaction in creating beauty.

Soon, she would paint the scenes she had seen on her journeys, paint them that others might know them, too. To those completely of Earth, they would appear as surrealistic, as fantasies, but she would know the truth. She alone.

Not alone. She started and scrambled to her feet, dropping her crocheting, glancing around the familiar room.

Had it been a thought, or had it been actual words? She frowned and closed the door of the stove.

No. It had been nothing but a stray thought—her own, she decided. For once, following translation, she was neither hungry nor thirsty, merely bone-achingly weary.

She showered, brushed her teeth, and gave her long hair one hundred strokes the way Grandma had insisted the girls do. It shone in the glow cast by her *Kahniya* looking, she thought happily, like the inside of a *florentia* shell, all filled with moving shades of brown and gold and amber and red.

Then, mounting the stairs, she took herself to bed. Alone.

As she slipped under the covers, not having bothered with the long flannel gown she normally wore here, she heard again the words *not alone.* Or . . . had she heard them? Had she merely sensed them? But if so, from where? Was it her *Kahniya?* Did they talk to their wearers? No one had suggested such a thing.

And then . . . *Mama, sing.*

She sat up, waved her wrist at the light despite the glow from her necklace, wanting more, wanting to see, wanting . . . what?

Mama, sing. . . .

And then she knew. With a choked cry, she cupped her hands over her lower belly, closed her eyes, and tried. It was hard. The words came thready from her throat, weak and unsteady.

"Toor-a-loor-a-loor-a . . ." and were joined by, filled in by, strengthened by, Jon's tenor, "Toor-a-loor-a-lie . . ."

Her voice faltered, trailed off as he rematerialized in the bed at her side, gathering her close. "Hush, now don't you cry. . . ."

But cry she did, clinging to him.

"Jon, you mustn't do this. It's too cruel. We've already said our goodbyes. I can't bear to have to do it again. Just go, please, go. I told you I'd wait, and I will. But your Octad needs you. You must take them home."

"They are home," he said. "As am I."

She gazed at him, uncomprehending. "But . . ."

"Glesta is a very powerful little girl," he said. "With her, the others had a full Octad. I was not needed."

He smiled ruefully. "It is a strange sensation, that of not being needed."

Lenore sat up and slid her hands into his hair. "Well, don't get used to it, Alien," she said fiercely. "Because you are needed. You are more needed than you can possibly know." She smiled. "Do you think I really want to raise our child alone for his first ten years?"

He stared at her, reached into her mind and saw the truth. She laughed at his expression. "Who did you think I was singing to?"

"Yourself," he said. "For comfort."

She shook her head. "I think we have one very precocious child in here," she said, sliding his hand over her belly. "He asked me to sing."

His warm fingers curled slightly as his warm thought curved into her mind, deeper, deeper, deeper, gliding along passageways open only to someone with the key of *baloka*.

"Two," he said.

"Two what?"

"Two very precocious children, *letise.*"

She closed her eyes and sank back on her pillow, overcome. He pulled her head onto his shoulder, wrapped her tightly in his arms.

"Jonallo . . . my love," she said. "There are no words. . . ."

"My *letise*, my love, we do not need words."

And as he captured her lips in a kiss, as they began the thrilling journey of joining both mentally and physically she knew he was right.

Shielder

CATHERINE SPANGLER

Unjustly shunned by her people, Nessa dan Ranul knows she is unlovable—so when an opportunity arises for her to save her world, she leaps at the chance. Setting out for the farthest reaches of the galaxy, she has one goal: to elude capture and deliver her race from destruction. But then she finds herself at the questionable mercy of Chase McKnight, a handsome bounty hunter. Suddenly, Nessa finds that escape is the last thing she wants. In Chase's passionate embrace she finds a nirvana of which she never dared dream—with a man she never dared trust. But as her identity remains a secret and her mission incomplete, each passing day brings her nearer to oblivion.

___52304-3 $5.50 US/$6.50 CAN

THE BLACK ROSE

JAN ZIMLICH

Though Lucien Charbonneau was born a noble, he's implemented plans to bring about galactic revolution. He wears two faces, that of an effete aristocrat and that of someone darker, more mysterious. He has subtle yet potent charms, and he plays at deception with the same skill that he might caress a lover. And though Lucien is betrothed, he swears not even his beautiful fiancée will ever learn his heart's secret, that of the Black Rose.

Alexandra Fallon has of course heard of that infamous spy, but her own interests are far less political. When interplanetary concerns force her to marry, the man who comes to her bed is in for a rude awakening. But the shadowy hunk who appears lights a passion hotter than a thousand suns—and in its fiery glow, both she and Lucien will learn that between lovers no secrets can remain in darkness.

Starlight, Starbright

Saranne Dawson

Serena has always been curious: insatiable in her quest for knowledge and voracious in her appetite for adventure. No one understands her fascination with the heavens and the wondrous moving stars that trace the vast sky. But when one of those "stars" lands, the biggest, most handsome man she has ever seen steps off the ship and captures her heart.

His mission is simple: Bring Serena to the Sisterhood for training to harness her great mental power. Yet Darian can't stop thinking about the way she looks at him as though he is the only man in the universe. Despite all the forces that conspire to keep them apart, Darian knows that together he and Serena can tap the power of the stars.

___52346-9 $5.50 US/$6.50 CAN

THE MAGIC OF TWO
SARANNE DAWSON

Quinn knows he seems mad, deserting everything familiar to sail across the sea to search for a land that probably only existed in his grandfather's imagination. But a chance encounter with a pale-haired beauty erases any doubts he may have had. Jasmine is like no other woman he has known: She is the one he has been searching for, the one who can help him find their lost home. She, too, has heard the tales of a peaceful valley surrounded by tall snow-capped mountains and the two peoples who lived there until they were scattered across the globe. And when she looks into Quinn's soft eyes and feels his strong arms encircle her, she knows that together they can chase away the demons that plague them to find happiness in the valley, if only they can surrender to the magic of two.

___52308-6 $5.50 US/$6.50 CAN